Making Faces

Making Faces

A NOVEL

JOHN BULLOCK

John Bullock (signature)

Dear

If this copy actually reaches you, may your charm,
wit, and intelligence find something of interest in these
pages. It's a great pleasure to (get to) know you.

GHOST ROAD PRESS

Fondly,
John
xx

Library of Congress Cataloging-in-Publication Data.
Making Faces
Ghost Road Press
ISBN (Trade pbk.)
13 digit 978-0-9796255-2-7
10 digit 0-9796255-2-1
Library of Congress Control Number: 2008920342

Cover design & author photo: Patricia Cue
Book design: Sonya Unrein

Ghost Road Press
Denver, Colorado

ghostroadpress.com

Acknowledgments

Eternal gratitude to Bob Pope for his inspiration, encouragement, and friendship. Without him...

Love and thanks, past and present, to Marc Richmond, Leigh Chalmers, Kate Rhodes, Sharmila Voorakkara, George Garrett, John Casey, Ann Beattie, Deborah Eisenberg, Ron Riekki, Michael Drew, Laura Dave, and Carey Snyder.

And to Matt Davis and Sonya Unrein, for taking the leap.

For Tom

Para Patricia y Julia

And for Mum and Dad

1

When you're born into the bed and breakfast game, you learn to be quiet from day one. A crying baby's bad for business. Everyone else can make all the noise they want, but not you – you live for *our guests*, and everything you do from the crack of dawn to last thing at night revolves around them. You can't fart in bed without muffling it with your covers, or take a dump without running the shower. You learn to walk lightly, cough softly, to keep your voice down. If you're angry, tough. If you're ill, stay in your room. Keep the germs to yourself. One of the old bids might catch a dose and come down with pneumonia.

And another thing: you've got to like people. You've got to treasure their foibles. You've got to enjoy having them treat you like something they stepped in on the prom. On top of that, you've got to love the kids they bring with them.

We didn't. At least, Mum and I didn't. Dad was better at pretending. He was a greengrocer. He still ran the same shop that Mum had gone into twenty years ago and seen him tending his veg. She'd just started the B&B. For some reason they joined forces. Over the years, Dad kept the shop and helped out at home in the evenings, ferrying meals when we were pushed, but mostly doing the bar, which he wiped twice a minute, whether he had customers or not. Failing that, he'd be tinkering. He relaxed by keeping busy. And if busy was good for him, it was good for me.

My attic room was at the back of the house, far enough to shield me from the peak season hullabaloo. Fat chance. To make sure I didn't get a minute's peace, Dad rigged an intercom between my room and reception, a silver-and-black box the size of a fag packet on the wall next to the door. I was sure he'd fitted it with a spy camera so that he or Mum could blast me out of my skin whenever they wanted. Regardless of whether I was training my telescope on the strip of sea at the edge of my window, or gluing Durex wrappers to my beachcombing collage, that buzzer could go at any moment. Next thing you know, I'd be up and down those stairs putting fresh lavender soap tablets in the bathrooms or mending the ballcock in one of our communal loos.

But mostly I'd be lugging up suitcases from reception, where the smell of morning tea and toast lingered through the afternoon and seemed to stain the light that filtered in through the front net curtains. Itching to get settled, the new arrivals would be waiting in reception, plucking sightseeing pamphlets from the racks and browsing them idly before putting them back in every possible slot but the one they'd taken them from. Even before I arrived to help them to their rooms, they'd begun leaving their mark. Things went downhill from there.

One afternoon I was in my room making a list of who would and wouldn't come to my funeral if I topped myself, an idea I'd been toying with all week. (Being fourteen, I was a miserable sod.) The list had started out long, but the more I thought about who I'd included, the more names I crossed off. On the final shortlist were Mum, Dad, Uncle Norm, Uncle Ern, Auntie Vi, and Lance, my sort of best mate, who, since getting his face burnt off by a firework had taken up grave rubbing. He'd visited every cemetery in Farthing – no small feat considering we had more of them than we had phone boxes. Farthing's always been a hotbed of geriatrics, or crumblies, as we called them. God's waiting room. And the only town in England with a death-to-birth ratio of fifty to one. Space wasn't the problem. With the South Downs on our doorstep, we could've buried half of Europe if we'd wanted, imported corpses to raise revenue. But the council couldn't even clear the washed-up seaweed off of the beach in summer till it had stewed so long that it stank out the town and sent everyone up in arms. So there wasn't much likelihood of it tendering for corpses from across the Channel. Or the North Sea. Or the Irish Sea, come to that. Anyway, my only hope for the afterlife was that Lance would do a rubbing of my headstone and frame it for posterity. The pride of his collection. But what moving epitaph would Mum and Dad choose in my honour? Good riddance, probably. Thank Christ he's gone.

Uncle Ern, Mum's older brother, jumped ship to Australia in the sixties and hadn't been back since. I'd never met him. As far as I knew, he'd never written. The odds of him flying halfway round the world to watch a kid he didn't know get dropped into the ground were slim. So I wrote him off. The shortlist was now down to five predictables, none of who had oceans to cross, and none of who were famous. A crap turn-out. Hardly worth the dying.

The buzzer went. Mum needed some cases moved. Instead of smashing the intercom with a hammer, I punched the wall next to it hoping the pain would make me feel better, send sparks through my veins like it usually did. But it just made me madder.

On the first landing I caught a young boy and his sister sprinting from one end to the other, making all kinds of racket. So I blocked their way.

"I'll chuck you out if you don't stop," I said.

The mop-haired boy faced me off. "You're not my dad."

"Yeah," said his sister, stepping up beside him. "Our dad'll chuck you out if you don't leave us alone."

"No he won't," I said. "This is my house. I can do what I want."

They ignored me and bolted off down the stairs. I chased them into reception. Mum was showing a middle-aged couple the wall of watercolours done by her amateur painter friends. She sold them on commission. Tacky as they were, in the peak season they sold like Bank Holiday cockles.

"What on earth?" said Mum.

"I won, I won," shouted the boy.

If it hadn't been for the guests I would've lamped him. "Don't run, I said."

"Matthew, what do you think you're doing?"

"Ask them," I said, pointing at the boy.

"We weren't doin' nuffing," he said. Again his sister came up beside him.

"Dad said it's a safety hazard," I said.

"I'll be the judge of that," said Mum. Then to the kids: "Where's your parents?"

The boy shrugged at his sister, then at Mum. "Dunno."

"Well, go in the lounge or something. There's games. Ker Plunk. Matthew, these cases need to go upstairs."

The kids smirked. I felt like a dwarf, and vowed to get my own back. But even brats like those were *our guests*, and you didn't upset them, or even go near them, not unless you were on waiting duty or were called on to unjam a door they'd got stuck behind.

After the kids went in the lounge, the new arrivals signed the register while Mum picked a key from one of the hooks.

"Mr. and Mrs. Walker," she said in her fake polite voice, "this is Matthew."

I'd been shaking hands with strangers since before I could talk. My right hand was thinner than my left. "Welcome to the Remora," I said, with my best fake smile. (We were all liars, the lot of us.) I shook the man's cold, bony hand, and then the woman's, which was soft and warm as a fresh roll. She was nice. I felt like tickling her palm.

"Please follow me," said Mum. She led the way.

The suitcases sat there.

"I can't take both of them," I said.

"It's all right," said the man, picking up the bigger case. "Just my wife's, if you don't mind?"

We trudged upstairs in a line, Mum first, then Mr. Walker, Mrs. Walker, and me. What sticks in my mind is the scent of coconut that trailed from Mrs. Walker, a smell I'd not come across before, and one which made her seem wildly exotic, as though she'd just wafted in from Tahiti. I stared at her arse, not six inches from my nose, at her skirt kinking from cheek to cheek with each upward step. Smiling to myself, I imagined the fuss I'd cause by sinking my teeth into her rumpy flesh. Instead I lugged her case to their room – on the same floor as mine – dumped it on the bed and snatched glances of her figure while Mum reeled off the short list of Farthing's attractions: fish, pier, prom.

Maybe it was the coconut, I don't know. All I know is that Mrs. Walker's arrival was the starter pistol I'd been waiting for. After years in the blocks, I was finally sprinting to manhood.

That night I went to sleep with two fifty-pence bits taped to my dick. The plan was I'd gain an inch or more by morning and, with such consistent growth, be man enough to give Mr. Walker a run for his money by the time the week was up. Measuring myself the next morning, however, I found no sign of growth. Perhaps an inch was more than a night's work. Thus began my nighttime ritual of coin strapping. According to my estimations, come my next birthday I'd have the biggest dick in England for a kid my age. I daydreamed of regional contests in which I'd put all my opponents to shame, rising swiftly through the ranks to the national finals where I'd wipe the board with the best of them. Interviewed afterwards, I'd put my magnificent growth down to the same seawater that was once thought to cure everything, proving that the magic of the seaside, far from being on the wane, was clearly more potent than ever. Upon my subsequent election as Minister of Seasides, I would educate the public on the restorative power of our bright and briny, citing my ample organ as proof.

For the week she was with us, I couldn't get Mrs. Walker out of my mind. Serving her bacon and egg in the morning, I'd linger at her table just to hear her voice, even if what she said wasn't directed at me but at her knobhead husband. After having her on my mind all day at school, I came home that Tuesday and checked the visitors' book to find out her name. Carol. He was Jeremy. His flowery signature belonged on a scroll. I checked the hooks; their key was missing. Must've gone out for the day. I went straight to their bedroom door and knocked. Nothing. Again. Nothing. I slid my plastic strip in the bottom of the door and drew it up to the catch, same as I'd done before with most of the other locks in the house. With a few jiggles I was in.

The rattling of the door lock brought me round. For a brief bewildering moment I had no idea how I'd wound up flat out on the bed with a coconut-scented nightie over my face, satin blocking my nostrils, flapping in and out of my mouth. As if by reflex, I pulled the nightie off my face and stuffed it at my side. Next thing I knew, Carol was in the doorway. One minute she'd saved me from suffocating, the next she'd nearly given me a seizure. And she wasn't looking so smart.

"What on earth are you doing?" she said, scanning the room as if expecting a crowd, as if some party had mistakenly been given her room.

Grabbing my stomach with both hands, I rolled on top of her nightie hoping she wouldn't see it, hoping the sight of my pain would arouse her motherliness and stop her from grilling me.

"I said, What are you doing in here?"

She hadn't brought any kids on holiday with her. Bet she didn't have any. No mum in her right mind would grill a youngster in agony. She was frigid. Eggless. Needed a good seeing-to.

"Just you wait till I tell your father."

"It's me guts," I said. "They're chronic."

I pushed her nightie to the floor, then struggled to the edge of the bed and managed to get to my feet, weak and wobbly and clutching my guts, mindful of my agony. "I'm checking the windowsills for rot," I said – this was back when we had wooden frames and sills, before Dad fell for double glazing. "I'm sorry. I wouldn't be in here, it's just—" I groaned and doubled over, then made for the door, hoping to convey that this new fierce attack might well involve vomiting, and that the sooner she let me go the better.

After tossing and turning that night for what seemed like an eternity, I studied the sky through my parted curtains, imagining the North Star as something big and bright I could chain my bike to. I was too scared to watch for the neighbours' lights coming on. Dad had tapped into my mind and could tell where I was looking and what I was thinking. He'd be up those stairs to throttle me if I so much as glanced at someone's window. For hours I weighed the odds of Carol keeping quiet versus Carol spilling the beans. Why should she protect me? I wouldn't, in her shoes.

When the buzzer went the next morning, I was wetting my soap and flannel to make it looked like I'd washed.

"Mrs. Hodges is sick," said Mum. "You'll have to do the breakfasts."

"What about school?"

"You'll be done in time for that."

"Can't Dad do it?"

"If he hadn't left his lights on all night. The battery's dead. Now-will-you-get-down-here."

In the kitchen, Mum was doing her headless quickstep, like a kid with a dart in her eye. I put the long plastic apron over my neck.

"I've got a new biology project," I said, wrapping the apron strings around my front and tying a double bow. "You watch, I'm gonna get an A."

"Table six," said Mum, pointing to the four steaming plates of fried sausages, fried bread, fried eggs, fried bacon, and tinned tomatoes. Any other day I'd have died for a plate, but that morning the thought of jellied egg on my tongue made me gag.

"Tadpoles," I said. "Did you know they grow their back legs first, then their front ones, then they lose their tails? That's when they stop being tadpoles and start being froglets. The next step is being a proper frog."

The toaster popped. Mum's cheeks were flushed, the same hot pink as the rash on her chest. She dabbed her cheeks with a tea towel.

"That makes me a humanlet," I said, sliding the hot plates onto a tray.

She came over and sniffed me. I held my breath so she couldn't smell it. "You haven't washed."

"I have."

Mum looked agitated, as if a bug she'd been about to stamp on had just given her the slip.

"No wonder you've got no friends," she said. "That hair. I'll see if Vi can do it Sunday."

"What's iodine?"

"It's for little boys who don't wash."

"How come Gerald Durrell says tadpoles need iodine so they can grow into healthy frogs?"

"Matthew, just take the plates."

"Who *is* Gerald Durrell anyway?"

"He's at table six, crying out for his bloody breakfast."

If Carol Walker had told her gutless wonder of a husband about walking in on me, he'd have a field day pulling me up in front of the other guests. "Ladies, this boy's got wandering hand trouble, so hide what you don't want him finding."

Backing through the swing door with the fully loaded tray, I pictured Dad jumping on the car's bonnet and screaming at it to start. I forgot about the tray. It tipped. Tomato juice trickled onto the carpet, which luckily was dark enough to hide it. I rubbed it in with my heel.

There they were, plotting by the fireplace over their cups of tea. I kept my head down and swung left, made a beeline for table six – a mum, dad, and twin young girls with matching freckles and fringes. Secretly I begged them all to take their food without questioning me. I checked the table. They had both sauces – brown and tomato. Salt and pepper. Serviettes. It looked good. Then, just as I was leaving, the dad had to open his mouth. "Eh, kidda," he said, like a bouncer from Mansfield, "I'm allergic to marties. Got any beans back there?"

"I'll have a look," I muttered.

"Do what?"

"I'll have a look!"

Two more breakfasts were waiting when I got back in the kitchen. Mum was doing a stack of toast. She waved her butter-and-crumb knife at the plates. "The one with no sausage, extra bacon, and extra fried bread's for him." I put my feet together. If I could spin like a drill I'd go straight through the floor to Australia. Suddenly, there I was, chatting a couple of surfer birds up in fluent Kangaroo. It was hot, the sand twinkling in the sun. I wanted to live there. Then, as if through a fog I heard "Walker. And come back for the toast."

The Walkers were still mumbling to each other with their heads bowed. The husband must've caught me in his peripheral. He broke off from Carol and sat back, arms folded, and smirked as I approached. His shiny forehead was unmissable. If only I had a crossbow. A bolt from the blue. A peg for Carol to hang her key on.

"Well, well," he said. "If it isn't our little handyman."

Carol must've kicked him under the table because he cut her a sharp look. She glared back. Her lips were clamped, her wide eyes transmitting things. I put her plate down first.

"Thank you," she said.

"Your dad about?" he said

"No."

"Where is he?"

"Jeremy," Carol protested.

"Out," I said. Even through the bacon and sausage steam, I could smell Carol's coconut. She had her hair side-parted and tucked behind her ears. It curled into her collarbones. Her necklace was a string of chunky coloured cubes, some wood, some glass. He'd probably been all over that neck.

"I was only asking."

"Well don't," she said.

He looked at me. "Tell him I'd like a word in his shell-like."

I wondered if he could hear my heart thump, see my pulse in my neck. "I'll get your toast," I said, and left.

It was a light morning. Two crumblies in crêpe dresses by the window wanted boiled eggs with soldiers; at the other table, a chinny salesman with a centipede tash wanted porridge with treacle. Being used to strange orders, Mum had everything you could think of tucked away in her cupboards. Soon as I gave her the order, she put water on for the porridge and buttered bread for the soldiers, cutting the slices into fat strips.

"This takes me back," she said. "Remember when I did these for you?"

She was always reminding me of the nice things we'd done when I was little: picnics at Climping, go-karts at Lancing, pedalos at Littlehampton. Either she'd lost her grip on reality or I'd spent my first decade in a coma. If she *had* taken me anywhere nice, those happy memories had been erased by humiliating trauma. For instance. We were at the local pitch and putt. At the kiosk, Mum paid with a twenty-pound note, but the man only gave her change for a tenner. When she asked for the right change, he wouldn't have it. Mum was sure he was trying to diddle her, and said so: "Check your bloody till if you don't believe me." The family behind us jumped ahead as if we weren't there. The kiosk man ignored Mum and started serving them. Mum went ballistic. The family took their clubs and balls and walked off to the first tee. I felt like running ahead and giving the dad a few digs with my seven iron, see how he liked that. In protest, Mum refused to play. Dad followed suit. I don't know why he didn't just let her sulk and then take me onto the course so the two of us could still have a game. It was a shame. She'd made a nice picnic – cold sausage rolls and mustard; coleslaw and potato salad; fruit scones and yoghurts. A big bottle of pop. Instead we sat side by side on a bench like a trio of mutes, pretending not to watch the other family. I tried to eat, but nothing tasted right. I was up half the night with heartburn.

Instead of being born with a volume control like everyone else, Mum came fitted with an on-off switch. Loud or silent, there was no in-between. If she wasn't bawling down the intercom, she was drifting ghostlike to her room for one of her morbid retreats, when for days she'd lie in bed with the curtains drawn and the telly on low, ignoring my knocks at her door. It must've been during one of those black absences that she dreamed up her fairy tales of what she'd done for me as a kid.

"You never made me soldiers," I said.

"Oh, like I never did your washing and ironing, or scrubbed your back in the bath."

Trust her to have the last word.

We'd had the two-tone beige-and-brown Princess for centuries. Its black vinyl roof gave off toxic fumes when the temperature hit seventy. At eighty it melted. But it never let us down. Perhaps this time it wasn't the battery. Perhaps it was finally dead. What if we'd have to get a new car, one that you didn't have to slide down the seats in and pretend you weren't there? The shop was a good twenty-minute walk. If Dad got breathy and needed a seat, it might take him double that, by which time the Walkers would be finished and I'd have left for school. And he'd be none the wiser.

The family from Mansfield was still stuffing their faces when I took them their toast. The dad frowned and pointed to the teapot. Yes, I said, and put their teapot on the tray. Next stop the Walkers. I'm sure I saw egg on Gutless Jeremy's chin. I pretended to be up against it, working like a navvy to keep things afloat. Surely not even he was cruel enough to shop a browbeaten kid like me.

"So when's he back?" he asked.

I shrugged.

He tilted his head as if expecting me to answer. After realising I wasn't going to, he went back to his breakfast. For a moment I thought he'd given up. He carved into his yolk, lifted his fork to his mouth. He was about to pop it in when he paused, egg dangling, goo on the back of the fork. "I'll leave him a note then."

"For Pete's sake, Jeremy," said Carol.

The tension between them was perfect: it gave me the chance to wriggle free.

Dad still wasn't back by the time I left for school. Mum said he'd phoned again. The car wouldn't start, even with a jump, so he had to have it towed. When I thought of the day ahead, I saw that same empty Australian beach, only this time it wasn't sand twinkling but broken glass. Beckoning me in the distance was Ursula Andress, in her *Dr. No* bikini. I had a rod-on. But I was shoeless. All I could do was stare.

Mum was in her studio when I got home. Even if I wanted to go in and see her, her studio was completely off limits, unless there was an imminent evacuation she needed to know about. And even then, if she was having a bad day, she'd go up the wall at being disturbed. So instead I went straight to reception to check for messages, which were normally left under the Barclaycard slider on the desk. There were no little white envelopes with Dad's name on the front, no folded slips of paper. When my three-figure pulse subsided, I went to my room, pulled out my tadpole project, and spread my folder and books around me. If Dad came knocking, my diligence might stop him from clouting me, or at least give me time to explain. I'd stick to the story I'd told Carol: I came over queasy and needed to lie down. As for going in her room in the first place, I'd say I saw water dripping from their windowsill when I was out in the garden and, knowing how busy Dad was, thought I'd use my initiative and save him the trouble. He might buy it.

That night over dinner he was still irate about the car, making his usual pin-length fuse even shorter.

"You're a scruffy sod," he said, looking at me.

"What now?"

"That shirt."

I was trying to be good by drinking my glass of veggie water, or jungle juice as Dad called it. Vegetables lost all their goodness when you boiled them, so he made Mum split the sewage between us. There was always grit in it. She said there was nothing wrong with the vegetables and wouldn't drink it, which meant a double dose for me. And not being a tadpole, froglet or frog, I hated it.

My shirt was inside out. There were clumps of white cotton instead of buttons.

"How old are you?" he said.

"Ninety-four."

He slapped my arm. "You'll get such a bloody hiding. . . How hard is it to put a shirt on?"

"Not very," I said.

"So put it on properly."

I took my shirt off then and there, right in the middle of dinner. It was the first time I'd sat bare-chested at the table, at any table. I felt tribal.

Mum pushed her chair back from the table. Without a word, she got up and went to the sink.

"He needs to learn," said Dad, answering a question she hadn't asked.

But Mum wasn't annoyed with him for picking on me; she was annoyed with him for being him. I didn't come into it.

I turned my shirt the right way out and put it back on.

"That's better," he said. Then he gave me his baffled look, as though for a split second he couldn't quite put his finger on who I was or what house he was in.

I got on with my dinner. The mood he was in, if Gutless Jeremy *had* told him what I'd done in their room, I'd be chopped up and taken out in Tupperware.

When the Walkers lugged their cases to a waiting taxi three days later, I bounced on my bed like a blind trampolinist. All week I'd felt like I had a deer on my back; the second they left, I felt so light I thought I'd float away, and was sad when I didn't. Still, I couldn't rest. Just because they'd gone didn't mean they hadn't shared their story with Mum or Dad when they cleared their bill – a real humdinger to wrap things up. Scared as I was, I'd rather the truth come out so I could suffer Dad's hiding and put the hell of not knowing behind me.

That nothing ever came of the business with the Walkers must have been on account of my nightly bellyaching to God. It was the third time I'd played that joker. So far He'd stopped the Sadler brothers from grassing me up for smoking, plus convinced Dad that the cracked headlight on his Princess had been done by some yob in town rather than by me with a spade handle after he'd made me scrub the front of the shop when I'd promised to meet Lance. As for God, it was handy to know there was someone who'd sort things out for you when you'd run out of options. He didn't mind helping as long as you didn't hassle Him too often. In that way we weren't so different.

2

Most of the other houses on Ham Road were white two-storey Victorian jobs with bay windows, high ceilings, and tiled fireplaces – the typical seaside kind. Groin-high walls divided one garden from the next; another longer wall boxed in each garden from the road. Outside every house was a gate break in the wall, only most houses didn't have gates, just a ten-yard path to the doorstep. Some of the B&B owners had done away with their walls and tarmacked their gardens for extra parking. As for the others, it was as if an enterprising pikey had brought a dump truck full of pea shingle and sold it as a neat alternative to grass – a quick rake and you're set. And for the rest there was always concrete: fountains, rockeries, and ponds; gnomes and miniature windmills; or just a few yards of ready mix. As far as flowers and plants went, you could count the traditional gardens in the road on your fingers. Starting with ours.

We lived in the Remora, a superior three-storey guesthouse at the sea end of Ham Road, a stone's throw from the prom. Our garden feature wasn't a concrete gnome or a miniature windmill, but a two-wheeled long-handled trader's barrow that Dad nicked from Borough Market, where he drove in the early hours for his fruit and veg. He took Norm along on a mission to pinch the barrow. Rather than upset Dad by saying no, good old Norm – Mum's bachelor brother – agreed to ride shotgun. That cowboy raid was probably the highlight of Norm's life, the one and only night he'd not been in his own bed at three o'clock of a morning. As for the barrow, it was Dad's little baby. He choked it with creosote. For the first couple of weeks, I'd get back from school to find it had crept round slightly, like a sundial shadow. Eventually it came to rest in the left front of the garden, handles facing the house, barrow tipped forward to show its wares. As well as the lupins, irises, and hollyhocks that vied for space in our borders, each spring the barrow gave birth to a contained explosion of colour – geraniums, marigolds, pinks. The list went on. And every year it changed as Dad tried out his stock of combinations in search of the perfect display. That barrow set us apart, he said, let the town know who they were dealing with. Like it didn't know already.

The Remora had eight guest rooms plus a couple of luxury en-suites to attract the cameo-and-cravat types, the latter refinement fuelled by Mum's delusion that she was in fact running the Ritz and not the same germ-ridden knocking shop her grandparents had run at the turn of the century. Back then, in the peak season, Londoners flocked here in droves in the hope that the seaside would work its fabled magic on them. Something must've gone right for them or they wouldn't have come back every summer with another wallet of savings. And with them being so intent on spending, a seasonal army of workers was drafted to help them lighten their loads. These youngsters came from all over to staff the hotels and tearooms, the pubs, theatres and plea-sure palaces, the beaches and municipal gardens....From Easter till September there was work for all. But the plush hotels didn't want their cooks and waiters taking up prime customer bed space, let alone run-ning amok on their nights off, so places like the Remora became their seasonal homes from home. And what homes they were.

Along with the other rooms on the top floor, my attic room was once home to a bevy of brown-toothed scrubbers living off dried crusts and crackling, or whatever they smuggled from work in the folds of their underskirts. Many were fresh off the farms. Except for the odd smooch in the cow shed or grope in the hay, they were as green as the fields they looked out on. And some stayed like that, found lodg-ings in one of the single-sex boardinghouses that insisted on referenc-es and curfews to keep the rabble out. Others weren't so prim. They brought their innocence to the seaside like any trader, as goods to be sold or bartered, and, like their fathers who carted in the fruits of their harvest from the surrounding Downs, had no intention of going home with it. It was there for the taking, and there was no shortage of tak-ers. Madams prowled the doss-houses for these gullible bumpkins, all ears to their promises of easy money, not knowing what they'd have to go through to earn it, or that they'd never get to keep what they earned. All in all, a far cry from the sweet life they'd pined for during their lonely nights on the farm.

The men lived on the floor below. Beer-soaked by bedtime, their only needs were a wet willing hole and a patch of floor to curl up on. As for the barrow boys, the slower they were to learn the ropes, the sooner they were singled out by the local Fagins, who didn't exactly roam the doss-houses like kindly uncles handing out free mugs of Horlicks. Extortion, racketeering – you name it, they milked it. Not that the boys were forced to pay. The choice was theirs. Either they shut up and did what they were told, or they ended up as dog food beneath the pier.

But those days were long gone. When the four Dance kids – Mum, Norm, Ern, and Vi – inherited the house in the mid-sixties, it hadn't seen a visitor, or a paintbrush, in years. Despite being a devout smoker, Granny Dance would've likely lived to get her birthday telegram from the Queen if Fate hadn't elbowed its way onto the stage one night and pulled her plug early.

After cashing her family allowance one Thursday, Granny left the post office and stopped for a minute on the pavement to fiddle with her purse – finding a couple of bob for her lunchtime stout? Who knows. Whatever she was doing, while her head was down, a section of not-very-well-put-up scaffold attached to the front of the post office buckled, sending a long, rusty pole twisting and pitching some forty feet to the ground. Five-feet two inches above the pavement, its fall was broken by Granny's bent neck. Granny and pole hit the ground. Coins spilled from her purse, circling the feet of baffled shoppers. Apparently warnings had been shouted, but Granny was as deaf as a snake. Not being one of God's gentler creatures, her cremation attracted such little interest that Mum felt obliged, as the box slipped through the curtain, to do all she could to cry, in a bid to drown out the tearless silence. It didn't work. Her eyes stayed dry. There was the money to think of. Befitting the scale of the accident, and the negligence that had caused it, a "considerable sum" was in the offing, though the specifics were unclear. It was only right: a considerable sum was just what her dear old mum deserved. Bless her heart.

Ern wanted nothing to do with the house. They could demolish it or make a museum of it for all he cared. The same went for Norm. Not one good memory between them. Cash in hand, Ern booked a boat ticket to Melbourne, taking only what he could fit in a kitbag. Back then Australia was so desperate for nice white people you could sail there for a tenner – "ten-pound tourists" they were known as – as long as you agreed to stay at least a couple of years. Being a plumber, Ern could work anywhere. Why rot in Farthing when you could have sunshine and sandy beaches? So after a few pints in the pub, he and two mates made a pact: they'd go together. After all, thousands of other Brits had done it, why not them?

The night before Ern left, he and Mum had a row. It wasn't unusual; they'd never been close. Ern was the oldest. Mum was next, by a year. Vi was the youngest. She and Ern were alike, and he'd always looked out for her, always made sure she got her share, which was mostly all right with Vi, except that the older she got the more she wanted to stick up for herself. But Ern wouldn't let her; he always stepped in. Hence his row with Mum. He said that the minute his boat set sail, Mum would treat Vi like a skivvy and make her life hell. "If you were that worried about her," Mum said, "you'd stay. All that mollycoddling hasn't helped her. She needs to grow up." Unsurprisingly, from the minute Ern set foot in Melbourne, he wrote to everyone but Mum.

Norm, on the other hand, was a homebody. Besides, his skin didn't take to salt water, and was quick to burn. Hundred-degree beaches weren't for him. Some said he'd had enough sun already, that he was over-ripe. Left too long on the stalk. A born plodder, he was the one they all got on with, the one everybody loved. Even Mum. With his share of the payout he bought a toy-town cottage in Shoreham, got a job in the new Bryce's, and settled down to a tidy life of cocoa and carpets.

As for the house, any sane person would've torched it and cried arson, taken the insurance cheque to Polperro, bought a matchbox cottage overlooking the harbour and spent the rest of her days in a rocking chair by the window watching the fishing boats chug home. But not Mum. She had a new reputation to make, and a nice lump of money to make it.

She and Vi worked together to get the house back on its feet. They would run the new business as partners, fifty-fifty. While Vi swanned in and out of junk shops looking for half-decent beds and furniture, Mum slung out the carpets and had the whole place fumigated. She washed ten tons of grime from the walls and went berserk with the bleach. Months later, the prep work done, she set about slapping a thick coat of paint over the past. Kissed the knocking shop goodbye. She even came up with a name for the house: The Remora.

On a walk into town one afternoon, she paused on South Street to watch a sign writer up a ladder over the doorway of Banyard's, the greengrocer's. Noticing the new pavement display stacked with pears, plums, grapefruit, and oranges – and with broccoli on special – she went over. The sign writer had just put the finishing touch to the first letter, a gold cabaret B. Against the glossy-green fascia, it looked just the job, and just the kind of up-market touch Mum wanted for the Remora. Must've changed hands, she thought. Not that it mattered; she'd only ever gone into Banyard's if she hadn't found what she'd wanted in town. Chances were you wouldn't find it in there either, but it was your last chance before trundling off home.

As she went inside that morning she expected to be met with the same dismal Novembery light, so weak it fell short of the corners, and the same smell of damp that seemed to swarm all over you and settle in your bones if you stayed in there long enough. When she saw not the crusty old codger with nose hair at the counter but a neat chap no older than herself, she assumed the damp had finally gotten to Banyard and that he'd retired with arthritis. The new shop wasn't in the least bit Novembery: fluorescent tubes threw sharp light into the well-swept corners. If any creepy-crawlies had lurked there in the past, they'd found a new home now. Having just finished revamping the Remora, Mum had a keen eye for clean windows and fresh paint. This ceiling was white, the walls a bright, breezy yellow, slapped on so thickly, she supposed, to hide the state of the plaster – a trick she knew well. The cloying dampness was gone.

She asked who'd done the shop.

"Me, with me own bare hands," the man joked. "What's the verdict?"

"Not bad for a man," said Mum.

"I'm the new owner. Bowen," he added, offering his hand. "Stanley Bowen."

"Jean Dance," said Mum, shaking it. "Handy then, are you?"

"Why pay someone if you can do it yourself? That's my motto."

She turned and motioned to the sign writer's ladder. "Not signs, though."

"That's a knack, that. Know your limits, I say. It don't pay to go making a fool of yourself."

"Well, nice meeting you," she said, and made to leave.

"Hold up," he said. "Broccoli's on special."

"So I see," she said, smiling, and went back outside.

Two days later, as per their arrangement, Gordon the sign writer showed up at the Remora to see what Mum had in mind. Something classy, she said, in black and gold. And did he know anyone who could knock up a frame to hang it from? He'd see what he could do. Like the new chap at the greengrocer's, Gordon seemed able to turn his hand to anything. Mum was glad to be bumping into a bunch of doers rather than sit-arounders, the sort who spoke her language, or the language she was busy learning. Things were on the up. Gordon came back the next weekend with the frame for the house sign and a spade for the hole. When he offered to paint the frame for her, Mum remembered the greengrocer's do-it-yourself motto, and said no. If she was a dab hand at anything, it was painting. By the end of that day, the frame stood square and tall at the front of the garden. The last thing she did before going to bed was hang the new sign.

Open for business.

Albeit sparsely furnished, and with only three half-kitted-out guest rooms. But it was a start. And besides, there was no rush: Mum wasn't going anywhere.

Vi took a fortnight to come up with the beds for the first three rooms. As for the bedside tables and chests of drawers, she had three grotty versions of each delivered to the Remora. When Mum saw what the men were bringing in, she told them to take it back where it came from. A load of old tat, she said. No amount of rub-downs and varnish could save them. Vi threw up her hands: "If you don't like them, find some yourself." And when Mum tried to sell her the idea of divvying up the duties, suggesting that Vi take care of the upstairs and every-thing that went with it – they both knew she was no cook – while Mum did the downstairs, including cooking and serving guests, Vi hit the roof. If she'd wanted to be ordered about, she said, she'd serve after-noon teas at one of the posh hotels on the seafront. So they fell out. But only because of Vi's contrariness – a chip off of their old Mum's block. (Where was Ern now?) Vi seemed to think that now they'd come up with the idea, they could snap their fingers and watch the house mag-ically transform itself into their dream design.

After that first falling out, and with the worst part of the overhaul done, Vi started going out each night and coming home at all hours of the morning – if at all. On her quiet nights in, Mum had a think. Either Vi changed her tune and began pulling her weight, or Mum would go it alone. It was ultimatum time. As it turned out, Vi didn't need to be pushed: she'd already decided to jump. She'd met and gotten "friendly" with a chap who ran the bookies over on Redland Road. They were serious, said Vi. So instead of Mum having bad news for Vi, Vi had what she thought was bad news for Mum.

She'd found better things to do with her share of the money. Mum didn't argue. Far be it from her to say how hasty it all sounded, or question what kind of a gold-digger Vi had thrown her lot in with after a gin too many. She was old enough and ugly enough to know better. And if she didn't, well: more the fool her.

3

Carole Walker might've changed everything, but she wasn't my first. I'd been a master sneak long before my bollocks dropped. There wasn't a door lock in our house I hadn't jemmied. By the age of nine I could've written a book on women's holiday undies, which were mostly the same peach-coloured nylon as Mum's, though sometimes I'd hit the jackpot and pull out some lace-trimmed knickers – more the sort I'd wear if I were a bird. I'd find out which room the guests' daughters were staying in, wait till they went out for the day, then nip in and poke through their drawers. But it wasn't just the undies. If strangers could come into our home and see us warts and all, we had the right to know who we were dealing with. After all, it was *our house*. Besides, what did they expect? They'd have done the exact same thing if they'd grown up in a B&B.

Mum and Dad's private quarters were downstairs at the back of the house – an en-suite bedroom, a large sitting room with a dim brassy light that made me think of the Blitz, plus a cold undecorated storeroom that doubled as Mum's studio. Whenever I went in the storeroom for napkins or a new jumbo jar of Branston, I'd be hit with the smell of turps from the jars where Mum kept her brushes. Her side of the room was crammed with paintings, but I couldn't make head or tail of them. Nothing looked like anything. She didn't have a clue. Why waste your time doing things you're no good at?

Theirs was the first room I nosed about in, hoping I'd find a key to their lives with every new rummage. Dad's bedside table drawer smelled different to Mum's, more medicinal and woody, like the old chemist's he sent me to for his bottles of pills. Mum's had a faint tang that reminded me of my summer bike rides to the golf course – a scent I later learned was chamomile – which came from a bell-shaped bundle of flowery fabric, tied at the neck with red ribbon. Dad's monogrammed hankies, his unused pipe that lived in a velvety drawstring bag and looked more like the property of some octogenarian belt maker named Cobbett than a middle-aged greengrocer called Bowen, and his tin cigarette case inscribed with a map of Burma and the name of some campaign regiment he'd never served in 'cause he was too young for the war – none of these were half as intriguing as Mum's bits and bobs. After my first couple of visits, I stopped looking in Dad's drawer altogether. I knew enough about him already.

But no matter how hard I searched Mum's drawer, there was nothing to explain why she spent most of her time, when she was at home, either in her studio or in bed, or acting as if her real home were elsewhere and that she was only with us because she had to be. Or why she always seemed sad, except after dinner, when the kitchen had been bleached to perfection, and she'd slip into her fur-collared coat, wrap her head in a scarf, pull on her black woollen gloves, and go out.

When I first came upon the two black-and-white photos, one of primary school kids – about seven or eight; my age at the time – and another of early teenagers in secondary school, I thought I'd found the answer. Neither photo was dated. I scoured each one trying to find Mum's young face, back when her happiness was a simple formula of jam roly-poly and hopscotch. But every time I went through her drawer and studied those photos, I plumped for a different girl. Never could I say for certain that Mum was the dour-looking kid with pigtails or the podgy one squinting behind thick-rimmed glasses. Which nagged at me. I lay awake wondering why I couldn't recognise her. Despite being able to spot her then from a mile off – she walked like she was straining to see over a hedge – she was still as much of a mystery as the girl in the photos.

4

Three days after my thirteenth birthday, I pinched a pair of Mum's tights from her drawer. My legs, arms, even the pit of my stomach trembled as I ran back up to my room. Sliding my hand into the flesh-coloured waist, I felt the nylon cling to my fingers and then crackle over my knuckles as my hand sank deeper. I took off my pants and jeans, my socks and shirt. Naked, the tights dangling from my hands, I looked around my room. Everything was the same. I sat on my bed and bunched the nylon of one leg the way I'd seen women do on the telly. I threaded it over my foot till it gathered at my ankle. Same with the other foot. As I stood I got a head-rush, oxygen slow to follow me up. I closed my eyes and waited. Opening them, everything still looked the same. Easing the tights higher, it felt as though I were wading into water, but not the cold murky water of the Channel. This water was clear, almost tropical, and the same temperature as my skin. And instead of sloshing around me, it shaped me and clung tight.

When I came, seconds later, it felt like fish were spurting out of me. Like I was giving birth to fish.

5

While Mum looked after the Remora, Dad ran his greengrocer's in town. If he wasn't driving to market at two in the morning, he was holding the fort while Mum went to one of her meetings at the water-colour club – she was something official, like bursar – or wherever else she disappeared to. And if he wasn't doing either, he'd be rearranging the shop, moving this here and that there in his relentless quest for The Perfect Display. The next time a regular came in, she'd find onions where the apples had been, or celery instead of bananas. He was always redrawing the map.

Businesses are unpredictable – everyone knows. Especially ours. You can't control how many orders you'll get or how many punters'll come down each season. Sometimes I wonder whether Dad chose his living just so he'd always have something to moan about, to justify getting stressed.

Whinge as he did about being in two places at once, he was born on the go. Even when the work day was over and there was nothing left to worry about, he couldn't sit in front of the telly for more than five minutes before he got the fidgets.

One night Mum and I were waiting for *Kojak* to come on. Dad said that any man who sucked lollipops at that age needed his head tested, but Mum and I loved him. Other than the news, *Mastermind* was the only programme Dad could sit through without ruining our night. He'd be more anxious than the contestants. He had a sixth sense for pressure, no matter whose it was. And what he really didn't like were smart-arses. Bus drivers, ticket collectors, flower sellers; people who thought they were "special" got a mouthful, especially when they answered wrong. "Wake up, sunshine," he'd say, "it's not your world." But if Magnus Magnusson announced that the new contestant was an accountant, a chartered surveyor, or a bank manager, Dad's awe was so fierce he had to loosen his belt. They were Professionals. They got hampers at Christmas. Bottles of plonk. They were clearly superior beings. After all, they'd been selected by those in the know. Wasn't that proof enough?

So rather than suffer *Kojak*, Dad decided the coal bunker needed sweeping, even though it hadn't been used for centuries and there was nothing in it to sweep. (I knew: I'd hidden in it when he'd come after me once for calling all the guests wankers.) So off he went with his dustpan and brush, torch to the ground. A while later, he came back empty-handed. He looked pasty.

"Where is it?" he said, going straight to the window. He cupped his hands to blot out his reflection.

I went over. It was pitch-black; I couldn't see a thing. "Where's what?"

"Bloody fox," he whispered, like it could hear him.

"Did you get it?"

His face was pressed so tight to the glass I thought he might go through it. From the outside he would've looked scary.

"Where is it?" he said.

He didn't go back out.

What Mum didn't know when she walked into Banyard's that day and saw the new chap behind the counter was that he, Dad, was no ordinary whippersnapper, no short-sighted flash in the pan. Nor did she know that Dad's buying out Banyard and setting up on his own was a well-engineered dream come true, and Dad's first great mark on the world.

Work wasn't hard to come by when Dad left school. He wasn't fussy about what he did. And as he still lived at home, he only needed a bit of pin money. Old Banyard offered to take him on, teach him a trade he could make a living at, if he wanted. By the time Dad stuck his nose in the door, the shop had seen better days. Banyard was in his early sixties and ready to retire. Not up to a major refurb, he sat back and relied on a handful of regulars and whatever passing trade happened by. By then he'd gotten so doddery that most of the straightforward day-to-day jobs like sweeping and stocking the shelves were more grief than he needed. So when Dad walked through the door all bright eyed and bushy tailed, he must've seemed to the old man like a blessing from a God who'd finally found a battery for his hearing aid. He'd sent this small bolshy kid as his saviour? Oh well, mysterious ways...

It didn't take Dad too many chats with the old man before he started having designs on the shop, started seeing what little lung power it would take to refloat the business and get it back on tack. More than that, though, Dad wanted to put his personal stamp on the place – take it over, tear it apart, and make it into something completely his own, something he could stand proudly in front of and say, I made this, it's mine.

Without mentioning his plan, Dad hopped on the bus to Brighton, went into the first greengrocer's he saw. After grilling the owner about where he bought his stock, what sort of a living he made, and what he thought were the main dos and don'ts of the trade, he moved on to the next. The owners were a mixed bag. One told Dad to sling his hook before he chased him out with a broom. Another said, "You buying or nosing?" So Dad bought a pound of cherries. The owner changed his tune and ended up giving Dad more handy hints than the rest of the owners put together. And a timely reminder to go with it: never expect something for nothing; every favour has its price. By the time he was on the bus home that night, Dad had visited eight shops. After work the next day he paid his first ever visit to a library (though not his last). The girl at the desk showed him where to look, and in no time he was cross-legged at the foot of the stacks thumbing through every book with the word "Business" in its title, jotting down professional-sounding phrases like "seasonal adjustment," "cautious expansion," "timely growth." It was all double Dutch, but it looked good, and that's what mattered. He knew he was onto a winner.

His plan took shape. There was no competing with the supermarkets; they'd always have the edge. But what they couldn't do, and what no one else in Farthing was doing on a regular, reliable basis, was deliver fresh produce to their customers' doorsteps every day of the week. With more hot-footed probing he discovered that most of the big accounts – the hotels and nursing homes – dealt with out-of-town suppliers, most of whom delivered to the area only twice a week. Plus, the distances they had to cover meant they were often late. As Dad put his plan together, one bit of advice rang in his ear: "Forget paying for someone else's graft," said the kindly greengrocer from Brighton, "and get up Borough Market yourself. Best gear, best prices. And if your gear's good, the punters'll pay. Believe you me." Dad liked the idea of going to the market himself, if only he knew where it was. So the next time he saw the wholesaler's van, he had a word with the driver.

"Know it?" said the bloke. "It's me second home."

"So where is it then?"

"London Bridge, mate."

"What, as in the falling down one?"

"As in."

"But that's miles."

"You don't say."

Dad wasn't put off by the prospect of driving to London most nights. If anything, it had the opposite effect: for a kid who'd never been there, it sounded too glamorous to be true. He had business "up town." How many could say that?

His plan fell into shape as he wrote it, first roughly, then in neat – nine times all told, till he was satisfied that he couldn't make it any neater or argue his case any stronger. All he had to do then was convince Uncle Rex.

Rex had set out with little ambition other than to have his own bakery. At first he limited himself to fresh bread and pasties, and a few pies for luck. It didn't take long till he was bored of churning out the same old stuff to the same old faces. He began to wonder about all the punters that weren't coming in during their lunch hours. There was an industrial estate up the road with a couple of big factories, plus the Prudential offices around the corner. So he had some leaflets done, paid his little nephews to paste them onto every surface they could find. He put a sign outside the shop advertising homemade sandwiches – "Choose your own filling." Things slowly picked up; new faces came in. He took classes at the local college and learned to do desserts. Soon he added Bakewell slices and egg-custard tarts to his list, plus apple turnovers, jam doughnuts, and cream horns. Trade tripled. He was selling so many sandwiches that he had one part-timer working flat out all morning to make enough for the lunchtime rush. Next came Cakes for All Occasions. Rex's Mum had a widow friend, Mrs. Light. She had a flair for icing and a soft spot for weddings. Nothing made her happier than seeing a newlywed couple sink their knife in her icing. The more tiers the merrier, for her. Rex advertised his new service and started taking orders. Word spread. Mrs. Light sprouted wings. By the time the next year was over, Rex's humble little baker's was more like a cottage industry. He bought a Jag to celebrate.

On his walk over to Rex's, Dad couldn't leave his plan alone, kept teasing it from his pocket and unfolding its creases, doubting, as he mooned over the facts, that anyone with half a mind for business would take him seriously. He recited every nugget of information, every hard, saleable fact. It wasn't a whim, he told himself. The whole thing more than added up.

Rex was on his way out the door when Dad arrived that morning, spry and impromptu, looking, in his old dad's jacket and cheese-cutter cap, like he'd come for an interview. Which he had. Surprised that young Stanley had walked all the way over to see him, Rex worried for a moment that he'd forgotten the boy's birthday. (Throughout the fourteen years since his brother Alf had passed on, Rex had done his best to replace him, to be a dad to the boy – going to his Saturday football matches, letting him help in the shop for pocket money...) But that day the boy looked almost scared of him. He didn't know that Dad had so much riding on his visit that he could barely stay on his feet. Whatever it took, he'd have to get out his now not-so-crisp plan and win Rex over.

In a voice he'd practiced for the occasion, one that had him wise to the world and twenty years older, Dad cleared his throat before announcing to Rex that he'd come on business. Rex tried not to smile. Still, there was no knocking the boy's front. And he was dead serious. So Rex put his car keys in his pocket and took Dad through to the office.

"I've got a plan," said Dad.

"Well, that's a head start on most of them," said Rex. "What sort of plan?"

"A business plan," said Dad, reaching into his back pocket. "I wanna be like you."

Rex laughed. "I always said you were a one-off. What's wrong with being a footballer?"

"Not me," said Dad, handing his folded plan to Rex. "I'm gonna be a greengrocer."

Rex unfolded the plan. "Make something of yourself, ay?"

"Yes sir."

"Lad, it's me. Save your sirs for your customers."

"That's what I want to talk about."

Rex did more than listen. On the strength of Dad's plan, and without his knowing, he paid Banyard a visit. Whatever arrangement was made, Rex asked the old man to say nothing about their chat to Stanley. From there he went to the bank to find out how much cash he could raise by using his bakery as collateral. The boy's twentieth birthday was coming up, but he wasn't going to hand him Banyard's on a plate. No silver spoon treatment here. The hard way was the only way. If Rex had done it, so could Stanley. He'd buy into the business as a sleeping partner and see how the boy coped. In time, once the boy paid him back, he'd leave him to it. Alf would be proud of him – of them both. Nothing could be better.

So while Mum was clearing the way for her new life, Dad was only a mile up the seafront doing the selfsame thing. They probably stopped at the same time to rinse their mops, wash their hands, and put the lid on the day. Maybe they ate their takeaway cod and chips at the same late hour, their hair specked with emulsion, their arms and shoulders burning. And both too tired to think of tomorrow.

6

When Lance told me the Harlem Globetrotters were coming to Brighton Centre, it was like a spaceship had crashed in the garden. They belonged on Saturday morning telly. How could they possibly know about Brighton, let alone want to visit? But they did, and Lance had convulsions. He talked his mum, Lorraine, into buying us tickets. I was a good influence on him, she always said, so he used that to persuade her. Even if it wasn't true, it came in handy. Lance was brilliant at memorizing what other people said and then using their words against them. It always worked. And it worked with his mum and the Globetrotters.

The Saturday after the show was announced, Lance and I got the bus to Brighton, bought our tickets, stood under an awning for what might've been five or twenty minutes, a ticket each, gawping in disbelief.

"Just think," I said, "there's Meadowlark Lemon in his world, and then there's us in ours. The only thing stopping us from meeting him is this ticket."

"Yeah," said Lance. "And Curly."

After he took my ticket for safe keeping and put them both back in the envelope, he spat on the pillar next to us and off we went. His spitting was automatic. We first met when we were five, and he was doing it then. He couldn't stop. It was as though he kept seeing little fires around him that needed putting out.

We messed about on Palace pier, with Lance talking about the tickets as though we'd been shown a five-second clip of our future, which looked so amazing we couldn't wait to get there. Lance kept shouting "The Harlem fucking Globetrotters!" at the sea. He wasn't good at keeping things in. We'd probably be totally different for the rest of our lives. That lucky feeling lasted about half an hour until we got thrown out of the amusement arcade for banging the shove-a-penny machine, trying to nudge the coins over the edge so we could win enough to buy candy floss. The bouncer grabbed us by the collars and marched us out. Lance protested, saying that the machine was losing them money and that we were doing them a favour by fixing it. I don't know why he bothered. Even though he was a great liar most of the time, he could be really lame, and that day was one of his lamest. After that, with no money to do anything, we threw pebbles at each other until our bus came, then went home.

On the bus, he kept taking the envelope out of his jean jacket pocket so we could check the tickets, just to make sure we weren't seeing things, that while we weren't looking they hadn't turned into front row seats for Showaddywaddy.

But it *was* weird about the Globetrotters. During a quiet stretch of the bus ride, I thought about where they came from – Harlem, wherever that was – and how different it must've been to Farthing, to Brighton, to every town on the coast. So for less than a tenner, we'd all be under the same roof? Just because we'd got the bus and bought tickets? It might've been blatantly obvious, but it was still bizarre. And then I started thinking that if that could happen just by buying a ticket, how easy would it be for other worlds to come together the way they did at home, with strangers traipsing in and out of our lives every season, bringing along their own versions of life? Even the crumbly sitting a few rows in front of us on the bus had his own version of life. It didn't make sense that we could all be so close without knowing a thing about each other. Not only not knowing, but not wanting to know, wanting to keep yourself in a box. As if life wasn't lonely enough.

Lance saw me looking at the crumbly further up. He drew a little line in the air in front of us, with one eye closed, like he was painting a tendril with a lick of his brush. I laughed, knowing he was taking the piss out of the three carefully combed hairs across the old man's head, which must've taken him hours to get right.

"Don't you think it's weird?" I said.

"Why? Everyone goes bald."

He kept pretending to paint.

"It's like all these different worlds, and they're only about this far apart but they never bump into each other. Why not?"

"It's obvious," he said. "Because the hypotenuse is adjacent to the trapezium which is parallel to the—"

"I'm being serious."

"You always are," he said. "You'll turn into one of them boffins if you don't watch it."

"Don't you wanna know what other people get up to, how they live?"

He looked around, as though startled. "Shit," he said, "you could've told me this was the boring wanker bus."

"You can talk."

"Me? I'm not boring. Anyway, I've got enough on my plate."

"Such as?"

"Such as working out how I'm gonna shag Mrs. Pike."

Mrs. Pike was our school librarian. She was married with three kids. Not only was Lance never going to shag her, he wasn't going to shag anyone. He lived in a dream world.

We got off the bus and went into Dice's for weedkiller. Shiny lawn-mowers were lined up in the window like at the start of a race. I asked the shop assistant whether the weedkiller she was showing us was the exploding kind. "No sir," she said, "it's for everyday use. It's perfectly safe." "Oh," I said, "but it's the exploding stuff we want." Lance kicked my ankle and told the woman we'd have a ten-pound bag of it.

"*You* will," I said.

"No, *we*," he said. "You promised, remember?"

He meant his plan to blow up the electricity pylon over the rec. He couldn't do it alone, he said. (He never did anything on his own.) I had to help him. If I didn't agree to help, I'd never hear the end of it. So I agreed. It wouldn't be our first damage together. So far we'd smashed the windows of allotment greenhouses plus some truck windscreens over Fry's Yard. But explosions were new ground. I couldn't see how we'd blow a hundred-foot pylon out of the ground, but Lance said it was a breeze. He also said the two of us could pull off a modern-day Great Train Robbery, even though I said I didn't think trains still car-ried mailbags full of cash. He called me a dildo.

The further we walked, the more our arms ached, the more fed up we got. Before long we were handing the bag to each other every twenty, thirty yards. It killed the joy of getting the tickets. "This is stupid," I said. He didn't answer, just tossed the bag out of his hands like it was a shoe. I felt wimpish.

Then, as usual, we started arguing about my dad, who always came up whenever we talked for more than a minute. Instead of just let-ting me moan about him, Lance always had to offer his advice, like blink blink he was old grasshopper off of *Kung Fu*. What got me was that he didn't have a dad, so he didn't know anything about having one, which meant he definitely didn't know anything about having one like mine. As soon as he put on his Wise Son voice, I wanted to push him in front of a bus.

"He only does it because he loves you."

"When you can walk on lice paper," I said.

"It's true! He wouldn't do it if he didn't care."

"You velly rise."

"It's the only way he can show his affection."

"Seriously, I'll kill myself if you don't shut up."

"You always make it sound like he hates you," he said.

"Consider me dead."

He passed me the sack of weedkiller. It felt much heavier than when I last had it. At that rate, by the time we got to his house it would weigh as much as me.

"If you were a dad," Lance said, "and your kid was just like you, what would you do?"

I thought for a moment. "You know the spire thing right at the top of the Odeon?"

"No."

"You do. I've said about it enough times."

"No you haven't," he said. "I would've remembered."

"You don't listen, that's your trouble."

"So what about it?"

"I'd climb to the top of it and jump."

"Why?"

"That's if I had a kid like me. If I had one like you," I said, "I'd feed myself to the sharks."

"What sharks? We don't get 'em round here."

"'Course we do. They're everywhere."

"Liar," he said. It was obvious he wasn't sure.

Then he said, "I'd be one of those horror stories where they keep their kids in the cellar and throw 'em potato peel, then about once a year they get the hose out and blast the shit off 'em."

"Nice," I said.

We walked on. Up ahead, steam was spewing from the brewery

chimney. The smell of yeast and hops was so thick it got stuck like rice at the bridge of your nose, and wouldn't shift. When they brewed in the summer, that smell battled with the perfume of washed-up seaweed, and, if you were over the other side of town, with the slaughterhouse, which kicked up nicely in the heat. Imagine a bubbling cauldron of cat food. Horse soup. That's what it was like. And they wondered why everyone went abroad.

"I don't know why nothing's ever good enough for you," he said.

"Where d'you get that from?"

"Moaning about your dad, for starters. He's all right. You go places. He tells you things."

"Tells me things! My head's full of him. I've given up trying to hear myself think. And where does he take me? Up market or on deliveries. It's slave labour. If we were living in the industrial revolution, like old Coatsy keeps going on about, he'd have his own factory and make me work eighteen hours a day."

"At least you've got a dad," he said.

"For fuck's sake," I said, shoving the weedkiller at him. "You're like a stuck record. 'At least you've got a dad.' Give me no dad and a mum like yours any day of the week. At least your mum's normal. Mine only talks to me when she wants to moan about dad. 'And how was school today, Matthew? Did you kill any teachers? Did you eat any friends?' Nothing. She'd take more notice if I was a ghost. At least your mum isn't an advert for the walking dead."

"She's a hand model."

"I know."

"She does adverts for jewellery and nail varnish."

"I know!"

"Her hands aren't like ours, they're investments."

"Give me strength," I said.

"You're just like Marvin the Paranoid Android," he said, and raised the weedkiller to his shoulder. When his other arm ached from having to hold the bag steady, he passed the bag back to me. My arms still ached from my last turn, so we stopped and sat on a bench opposite the station. Michael Crawford's grin went by on the side of a bus. I was enjoying the smell of hot pastry from the baker's, picturing the steam from the fresh sausage rolls, wishing I had some money to buy one. A car screeched further up the road. The driver blasted his horn. A dog was weaving in and out of the road. Then it took a liking to one of the council's flowerbeds, and left the traffic in peace. I felt really hungry.

We got the bus for the last mile or so. My *Live and Let Die* daydream of trying to escape with Jane Seymour through the tall grass, or the sugar cane, or whatever it was they were running through, took my mind off the grim landscape of car showrooms, bulldozered rubble, and warehouse-sized concrete patios. In places, the grey ground matched the grey sky so perfectly you couldn't tell one from the other. And then some of the more exposed patches between buildings were grainier than others, depending on how much light came through. It was like being a bank robber: seeing the world through a stocking.

I don't know what jogged my memory, but it was then that I remembered the fish. Mum made me promise not to forget to pick it up from Bill Turret on my way home. The bus was going the totally wrong way. And not just that. I didn't have the energy for another episode of Turret's Inquisition. He knew my shoe size and everything. My favourite colour, football team, book (I didn't care about football or books, so I had to make them up). When I was in the right mood I could cope with him. But not then. Lance had already drained me.

We went through the side gate to Lance's garden so his mum wouldn't ask what we were doing with a bag of weedkiller. Lance put it behind the bird bath, which made it about as invisible as a giraffe hiding behind a pencil. I didn't care. My biceps were killing me. I needed elbows that bent both ways so I could stretch my arms back into shape.

His mum was a lot tastier than mine. Her eyes were big and brown and shone like a horse's. If you looked into them in the right light, you could see a tiny version of yourself standing in a field of yellow flecks, talking to you. Like one of *The Tomorrow People*, I gripped my belt and transported myself to her bedroom at night, or to one of her many photo shoots, where I stood envying each ring the assistants slid onto her finger, every bracelet they clasped to her wrist.

For years I'd used every ounce of telepathic power to make Lorraine fancy me. How many times had I transmitted the fact that just because I was Lance's age, he was a baby, a fatherless sap, soft in the middle, whereas I was all man? I could mend ballcocks. I could open doors that no one else could open (especially toilet doors). I was everything a woman with expensive hands needed. It was about time she realized.

Apart from depression and furry slippers, the only thing my mum and Lorraine had in common was that you always knew where you stood. They repainted your day. If they were happy, you felt like you were in perpetual motion, in a weightless wonder that would never end. Only great things would happen for all eternity. If they weren't happy, it was like you were sharing a stranger's oxygen mask, surviving on borrowed air. Unlike my mum, Lorraine wasn't always out or busy or locked in her room. She didn't treat Lance like a flea in her ear, even though he was the biggest pain on the planet when he wanted to be. She also didn't blow hot and cold. She actually sat back and laughed. Even though her hands were precious, she didn't mind shoving them up the back of your shirt when you were eating dinner, and tickling you. She was the closest I'd ever been to a model. Well, a human one.

As much as he went on and on about my having a dad, Lance had no idea how lucky he was. Having a mum like his was almost reason enough to want to be him.

I hated the way they cuddled on the sofa whenever I went round for tea and stayed to watch telly. Talk about playing gooseberry. Hard as I tried, I couldn't stop watching them from the corner of my eye – her stroking his forehead, him narrowing his eyes like a cat. When would I get my turn? Sometimes when they'd be getting off with each other on the sofa, I nearly cracked and blurted out every secret he'd ever said about her, like how she'd stop singing in the bath and then fart the next few words and then start singing again. Times like that, I considered doing whatever it took to get her to dump him. But I couldn't. I was a friend, and a guest. And I was born to know my place.

After not opening the tin for our tinned ravioli that night – Lance was the house's tin opener – Lorraine sat with us at the table while we ate, covering her ears whenever Lance went on again about how brilliant it would be to see the Globetrotters.

"You're making me wish I hadn't bought them for you," she said, as Lance took the envelope out of the fruit bowl and made us all look at the tickets again.

"Have you got any fish?" I said.

"Fish?" said Lorraine.

"Fish," I said.

"What sort of fish?"

"Cod or haddock, either one. Frozen'll do."

I could see her mind's eye open the chest freezer and peer inside. "What about fish fingers?"

"Not really," I said. "It's for the guests. They like it with parsley sauce. Or with mushrooms and melted cheese. That's mornay. It's French."

"I might have a few fishcakes."

"No, it's all right," I said, even though it wasn't. Mum would go up the wall when I got home. Why didn't you phone? Why didn't you phone? I could feel the earache already.

"After we see 'em," said Lance, still stuck on the Globetrotters, "I'm gonna start a team down the sports centre. After that I'll get a league going."

I looked at Lorraine. She was smiling. She didn't believe him either. When she looked away, I studied how neat and unlined her face was, how tight her skin was to her cheeks and under her chin, unlike Mum's, which you could grip in chunks with a clothes peg. Why wasn't Lorraine a whole-body model? Why just her hands? Every inch of her was perfect.

"Time for my bath," said Lorraine. What music. It meant that in a while she'd be back down in her dressing gown, which sometimes fell loose, even though she always caught it just in time to re-tie it. My teeth melted at the sight of her model-quality knees. It was torture. I'd sit in the armchair wondering if I was the only kid watching Bob Monkhouse with a rod-on.

As soon as we heard the bath water running upstairs, Lance got a hacksaw from the toolbox in the broom cupboard and called me outside. It was nearly dark, but the patio light was on, which made the grass closest to the house look like the plastic parsley we used in the shop for displays. The rest of the grass was black. I took the weedkiller to the shed while Lance sawed a couple of bits of copper tube from what the plumber who'd fitted their new radiators was supposed to have taken away. After dumping the weedkiller, I looked across at the other houses, with their kitchen lights shining out onto the gardens, making the whole row seem homely. From where I was standing, the neighbours' houses were so invitingly lit that the people inside them could only have been happy. How could anyone be miserable in such a cosy house? If Lance hadn't been waiting for me, I'd've stayed out there all night, or at least until the last house light was switched off and everyone was wrapped in their duvets dreaming South Sea dreams. And I'd feel freer than ever knowing that no one could see me, the same unreachable feeling I used to get when I went into guests' rooms. The luxury of no one knowing where you were, no one being able to find you. A place you could be for as long as you wanted without anyone sticking their oar in.

Lance said it was too dark and too late to make bombs so we shared a quick fag in the garage. I buffed the chrome on his mum's wing mirror while he prattled on about all the different things we could blow up once we mastered the art. I barely heard him. My mind was full of Lorraine, humming upstairs in the bath, dipping her sponge in the lavender water then squeezing it over her glossy skin. Jesus.

7

Mum said Vi's initials stood for Verbal Diarrhoea. It wasn't the first thing that sprung to mind.

She wasn't a qualified hairdresser, but she cut hair – well, my hair; I don't know if she cut anyone else's. Mum said she wouldn't dream of letting Vi touch hers. But bar a good wash, mine didn't need anything special, just a bowl and a pair of shears, which Mum said even Vi could manage. What I always came away with was a fringe full of careful nicks designed to make it look natural. Organic, Vi called it. It looked daft. But I liked going to see her.

Within a minute of getting round there that day, Vi had my head in the kitchen sink, moaning as usual that she wouldn't touch my hair unless it was squeaky clean, and why didn't I ever wash it beforehand? On a chopping board by the sink was a half-skinned rabbit, its fur torn back, the inside of it only slightly rougher than the freshly peeled skin. I don't know how long it had been there, but the skinned part looked dry. There was fur on the knife. Roy, her lodger-cum-boyfriend, liked to shoot things. Vi liked rabbit. They were a match made in heaven.

"Guess who I had round the other day?" she said, fiddling with the taps. "The telly people."

The water was scorching. "Colder," I shouted. My ears were blocked, my voice distant and muffled.

She adjusted the water to bearable, then drowned me. I held my nose and concentrated on the shampoo bubbles crackling in my ears while she dug her nails in my scalp. When it was over, she rubbed my head with a towel and sat me down at the kitchen table. That day the blood blister was on her right thumb. It travelled around. She took the wet towel away and put a dry one round my neck. I wiggled my fingers in my ears to clear the water.

"Granada television," she said. "I couldn't believe it. Younger than me they were. Clipboards. Him and a her. 'We've looked everywhere,' the woman says. Redhead. Fat, but the nice sort. 'Ark at old Twiggy here! Anyway, 'Your house is just what we've been looking for,' she says. Course, you know me, red all over in a flash. My house what? 'Thanks very much,' I says. 'I do me best.' 'Indeed you do,' he says. Quite dishy. Turns out they got a film in the pipeline, not the war but after it. Tommy comes home and that. Make your hair curl the money they were talking! Set me right up. 'Would you be interested?' she says. Would I! Course, I didn't tell them that. Crafty, me. So, cool as a cucumber I says, 'I'll need to discuss it with my husband.' I mean, what they don't know won't hurt 'em. But then he gets all stroppy. 'Mrs. Dance,' he says. 'Call me Vi,' I says. 'Mrs. Dance,' he says, awkward sod. 'It's an excellent offer.' I'm thinking, what's he take me for, a biscuit tin? So I says, 'You're very kind, Mr ...?' 'Clive,' he says. Don't like him. Smarmy. 'Right-o,' I says. 'Well, Clive,' I says, 'my husband works on the rigs. Three on, three off. Trouble is, he's incognito just now, but I'm sure he'd be happy about it.' 'It's always best to double-check,' says the girl. Button missing right here. Honestly, you can't win with them. First he's not happy, then she's telling me to hold me horses. Always the same. Anyway, so I puts me foot down. 'No, Miss ...?' 'Call me Moira,' she says. 'All right,' I says. 'Moira. I know my Eddie,' I says. 'He'll be happy as Larry.' 'Larry?' says Clive. I coulda throttled him. 'It's a figure of speech,' says Moira. She'd had enough of him 'n' all."

Vi crouched in front of me to do her arty fringe. "Look at those long eyelashes!" she said, pulling away and standing straight again. "I never noticed them before."

"There's nothing wrong with them."

"They're like a girl's. Makes sense, I s'pose. Your mum wanted you to be a girl."

"What do you mean?"

"Your mum. She always wanted a girl. Course, then she had you and—"

"I'm not a girl."

"Don't bark. I never said you were."

When she was done, I blew the bits of snipped hair from under my nose. I itched everywhere.

"There you go," she said.

"What part are they gonna give you?" I said.

"Me?" The idea of it shocked her, or so she pretended. As if it hadn't crossed her mind. "What would they want with an old goat like me?"

"You'd make a good actress."

She pinched my cheek and shook it. "You've got some funny ideas."

Vi didn't have a husband. The man she went off with from the bookies all those years ago turned out to be on the make, just as Mum thought. Too honest for her own good, Vi had told him about her compensation, thinking it would make her more of a catch, and to show she wasn't a gold-digger, which was just as well: he was skint. He didn't own the bookies, he only worked there. The few coppers he earnt went straight on the two-thirty at Chepstow, the four-ten at Ayr… If there was a horse to back, he backed it. Dogs too. Anything for a flutter. The night Vi told him about her payout, he probably looked at the fruit machine, imagined a jackpot row of melons, and counted his lucky stars. As the years went by, every horse and greyhound in Britain got a share of Vi's payout. He had the odd winner, of course, but those only convinced him he'd hit a lucky streak again, and made him bet even heavier.

But Vi wasn't totally dim. The first thing she'd done with her money was put a sizeable lump down on a three-storey terraced in Redland Road, a sort of squashed version of the house she'd grown up in. The similarities ended there. The stairs of her new house were narrow and steep; you had to pull yourself up by the handrail for fear of toppling back down. And unlike Ham Road, Redland was more of an alley: barely two cars wide, with the facing houses so close you could see what colour the girl across the road was painting her nails. Nets were a must. But it was quiet, with a small park at the bottom and a pub at the top. She couldn't grumble. When she finally gave the bookie his marching orders – he'd moved in with her the first chance he got – she put an ad in the *Argus* and found lodgers for the three upstairs rooms, tossed out everything she had no use for, and shrunk her new life into the thirteen-by-nine ground-floor room at the front of the house. The incoming rent was enough to cover the mortgage and gave her a nice little wage on top. Best thing she'd ever done. And so began her new life as, well, a landlady, only on the other side of town.

"They're comin' back to take measurements," she said, whipping the towel from my shoulders. "It's not all crack, snapple, and pop, there's your film. Not in that game."

Mum said Vi's imagination was too vivid for her own good. Don't believe a word, she said. Why not? So what if she made things up? At least she had some life in her, which was more than could be said for anyone at home. And besides, Vi's version of things might've been truer than anyone else's, if only Mum would stop for a change and listen. But that wasn't likely. Twenty years after falling out over the house, there was still no love lost.

Once when I popped round on the off chance after school, Vi's neighbour Annie was there. She'd been in court that morning for drink-driving and had gotten a year's ban. They'd been celebrating with a bottle of Bacardi. The room was smokey. Bowie was blaring out. I turned the music down and sat at the table. Annie said she had no intention of stopping driving. They'd have to chop off her legs first. After a while, talk turned to Mum. Vi said she'd had it up to here with her. The latest upset apparently involved a lift to the dentist, which Mum wouldn't give Vi even though Vi had told her she couldn't get anyone else to take her. They were always bickering over something. When "The Jean Genie" came on, Vi raised her glass: "Here's to your mother's new nickname." Then she started singing, changing the chorus to "lives on *her* back" instead of *his*. And once Vi started, Annie joined in. Next thing you know there were loads of unfunny jokes about Mum rubbing Dad's spout, or rather, not rubbing it. She and Annie were doubled up. The more annoyed I got, the harder they laughed, as if the real joke was on me. In the end, Vi stopped and apologised. A bit. But it was still my fault for not taking a joke.

On the other hand, she was always glad to see me, or acted like she was, even if she had a migraine and wasn't up to much. When she felt bad, she'd lie on the settee with a bowl of hot, herby water beside her and ask me to soak her flannel, ring it out, and lay it across her forehead. I'd make her nettle or chamomile tea from one of the jars on the windowsill full of witchy roots and leaves. Another thing I liked about going round there was that she let me watch whatever I wanted on telly, which she said was the worst thing ever invented, even though she watched *Crossroads* and *Emmerdale* and every other soap going.

She'd been talking more about the telly people's plans. Then we heard the front door close.

"Talk of the devil," she said.

Roy came into the kitchen. I got up and put my hand out for shaking. He looked puzzled, as though no one had ever done that to him before. "Don't" was all he said. I took my hand back and sat down.

"And how's Roy?" said Vi, all lovey-dovey.

"Parched," he said, dropping his bag, the sort of thing you'd take down the river to put fish in. He was always either starved or parched, sometimes both; never peckish or a bit dry. And the most I'd heard him say were things like she is, it wasn't, they would, it can't, he didn't, they haven't, and I might. If you asked him what he thought of them closing the Lido, our open-air pool, he'd act like he hadn't heard you. Then, a minute or so later, in the middle of cracking a walnut, he'd say, "Told you," which he hadn't 'cause he never told me anything. Even when he brought back his rabbits or pheasants he wouldn't say a word, just dumped them on the table as though he'd found them on the doorstep with the milk. Then he'd stare at you blankly and pick his ear, like he was the origin of gormless. Mostly he drank tea and smoked roll-ups.

He lifted the kettle off the cooker ring, shook it, and got the long matches from the ledge.

"Look at Matthew's gorgeous eyelashes!" said Vi.

"Give it a rest," I said.

Roy struck a match and lit the burner.

"Careful," said Vi, watching Roy. "He'll have no lashes left he carries on like that." She looked around to collect her laughs, but there weren't any. Roy was holding the dead match in front of him like a dowsing rod.

He'd written two books on astral projection. I don't think he'd ever had a proper job. Vi said he had trouble with people. I asked whether part of his trouble was that he spent most of his time looking down on them. She didn't hear me. Another time she announced that Roy was a mystic. I told her we had one of them at school – well, not a mystic exactly, but he was from out that way.

"His name's Sid. He's a Paki."

"That's not very nice, Matthew."

"Nor's he. He's a swot. Every time the teacher asks a question, his hand flies up. It's not fair. He's not the only one who knows things. It's always 'Yes, Sid,' 'Well done, Sid,' 'Three bloody bags full, Sid.' They don't care if you've had your hand up for ages. It's always him.

And he sits right in front of them, mumbling, so you can't hear what
he says."

"Sounds a bit like sour grapes to me."

"He's a wanker. He wears tights."

"He probably feels the same way about you." Then, as if she'd only
just clicked, she said, "Tights?"

"Yeah. You know." I mimed pulling an elastic waist out and letting
it slap back.

"Well—" It tripped her up for a moment. She looked stuck. "Well,
they're warm. I s'pose if he's from a hot place, we must be like a
freezer."

"Don't you think it's weird?"

"Everyone's weird, Matthew." She said it as if I was dim for not knowing. Coming from Vi, it didn't only sound obvious, it sounded right, as
if people were made to be weird the same way whelks were only edi-
ble if you drowned them in vinegar. Which meant that if you weren't
weird you were, well, weird. Or something like that.

8

Angina or no angina, Dad had a business to run and customers to please. So after a few days of being rigged with wires and poked and prodded by so many nurses he developed close to a phobia of white, he checked himself out of the hospital, got a taxi to the shop, took down the Temporarily Closed sign I'd put in the window like he told me to, and opened his doors. He was still in his pyjamas. He phoned Mum and told her to bring him something to change into. "Given half a chance," she said. Against all sound advice, he was back in the game. With one big difference: me.

That was when I started going regularly to market with him, two o'clock in the morning, three or four times a week. No discussion about it. He'd decided, and that was that. Course, he wasn't likely to let on that this new arrangement had anything to do with the doctor telling him that if he didn't stop lugging sacks of spuds about, his ticker would stop for good. (He was forty-four. Life was meant to begin again by then, not end.) He said I'd be getting some priceless hands-on experience that would set me up for the future. I might not thank him then, but I'd soon see the sense of it the day he hung up his clogs and handed the reins to me – another undiscussed cert. When I moaned about being woken in the early hours, he said I should count myself lucky, that when he'd started out, the only example he'd had to follow was Banyard's, who was next to useless. Lazy wasn't the word. Banyard invented self-service. After forty years with his arse plonked on the same rickety stool, he was as wise to the business as young Dad. All he knew was that his stock got delivered twice a week in a van the shape of a loaf of Hovis, that he signed for each delivery, and that once a month he wrote a cheque to clear his tab.

Dad's first ever trip to Borough Market – and to London – involved several panic-stricken hours crisscrossing the Thames, praying for the patron saint of greengrocers to pop out of a hole in the middle of the bridge and take the wheel. If he had, he would've surely informed Dad that there was nothing actually on London Bridge – what with its being a bridge – but that there were plenty of things on either side of it, such as a famous old fruit and veg market under the railway arches on Borough High Street.

It was dawn when Dad finally found the market, by which time he had to double park with his flashers on and hustle his barrow through the concourse like a kid with the trots. He drew a bale full of short straws, paid silly money for leftovers. The traders loved him; they'd seen some green ones in their time, but none as green as him. Talk about putting his back into it! To cover up for being the last to get there and the last to load, he slung his stock onto his lorry faster than anyone they'd ever seen, bruising it to buggery as he went.

It was gone seven by the time Dad pulled away. He couldn't have been gladder to put the night behind him. If that was London, they could shove it. And by then, it didn't matter that half of suburbia was shaved and dressed and on its way in: Dad was heading south. Easing his old mule into fourth, he smiled at the clogged drain of inbound commuters, and purred as his outbound lane flowed smooth as an emptying bath.

The Happy Palace wound up getting their stock an hour later than they would have done if they hadn't changed suppliers. The cook came to the back door with a cleaver. Crates of dead ducks were stacked in the yard. When the cook waved his cleaver and hopped from leg to leg, Dad backed into them. Luckily he got his shoulder to the stack before they toppled, but it didn't calm the cook:

"I tol ev'one no chain'! Chain' dum! I call ol' cum'ny!"

Dad was ten customers behind before he started. The last thing he was about to do was fall to his knees at every drop and beg forgiveness. They could like it or lump it, or so one half of him said – the half that almost lost him his first customer. The Happy Palace cook was anything but happy. Saying that, standing at the kitchen door with a crate of cabbage, spring onions, and mushrooms, and being yelled at by some stubble-headed granddad in pink nylon, neither was Dad. If the Chink didn't soon pack it in, Dad would tell him where to stick his pak-choi.

But he didn't. He might not have been much more than a kid, but he was a kid with an old head and a future to build. Course, he despised the jumped-up hotel-and nursing home managers who on rainy morn-

ings insisted he walk his delivery to the tradesman's door at the far-
thest end of the building, while they, in the meantime, took a warm,
dry, leisurely stroll through the corridors. But he knew it wasn't for
long; they'd soon be won over by his faultless service and top-quality
stock. And when they were, they'd give themselves a hearty slap on
the back for being smart enough in the first place to pick him as their
supplier, which in turn would reflect brilliantly on Dad for having giv-
en them a week's worth of reasons to feel perfect.

In one breath he said I could buy the business from him eventually,
try building it up the way he'd done after taking it over from Banyard.
In the next breath he said he'd give it to me when he retired so as to
keep it in the family. I needed to get a feel for the basics – what to look
for, what traders to use, what prices to pay, and how to make up and
load the orders once we got back to the lock-up. Apparently he'd forgotten that I'd been helping him on and off for years, and knew exactly
which customers lived on which routes and what kinds of stock they
ordered. But this was different. This smelled of forever.

Maybe Mum would have a word with him.

When I got back from school that day, she was on the phone in the
kitchen. Her face was listening. Something wasn't right.

Greaseproof paper and a scraped-out bowl were on the side, along
with the big wooden spoon she used to clout me with. She'd already
licked it clean. The cook's prerogative, she used to say. I didn't know
what the word meant but it was obviously bad. So I never looked it up.
Another word I never looked up was cuckold, which I came across in
a book Dad had on Queen Elizabeth, the one with the electric-tan-
gerine hair. You can guess most words by their sounds. Cuckold and
cuckoo: it was obvious. The tang of warm mixed peel came from the
oven. Fruitcake.

"I'll tell you what," she said down the phone, "I'll bring the whole
bird if you like."

I put my bag on the table and got a glass of water. Nought point
three seconds of standing over the sink was enough: the chicken stank.
Mum must've been unwrapping it and then dropped it as soon as the
smell hit her.

She slammed the phone down. "They don't believe you, you know.
I told him, 'If you think I've got nothing better to do than make up

stupid bloody stories—'"

"It stinks."

"I know it stinks." She pulled out a carrier bag from the drawer. "I'll give them proof of purchase all right," she said, snapping it open. She held the bag over the chicken till it was covered, then lifted it out of the sink, dropping the bird into the bag at the same time. I picked up the bag it had come in and put that in with the chicken.

At the superstore car park I said I was tired and that I'd wait there and have a kip. No. If I wanted the new geometry set I'd been asking her to get me for ages, now was the time. It really didn't matter, I said; I'd make do with what I had. A right angle was a right angle no matter what colour plastic it came in. No, she said; if you need something for school, you need something for school.

Lugging the carrier bag into the store, I felt like I was returning a faulty head.

Mum was in her element. She could've found Customer Services blindfolded. Marching through the lobby part of the huge bright store, she touched up her hair in the mirror by the fresh flowers. Her hair was her friend – stubborn, argumentative, but loyal. I was half a head shorter behind her. Everything was heads.

"I rang earlier," she told the spotty school-leaver at the desk. His badge said Stu. He looked about as useful as suet. "My son has a chicken. Show him," she said to me.

"What?"

"Show this gentleman your chicken."

"It's not my chicken," I told him.

"For God's sake, Matthew." Mum snatched the bag from me and upended it on the counter. The chicken rolled out. Mum took out the wrapper bag stating the sell-by date. Just then, a girl popped up from beneath the counter – twentyish, with snaky brown hair and a white company blouse. She had a gold-coloured badge that said Shelley. And nice tits. Not like Mum's sacks of feed. (Why couldn't she wear bras that did something?) Shelley's womany confidence made me shrivel like a six-year-old clinging to his mum's apron. I wanted to kick Mum in the shins and ask Shelley out to the pictures. I wanted to lick the raisin-sized birthmark on her throat.

She must've sensed that Mum was more than her trainee assistant could handle. "Collect all the hangers" she said to Stu, and then faced Mum from a wise distance behind the counter.

As he left, Stu pointed at the bird. "That's enough."

"Stuart!"

He left.

"How can I help you today?" said Shelley.

"You can help, dear, by reading this."

Mum flattened the chicken bag on the counter next to the chicken and put her thumbnail under the sell-by date. She looked at the wall clock over Shelley's shoulder. It had the date under the time.

"The fourteenth," said Shelley, reading the bag.

"Correct," said Mum. "And where are we today?"

"You don't need to tell her the day," I said.

Grey juice started to leak from the chicken. Shelley called Stu over to wipe it up. He stifled his laugh with his hand. "I'm not touching that," he said.

"Stuart. Please."

He took the carrier bag from Mum and set about doing the same trick with the chicken that she'd done at the sink. This was secret knowledge. Where did it come from? How come he knew and I didn't?

Kitchen roll was found to mop up the juice.

"I was told on the phone in a hostile manner that if I wanted a refund I needed to provide proof of purchase. As you can see," said Mum, spelling out the supermarket's name on the bag letter by letter, "it *is* one of your chickens, one that should be fresh until tomorrow. At least. So why does it stink to high heaven?"

"I don't know, madam," said Shelley. "But..." She moved closer to it then backed away. Her nose was crinkled.

"Thank you," said Mum, taking Shelley's reaction as proof. "I don't like being called a liar."

"No one's calling you a liar, madam."

"Really?" She whirled round as if to catch her accusers spying on her from the soup aisle. Disappointed, she turned back.

"Would you prefer a replacement or a refund?"

"My money, thank you."

Mum told me to run and get what I needed and to meet her back at the checkout.

The geometry set I chose was a shallow rectangular tin box and smelled like Mr. Perrin's metalwork room, only cleaner. More like new pencils. I got a couple of scrapbooks too, for a new hobby I had planned. I ran back to the checkout sounding like the Tin Man with loose hinges.

Outside, the rain had moved on, but the sky didn't look empty, more like it was waiting to catch us all out. In the car, Mum put her handbag on my lap and moved the rearview a fraction in all directions before leaving it at the exact same angle it was before she touched it. She started the car, switched the wipers on. A kid pushing a long train of trolleys crossed our path. They'd veered the wrong way. He was sort of trying to shunt them back on target only he couldn't be arsed. Mum tapped the wheel. "When you're ready."

We were off. It was as though nothing had happened. She couldn't have cared less about the people in the store. The chicken stank and she wasn't having it. And if they wanted to make her feel stupid on the phone, they deserved to be pulled up for it in the flesh.

Mum wasn't one to sulk or hold grudges; she dealt with things on the spot and then forgot them. Otherwise, she said, you wasted too much energy dragging stuff around. "Do yourself a favour," she said. "Life's hard enough."

At last the air was clear. Next on the agenda was me going with Dad to market. She'd have to see my side.

"How long have I got to do it for? I've asked him a hundred times. 'You'll know when I tell you' he says. What sort of answer's that?"

"Don't talk to me about it," she said. "You've got school. I told him. As for your Auntie Vi. Talk about charity. Won't lift a finger to help herself. This dentist business isn't the first time. I said to her: 'Don't they have buses over your way?' That soon shut her up. 'I know half of Farthing,' she says. Yeah, the useless half. Not a car between them. Honestly, you'd think I sat around twiddling my thumbs all day the way she talks."

"She's gonna be on the telly."

"It's all fetch and carry with her. Telly? Says who?"

"Says her. They're using her house for a film. She's gonna be rich."

"She can get herself a car then."

"Wait till Dad sees my report," I said: "he'll go spare. I've already got a D for physics and economics." I ran through the list quickly in my head. "And woodwork."

She wiped her nose. "He can't lift like he used to."

"It's his own stupid fault."

"It's in the family," she said. "All his side's weak. Oh, a Sketchley's." She slowed up alongside a parade of shops. One had whitewashed windows. The posters said COMING SOON. "Another dry cleaners? Whose bright idea's that?"

A golden Labrador was staring at us from the hatchback in front. Mum hadn't noticed. I didn't want her to. She was knocking passersby – "Fancy going out like that." I made quiet silly faces at the dog. I wanted to wave but Mum would've said something. She ruined things without knowing it.

"Seeing the obvious was never your father's strongpoint."

"Can't you make him? He'll listen to you."

"To *me*? A parrot'd have more luck."

The car with the Labrador drove off. Mum didn't notice; she was too taken with the busker in his straw boater and striped jacket outside the pet shop, singing and playing the banjo. *Walk Elsie Our 60lb Tortoise* said the sign in the window next to him.

"Look," I said, "an elephant's heart. That's what they weigh."

"Facts and figures, you," she said, smiling at the busker. I thought she might wind down the window and toss him a pound coin, but she didn't. Instead she said, "Shame he can't find a proper job."

The cars in front of us moved on. We sat there like a lump in the throat.

"We're off," I said.

Mum snapped out of her daydream and put her foot down. Further up, a pedestrian light turned to red. Mum was still eyeing the shoppers.

"Light," I shouted.

She slammed on the brakes, stopped just as our bumper nudged the line of the crossing. Five or six school kids in uniform had begun to cross. The signal was beeping. The squeal of our brakes stopped them cold. "Stupid bitch," shouted one of the girls. I was about to give her a mouthful, but then didn't. If some stupid driver had nearly run me over, I'd've done the same. Or worse. I fished about in the footwell till the kids had crossed. With my head down, I could feel how red my face was.

"That man," said Mum, staring into the distance. She knocked the gear stick into neutral and wiggled it. "Talk about cut off your nose to spite your face. He's the king of it."

9

When Dad knocked at my door on those early mornings, I buried my head in the covers hoping he'd tire of waiting and leave for the lock-up without me. But at most there'd be a pause for him to smooth out his eyebrows or bang his ear – he was plagued by an inner tickle – before he was back with a different knock, hard and slow as a bear's. I sat up in the darkness, slid my legs out of bed, and groped for my clothes. To make sure I was awake, he stood on the other side of the door until I opened it. In my sleepy daze, I'd sometimes forget my socks or put my T-shirt on inside out. He'd notice. Nothing got past him. If you had a zit brewing, he knew it.

The Princess would be ticking over in the drive. While I fiddled about getting my shoes on, he sat in the car and prepared himself, as if a silent drive through deserted streets required the protection of some mystical guide. On our ten-minute drive to the lock-up, we said nothing. Instead Dad acted like he was retaking his driving test: mirror, signal, manouevre; feed the wheel...Maybe his mystical guide was filming him? Whatever was going on, I felt like I should be ticking off boxes on a clipboard, judging his every move. (Talk about the worm turning!) Once we got to the lock-up, he parked in the exact same spot every time, about a foot back from the bollard, so that our heads were perfectly aligned with the hanging basket. As much as I moaned to myself about how predictable he was, and how he wouldn't try anything new, it felt good to have your own space. He didn't need to put a sign up. Everyone knew he parked there. I never once saw another car in his place.

Our old Bedford lorry had thick canvas curtains and drop sides for easy loading. Rust holes over the wheel trims. The cab smelt of old pipe smoke and whatever we'd stacked in there the night before, usually something pricey and crushable like strawberries. It had a tray of cutlery in the gearbox, and a million miles on the clock.

On the way to market, I kept myself from falling out of the big vinyl seat by wedging my feet against the dash, and then drifted off to the dry whir of the engine that seemed to hate those morning drives as much as I did. Still, it never let us down. A24, M23. Through Purley, Streatham, and Brixton, the cab flickered with streetlight as we clunked and rattled past roundabouts and shopping parades, past phone boxes rammed with shopping carts, past pavements littered with half-eaten burgers and chip bags. You couldn't drive fifty yards without seeing a dole office, a tower block, an overpass. Life was either concrete or water. Never both.

Borough Market hit you like a dawn dip in winter – noise, light, damp from the arches. Hustle and bustle. An assault on all senses. Men bawled at each other as though they'd only just been given voices. But the noise wasn't the worst part. As soon as Dad parked up and found a barrow, I'd have to slip into my harness and be Matt the Mule for an hour while he fannied around with his pad and pencil, scouting for bargains.

No matter how nice the people seemed, Dad said it was all fake. Never mistake friendliness for friendship. They'd soon have the shirt off your back. He'd been going up there for twenty years, and he still thought like that.

Even though most of the traders hadn't set foot in a kitchen, fruit and veg was still man's work. Like barbecues. There might've been ten women tops in the whole market. Most worked the snack vans or sold polystyrene teas from flimsy tables that wobbled from the weight of the urns. I was the only kid. In other walks of life, that might've entitled me to special treatment, but not there. You were only there for one reason, to work. There were no short cuts. They even had their own pub on the corner, which stayed open all night long before pubs were allowed by law. I don't know if Dad ever went in there to see his mates. He didn't when I was there. Market wasn't for making friends. Come to think of it, nowhere was. He didn't have any.

Name a situation, he had a saying for it. God knows where he got them, or what half of them meant. For example: Enemies aren't cheap. Surely he had it arse about face. What he must've meant was that friends were expensive, what with them being so rare, and that once you'd found one you treasured them for life. As far as enemies went, it wasn't hard to hate people you didn't even know. People always do stupid things to set you off: jump the queue at the post office, smack into you in the street, tell you to get off your bike in the park. So whichever way you looked at it, enemies were cheap, and easier to make than a sandwich. Plus they were no use to anyone, therefore cheap to come by, at least in terms of demand and supply, which had been Dad's big thing ever since he tried to convince Uncle Rex all those years ago that he wanted a life in the trade.

Dad often did his buying at one stall and then moved on to another, leaving me to load up whatever he'd just signed for. It was a relief when he'd gone. Not having him constantly in my ear meant I could please myself. That's when I got the chance to see some of the traders' true colours. They were no different, just the usual backstabbers you'd find anywhere. And they were so at home with themselves they didn't care who heard them. Apparently Frankie Bell's business was on the skids because he was too soft to get rid of the lad he'd taken on to run it. Like Frankie, the lad came from a dodgy home, and Frankie wanted to give the kid a leg-up. But while Frankie was busy "diverting his energies" around town, the lad paid him back for his kindness by cleaning him out. At another stall, three blokes were saying how Don from Ilford had got too big for his boots since his win on the National. He'd roped in his daughter and son-in-law to run the shop while he golfed in the Algarve. They'd made a mess of it. That'd teach him a lesson about family.

By the time I caught up with Dad, not only was the barrow so loaded that when I stood between the long handles with my back to the mountain of stock, I could hardly shift it, but my head was so bunged up with gossip that I felt bloated and sluggish. I'd heard more than was healthy.

Everyone at the market stuck together. If you upset one of the traders, more than likely you'd upset them all. And if you did, they'd stitch you up quick as quick, till it wasn't worth your while going up there. Dad had seen it plenty of times. And like he said, people were friendly all the time they could afford to be. After that, you were on your own. Which was why enemies weren't cheap.

But he wasn't about to lose sleep over the ones who'd felt the pinch.

"Serves them right," he said. "If they don't know what side their bread's buttered, I'm not about to tell them. They've got the same two feet as the rest of us."

* * *

On his good nights, he talked about the seaside as though it were the house he'd grown up in, long since pulled down.

"That's why they started coming down here in the first place. Early 1700s that was. The sea was a cure-all. That's what they sold it as. Didn't matter what was wrong with you, a dip in the sea'd soon put you right. It's like the spa towns, Scarborough and all them. They started calling them watering places. Blokes went out in little cobble boats. In they'd jump, birthday suits, summer or winter, made no difference. And the women—" He threw his head back, the lump in his neck like a pig's knuckle: "—you know what they're like, always faffing. So what they'd do, they'd strip off in these little beach huts, put their clobber on. Soon as they were ready, a guide took them into the sea. Same thing with the bathing machine. Benjamin Beale that was. Margate. 1750s. Course, he didn't make a penny out of it. Died skint."

Then he leaned forward to check his mirrors, as if he'd see more out of them up close.

Sometimes I shut my eyes and listened while his voice painted pictures in my mind, and I saw all the places he spoke of – the beaches, the women with puffy dresses and parasols, the mutton-chopped men – as if I were standing on the prom all that time ago.

He said the more popular these watering holes got the quicker the locals came up with attractions: the Assembly Rooms for cards and dances; theatres and chapels and libraries. Apparently the sea was good for the teeth and glands too, according to Dr. Richard Russell, who eventually moved to Brighton – or Brighthelmstone, as they called it back then – and set about making it famous.

"They weren't daft," he said, "Dr. Russell and his lot, the town councillors. Business-minded, see," he turned to me, tapped his nut. "They spread this rumour saying that once you started going in the sea you couldn't stop. Might danger your health. They came up with all sorts of side effects just to scare everyone, make sure they kept at it. Course, didn't occur to them that they'd scare people off from coming in the first place, specially them that lived miles away and never saw the sea except on their holidays."

But Dad's good nights didn't last long. He soon started whinging.

"Self-catering's what put the knife in. Holiday homes." His anger sent his head this way and that, like he was trying to shake off a custard pie with his hands tied. I ducked to hide my laugh. "Weren't coming down here no more, not for a week or two like they used to. All bloody day-trippers. Cars, see. In and out in no time. None of that palaver with the railways. And that's another bloody farce." He raised his palm as though I'd tried to cut in. "Don't get me started." Then he fiddled with his matches, lit two, and sucked the flame into his pipe bowl. His half of the cab disappeared in smoke till he wound down the window and let it out. "See, now they could drive down here, stroll along the prom, give the kids a paddle, have a pint, wander up and down the pier, and still be home for tea. Didn't need to make a song and dance of it." He puffed. "That's when the rot set in."

Foreign holidays were so cheap then that no one was staying at home. You could pick up a fortnight on the Costa Brava for peanuts. It wasn't just toffs who spent their summers swanning round the continent; now you had bricklayers, forklift drivers, milkmen. And once one went, they all went. There was more money for everyone, and they wanted more goodies to buy. The latest version of Keeping up with the Joneses. Back then you were a nobody till you'd had a pint and a butty in Benidorm.

That was the early eighties. Trade had gone for a burton. Down our way it was all caravans and bungalows – the plague of self-catering. B&Bs did everything they could to drum up business: discount breaks, pensioners' specials... Anything to fill beds. Dad had seen trade come and go before; this was no different. People would soon get bored of flying and not being able to speak the same language and trying to make sense of that foreign money, all them frankfurters and potatoes. Before you knew it they'd be banging at our door again just like the old days, when a week by the seaside was something to aim at and not something you just settled for.

"There's no helping them that don't know a good thing when they see it." Or he'd say, "Mark my words: we'll be waiting when they start coming back. And we'll bump up our prices too."

He hated anyone who went abroad. They didn't think twice about what they were doing to seasiders like us. Centuries-old firms had gone broke. Families fell apart. Dad had friends who'd gone bankrupt all because people wanted a change – sandy beaches, watery lager, Spanish roast beef and Yorkshires. "All that grief," he said, "just for a postcard with a foreign stamp." I couldn't help thinking of my cartoon-coloured stamps from Trinidad, my Bulgarian dinosaurs. Who wouldn't want a postcard with a foreign stamp?

Only those with any spine held on for things to come full circle. Dad had the greengrocer's and was still supplying the local pubs, hotels, and restaurants, so even if business had dipped overall, he wasn't worried. We had concrete foundations. We'd ride the slump out. "See, them curry lot don't get it," he said, meaning Sid's family, the Bhargavas, down the road. "A solid business takes patience. It don't happen overnight."

I'd heard on telly that Maggie was a grocer's daughter, but she didn't talk like any shopkeeper I knew. Dad said it was her fault everyone was going abroad, that trade had bottomed out. He said she cared less about our seaside than the Bhargavas did. That's the closest he ever came to praising them.

10

For school I wrote history essays on the seaside, even when old Coatsy gave us topics like "Describe the Economic Impact of the Spinning Jenny." I'd start off trying to stick to the question, but always found a way to get sidetracked. My spinning jenny essay began:

> While the invention of the spinning jenny by James Hargreaves in or around 1767 had – along with other important developments such as the flying shuttle (John Kay, 1733) and, in America, the cotton gin (Eli Whitney, 1792) – tremendous long-term economic impact both on our textile industry and on our country as a whole, the invention of the bathing machine by Benjamin Beale in or around 1753 transformed the way we English view the seaside and marked the beginning of what can also be termed a 'revolution' of another, though no less important, kind. At least, not if you happen to live by the sea like we do.

My essays were mostly made up of what Dad drummed into me on our drives to market, with a few added facts from the library. I always asked him to read them before I handed them in, which he did, but not before reminding me how much he already had on his plate. Did I think he had a time-making machine that he could crank up and churn out a few extra days when things got tight? If I learned to follow my own nose, he said, I wouldn't need to keep asking him. It was never too soon. By the time he was my age he'd had three different plans for his life. He didn't run around asking everyone he bumped into if they liked his plans, if they were workable, if it was all right for a kid his age to be making those sorts of decisions. If he had, he'd still be at square one.

I'll never forget the night he read my spinning jenny essay. It was shortly after his lecture on Benjamin Beale. Stickler that he was, I'd double-checked every detail till I was sure the essay was sound, so that even if he read it on one of his grumpy nights when nothing was right with the world, he'd have to outdo even his own harsh standards to find fault.

He plonked himself down in his chair and sat an ashtray on one of its wooden arms. His chair was the sort of solid job you get in retirement homes, with one square of sponge for the seat and another for the back, all covered with prickly fabric. The pattern was like blue and grey sick. No wonder he was up and down like a yo-yo. A night in that would've been torture. He tapped out his pipe bowl in the ashtray. The powder was acrid. That was his signature scent: burnt tobacco and greens. Eau de Bowen. He thumbed down a wad of fresh tobacco. Before lighting his two matches, he stuck out his hand.

"It's only rough," I said, handing him the essay. "I can change it."

"This teacher of yours. He a handwriting expert on the side?"

He screwed his nose up and lit his pipe. Smoke rose, spread over us, hung. That and the electric bar fire made it hard to swallow without cricking your neck.

The reading began. His teeth clacked at his pipe stem while I counted the glass grapes in the fruit bowl, lined a place mat flush with the table edge, pushed it away, then lined it up again. Our three place settings were permanent. Mum wiped each mat once she'd cleared the plates, but only after Dad had swept the crumbs with his white nylon brush that lived on a hook by the family of wooden geese. Reading each word with his pencil, he paused to jot comments in the margin, sighed and reflected for what felt like forever, then handed it back. Ordeal over, I'd run upstairs to make his corrections, believing that if I followed his orders the essay would be a work of art.

But nine times out of ten I'd get my essay back with some version of SEE ME! on the front. Old Coatsy sat me down after the lesson. He had a bit of leg trouble – there was a lot of it in our town, even though it was flat. He dressed like an undertaker and had a permanent inch of tea in his mug. While my essay showed a good deal of thought, he couldn't understand why I didn't put the same effort into answering the question he'd actually set. He said he understood that the seaside was important to me, but not everything in the world revolved around it. But there's worlds within worlds, I said. Rather than take my word for it, he tried fifty ways to make his point, as though I just hadn't grasped it, even though there was nothing much to grasp. Rather than sympathise with his limp, I sided with Wally Crush, who was in my class, and whose uncle was a chiropodist, which made him an expert on everything. Wally had medical evidence, courtesy of a couple of textbook photographs, that Coatsy's dimpled car-vinyl nose was a sign of advanced syphilis. From then on we watched and waited for it to ooze what Wally was certain would be bubbling pus. That was the final sign. Once that happened, Coatsy would be dead within the week.

When I came home from one of Coatsy's lectures, Dad would go through my essay and scoff at the comments, saying what a fat load of no-gooders they were at that school, and what use were they in the first place if all they could teach were things they knew nothing about. "You can't know it if you haven't lived it," he'd say, another of his favourites that I wasn't quite sure about, although I got the gist: he might not have been totally on my side, but he definitely wasn't on theirs.

I spent most of my time at school trying to keep awake. As far as Dad was concerned, my real education took place between two and seven in the morning on our runs to and from market (usually four days a week, with a lie-in on Sunday), between four and six most weekdays when I'd ride to the shop after school, and all day Saturday. In the week we usually got home from market between half five and six, then unloaded the truck, storing boxes of produce in spaces chalked out for the big accounts. The Cranley Hotel, for example, took six boxes of icebergs, a fifty-pound sack of King Edwards, a sack of salad onions, a sack of Outspan, a gross of lemons, kiwis and honeydews...Their order was identical every day except for the weekends, when they doubled up. Dad had perfected his system. We set aside the bulk of the orders as we unloaded to save time and energy shifting stock from one place to another. And produce didn't take too kindly to over-handling. He'd give me a list of what he called "the frilly" – okra, avocados, sugar snaps; fancy stuff for the restaurants – and I put all the mixed boxes together while he loaded the bulk into the delivery van.

We'd pick off our main accounts first, most of which were either in the town centre itself or within a couple of mile radius. Others, such as the golf club and the Penthorpe Country Hotel, had to be done early, which meant making a special trip out Lancing way – twenty minutes there and back – to keep them happy. "Who plays golf in the soddin' dark?" said Dad as we bumped our way up the windy road to the club, hitting every pothole because he was too annoyed at having to go out there to bother missing them, so he punished the van instead, even though every thud and groan made him curse the customer, and the suspension.

A ridge fell away behind the clubhouse and appeared again in the distance, topped by a sand-colored path, the sort carved by hay carts in the past. They're all over the Downs. At that time of the morning the sky was priceless, bars of gold and purple and scarlet, framed by the fallen-away ridge, so that it really did look a picture, like something you'd jump at the chance to paint. I bet Mum's watercolour group had been up there.

Dad swung into the car park. "Couldn't buy that if you tried," he said, admiring the sky.

I looked. It was nice. After a while I said, "Would you rather be deaf or blind?"

"What sort of a thing's that to say?"

"If you had to pick one or the other." I pointed at the sky. "I meant *that*. It shouldn't be so quiet. It's like someone turned the sound down. But if you were deaf it wouldn't matter. It'd still look the same."

"Are deaf or blind the only choices?"

"Yeah."

"You're a cheerful sod."

He got out for a wee and a breather while I stacked the boxes by the clubhouse door. That morning seemed spookily quiet, the sort you get after massacres when the camera pans the battlefield. The wide gully of a fairway would've been great for a battle. It was the right shape, with high ground on both sides. (Ask any general about high ground.) Anything could've happened there.

"Do you think there was ever a battle here?" I shouted.

He was still admiring the sky as he weed. "With who?"

"I don't know. Anyone. Invaders."

He shook it, put it away, walked back to the van.

"I don't know what they feed that head of yours."

I closed the van's sliding door and got in the passenger side.

"Invaders?" he said, as though he'd never heard the word. "What do you take us for, the bloody Belgiums?"

Dad was in his element when we got back into town, driving the wrong way down one-way streets, parking in handicapped spots, jumping traffic lights . . . The town was his. There wasn't a cut-through he didn't know. The way he slung the van around kept me from nodding off. Being up against the clock brought out the kid in him. He seemed happy. Well, happi*er*. The system was working. He was focused. It was all go.

Because of those tear-about mornings, I knew the town nearly as well as he did. And when you know it that well, when you're out and about at all hours while the rest of the town's asleep, you can't help but get ownery. Like caretakers and security guards. You get to feel what the sea's like when the sun's down. How loud the dark makes it. How moody it gets...

By six o'clock there'd be lights on in the houses, usually the upstairs bathroom at the side, projecting a window-sized block on the neighbouring wall, with maybe a moving shadowy form. Some of the back gardens would glow with light from the kitchens. I imagined scenes, like a groggy florist sipping his tea, staring at the lingerie pages of his wife's catalogue, wishing he had the nerve to surprise her with something nice.

At the weekends we went on all the runs together, but on schooldays Dad dropped me off early so I could get ready and leave the house on time. It was always a close shave. I'd forget a book or go off without my sandwiches, and have to run back. At school I spent the next six or seven hours fighting sleep. I was a walking mains box full of nerve ends. The smallest things made me shudder, like the squeal of a tap in the loo. Other sounds that should've been deafening – the headmaster's megaphone for one – were dulled. Voices washed in and out of my ears, leaving behind such a fuzzy undercurrent that nothing made sense. Just getting through the day was a victory.

After school and during the holidays, I worked in the shop with Olive, Dad's assistant, whose main hobbies were word puzzles and emptying her pill bottles to see how many she had left and how many days there were till her next appointment. It never went well. She was always having to phone someone.

Up until recently she'd run a small B&B in Wick with her husband. But then his eye cancer went to his brain. She scattered his ashes along his favourite stretch of the Arun, up Amberley way, not far from the bridge where they went for cream teas. You could tell she was lost. "It got too much for me on me own," she'd say about their B&B, running her palms up and down the fronts of her thighs as though pressing her pinny. Her heart wasn't in it. So she sold up, found a nice little flat in Kingston, and got the bus each morning. She didn't mean to drop her silent-but-violents – they crept up on her. Not only did she guff all over the shop, she bent everyone's ear about how poor she was, how she didn't earn enough to save for a rainy day. I didn't have the heart to tell her that her rainy day was already here. She was living it.

Perched on Banyard's old stool with her mug of tea, she'd pull her Queen and Prince Phillip ashtray over, so blackened by years of stubbing-out that you could hardly see their faces, and leave her Superking in it to burn. I smoked more of her fags than she did, taking secret puffs when she was called into the shop. She went through her big envelope full of bills she'd paid but had hung on to in case the "authorities" came snooping. At the start of her lunch break she'd put on her spongy slippers with zip-up sides ("me feet do like to swell") and then forget to change back into her shoes for the rest of the afternoon. In order to keep sane, I learnt to ignore her. Instead I stared out the window, watching for girls, trying to guess by the way they walked which had been recently porked. The tiniest hint of a smile was enough to lift me out of my day. But once that smile faded, and the face disappeared in the crowd, the misery returned, and time moped off again like a jilted elephant.

11

The Bhargavas took over The Sunnyside about a year before. They were the first Indians in Farthing to own a B&B. They might have been the first Indian family full stop. Convinced they'd turn our precious Victorian seaside into a stinky little India, Dad got the hump from the start. He laid the blame for his recent heart attack at their door, even though the doctors said he'd had one coming for years, what with his pipe smoking, high blood pressure, and fatty diet, all of which he said had nothing to do with it. The whole point was economics. If the Indians brought any more of their lot down here, the bottom would fall out of the property market. He'd spent too much time and money trying to make a go of his business for some bunch of curtain-wearing foreigners to ruin it. Why couldn't they stick to their own seaside?

He came up to my room one evening. I was practicing headstands.

"You're as bad as that bloody lot," he said, jerking his thumb in the direction of the Bhargavas'. "'Fore you know it, they'll have us all on our heads."

I brought my legs to the floor, righted myself. Blood drained back into my system. My head felt cold when I looked at him.

"Where's that atlas of yours?"

I grabbed it from the shelf.

"Park your arse," he said, patting the bed, and for the first time we sat side-by-side like a dad and his boy, studying my world atlas to see where that bloody lot came from. I still remember his cardy smelling of greens, the harsh pipe smoke on his breath. And I remember wondering what his customers must have thought after catching a whiff of him in the shop. Mum was smart for spending as little time near him as she had to.

"Look!" he said, jabbing his finger at the saggy V of land on the page, "there's so many of them the sides are bulging." Then his finger slid in turn to the surrounding bodies of water – Bay of Bengal, Indian Ocean, Arabian Sea. "They've got an ocean named after them. What do we get? A bloody channel."

In the weeks of his recovery he'd stoke his pipe at the kitchen table and scoff at the doc's advice about exercise and changing his diet (i.e., more fruit and veg). Mum said if he still wanted his egg and bacon he could cook it himself, and that he was free to give himself another heart attack as long as he didn't try it on blaming her, which he would anyway, whatever she dished up. And besides, as far as he was concerned, cholesterol was in the eye of the beholder.

His favourite hobby was cornering me for another lecture on how the Bhargavas had made the value of our business – and everyone else's for that matter – plummet so drastically that we were no longer the hardworking owners of what he called "viable concerns." I looked up "viable" in my pocket dictionary. It said "sensible and reasonable." I thought, How could his concerns be viable? And if trade was plummeting (to fall or plunge rapidly), how come we were turning away guests in August? Still, Dad went on about their cooking, how you could smell it a mile off, plus the ridiculous sheets and shiny pyjamas the women wore. You come to the seaside to forget your worries, not to have a whole new family of them stare you in the face each time you set foot out of the house.

Dad wouldn't stop going on about what the neighbours must've thought when they saw the Bhargavas pile out of whatever jalopy they'd come down in. Who in their right mind would stay in a bed and breakfast like theirs when they could stay in one like ours? Even if Mr. Bhargava had come round one day on a peace mission and handed Dad a mug of diamonds, Dad still would've told him to bugger off. He didn't like them, didn't want them here. Bloody charabanc. Not that he reserved his anger just for them. Anyone who'd caught the sun was likely to get it, even if they happened to be staying with us and had got their tan down the road. Tans were for foreigners, or the jet set. Them that didn't lift a finger. I said, "What about road workers in summer? They're brown as berries." Dad shook his head. "You name me one berry that's brown."

It was true what I'd told Auntie Vi about Sid: he *was* a swot. The teachers couldn't get enough of him. Mr. Boyne, one of Sid's biggest fans, announced during a physics lesson that Sid hoped to go to university. Not having heard the word before, I took it to be the Indian version of heaven, up the road from ours perhaps, their gardens back-to-back. Boyne said we could all do with taking a leaf out of Sid's book, which was about the stupidest thing a teacher ever said to a bunch of fourteen-year-olds. After the lesson, Sid was bundled into the coat pegs and relieved of his satchel. Its contents were tipped onto the floor, his exercise books torn to shreds. Pages fluttered in the air. Everyone waited for him to cry or have an eppy, but he didn't, he just squatted against the wire mesh with his head in his hands till everyone went away. As for finding out about university, I'd ask Vi's Roy. If he hadn't astrally projected himself to the pearly gates – English or Indian – he was bound to know someone who had. Maybe he could show me how to leave my body for long enough to get to university. Even better: maybe he'd take me there himself.

All that Sid fan club business drove me up the wall. Any money you like, his dad didn't get him up at two every morning or make him help out with the breakfasts when they were pushed. If he'd had to fight like me to stay awake all day, he wouldn't have been so quick to wave his trunk in the air every chance he got. Instead he'd be hiding at the back of the class behind the Fat Andrews, counting sheep with me.

If he didn't have any friends, which he didn't, he must've had plenty of hobbies to keep him busy when he wasn't doing homework, if he ever let himself have time off. What *did* he do? Sit at night in the dark of his room like I did, waiting for the neighbours' upstairs lights to go on, hoping some girl would start merrily getting her kit off in the window? Did he have his own Mr. Tidy, who lived opposite us, and who I'd often see standing a few feet back from his window in what he must have thought was the cover of darkness, praying for the same chance sighting as me? I doubted it. Perhaps he just switched his energies from homework to a project of his own, like building mechanical seagulls that could fly to India and back faster than a magic carpet. Or maybe he just stood on his head.

He had an older brother and sister. His brother Gary drove an Escort van with blacked-out windows and *Hot Magic Mobile Disco* sprayed in glittery gold script down the side. He often drove by in his cap-sleeved T-shirt, wearing a diver's watch that sat on his wrist like a frying pan.

He always drove with his right hand draped over the wheel so that everyone could see that watch. His sideburns were a bit Elvis, but pointed. Other than that, he looked like an older, more normal version of Sid. I don't know what he'd done to his car but when it went up the road it sounded worse than the gearbox on our Bedford. You could hear it morning and night. But that disco. When I first saw the logo on his car, I was jealous. Music was too scared to come to our house. Once in a blue moon we'd watch *Sunday Night at the London Palladium* and other variety shows, but that was mostly at Christmas. Tell a lie. Dad once had a Connie Francis tape in the Princess. Someone must've lent it to him. But there was nothing to play it on, just a gap where the radio should've been. Knowing him he probably insisted they took it out when he bought it so he wouldn't be tempted. All those years with just his thoughts for company. No wonder he never smiled.

Once or twice I rode past Sid's house when his brother happened to be loading or cleaning out his van. Everything was on the pavement: crates of seven- and twelve-inch singles; mesh-fronted speaker cabinets; neat loops of cable; light boxes; amps and mics... A whole world of entertainment ready to go. Even if I fancied trying my luck at something like that, it would take years. I had three left feet. I couldn't drive. And you could fit what I knew about music on a spider's ear.

Sid's sister, Sandy, had black hair down to her waist. When she went to bed at night she must've lowered it to the floor and let it curl up beside her like a snake. She worked in Barnaby Rudge. They sold globes and suitcases and chess sets, though I never saw anyone in there, and I passed it at least once a week on my way to Thomas Cook for my holiday brochures. She drove a spotless white Fiesta. Even Dad said she kept it nice. She was taller than her brother, and wore ordinary clothes instead of dressing in shiny wrapping paper like her mum. Even with a job as depressing as hers, she was always smiling, and waved whenever she saw me. Her lit-up face made me feel guilty for hating life, for not loving everyone in it. Watching her fade from view down the road, I wished I could go with her, wished she'd introduce me to something that would make me even a fraction as happy as she was.

Sid, on the other hand, didn't try to make friends. Sometimes I'd come back from a bike ride and go past his house on purpose to see if he was out, but he never was. He was a hermit. It wasn't healthy.

Why didn't he do normal things like mow the grass (they had a patch the size of a snooker table), clean his sister's car, poke about on the beach, or yell to someone at the other end of the road like a grown-up? Whenever I saw him on his way to or from the corner shop, he'd be on his own, marching along with his head down, deaf to the world. It wouldn't have been so bad that his trousers stopped above the ankle if he'd worn quiet shoes instead of black plastic slip-ons. And because his trousers were so short and his shoes so shiny, you could see the split down the outside, especially when he wore his white socks. He got the piss taken out of him something rotten. If that wasn't enough, he had the best beard of any fourteen-year-old in history. And his parents let him out like that? If my bum fluff was anywhere near as dark as his, Dad would've tied me to the bathroom taps and made me shave. Best of all were his glasses, which were like portable windows with bright mauve frames. They looked homemade, a project he'd taken on in the evenings when he had nothing else to do.

He had the world's heaviest satchel. It pulled him over so that he looked like a watch stuck at half past two. Seeing as we both went the same way to and from school, I had plenty of time to see him struggle. That bulging block thumped so hard against his thigh it must've deadened the muscle, not to mention leaving his skin black and blue. At the start of his walk he'd be a perfect right angle to the ground, happy to bear the weight and thump of his satchel. But by the time he got to Brain's Electrics at the corner of Stoppage Road, half a mile away, he'd be carrying the satchel like a tray, keeping the strap from skinning his collarbone. Then, slowly but surely, his arms gave out. The satchel went back to slamming his thigh and tugging him over.

On the rare occasion that I was ready for school on time, I'd stand at the breakfast-room window and wait for him to go by. From the side of the net curtains I'd watch him bend into the wind and lurch his way across our window until he was out of sight, at which point I'd grab my carrier bag of books and follow him, at a safe distance. I'd take my mind off of the walk by guessing what might be weighing down his satchel – an ancient Indian sextant decorated with ruby-eyed snakes? A tin of hot coals to walk over? A portable bed of nails? He could've had anything in there for all I knew. Once or twice I almost got up the nerve to ask, but it took a lot to approach him. He looked like he'd only listen if you had something important to say, and I didn't. I wasn't a talker. I was just nosy. I wouldn't have minded if he'd been nosy with me. Isn't that how most things start?

12

In a bid to get his law made, Dad recruited B&B owners and other small fry businessmen for a meeting in the back room of the Anchor. Sitting a few rows from the front next to Uncle Norm, I cheered with the rest of the crowd when Dad got up on the podium. I had no idea what he was going to say, but the scene was pretty impressive – the crowd, the lectern, him. On our way over he'd said something about a sheriff, but I couldn't remember what. My mind was on Cindy Caplin. She was my age. Her dad owned the slaughterhouse. Her mum was a regular in the shop. The last time I'd seen Cindy was at the train station. She was dressed to the nines, off to Brighton with friends. Even though I was scoffing my chips on the steps, she wasn't so full of herself or so worried about what her friends might think that she ignored me. She asked for a chip. I held the bag out. She could've taken the biggest one, but she didn't. I was ninety percent sure it was a sign. If she was there in the crowd that night, I'd ask to walk her home. There were two things in my favour. First, she was no oil painting, so she couldn't pick and choose; second, everyone else in the crowd was her dad's age. I was the only stud.

Dad cleared his throat. Whatever was in there sounded down the mic like thunder with feedback. He stepped away from it. The feedback stopped. He was about a foot from the mic when he started to speak, as if scared of being bitten. Then he got his nerve up and moved closer.

"I might be a familiar sight to some of you," he began, wincing at the hecklers. "I'd first like to begin by saying that I'm not here tonight out of choice. As any of you who know me will vouch, I'm not one for the stage. But I do feel that if we have strongly held beliefs, and we see that those beliefs aren't being supported or upheld by the people we elected to do our bidding, then it's time somebody stood up and stated the case. Which leads me to my John Wayne impression."

Laughter. Someone behind shouted, "Show 'em, Bowen." I don't know if Dad heard. He looked at me for a split second. By the time it occurred to me to smile at him, he'd gone back to uncreasing his speech. The noise fizzled out.

"No, I've never been one for impressions. But what I want to talk about tonight is not completely unrelated: it still has to do with impressions, but of another kind. I'm talking about the impression some groups of people are making on our community, and the effect they're having. I won't mince my words. Business is harder now than it's ever been. We're all feeling it. I don't know about the rest of you, but our phone isn't ringing the way it used to, and what bookings we do get aren't for the week or the fortnight like they used to be, they're for the weekend, the quick break. All right, so we can't help that. Times have changed. If the Smiths and the Joneses think when they step off the plane in the Costa Del Doo-dah that they'll be treated like royalty, as they are at home, that's their lookout. We might not be able to drag them down here, but we *can* make sure we hold on to what we've got, what's always been ours. Let's not get sloppy. We need to be vigilant. That's the new job, and it goes hand in hand with the old. And if we can't protect what's ours, what can we do?"

"What about protecting your own, Bowen?"

Another big laugh went up.

"Go on, laugh," said Dad. "Laugh all you want. But I've got news for those of you who're happy to sit there and scratch your arses while your businesses go down the pan. And don't think it won't happen. It already has. Next time you walk around town, you count the whited-out windows. And while our friends and families are going under, the Singhs and Patels and the God knows who elses of this world are opening up on every corner and worming their way into our pockets."

His voice boomed out to the long crimson curtains on the partition doors, then ricocheted around the hall. Suddenly it was as if there were ten of him shouting from different corners. He told the crowd that if they didn't watch their backs our world would soon be a thing of the past, something you'd only see in a museum. Next time you looked out your window there'd be so many darkies you'd think you'd died and gone to Tooting, or Wandsworth, or wherever it was they all lived. If we weren't careful we'd have muggings and looting and riots. They'd set Farthing alight. And just you wait: people would kick themselves for sitting back and letting them ever get a foothold in the first place. We were happy enough sending a task force of troop ships to the Falklands to defend a couple of flocks of sheep; what about the mess we'd let happen at home? Where was the government on that?

The crowd loved it. Pints were raised. *Sporting Life*'s were rolled up and waved. A cap or two was thrown. The hooting hurt my ears. Everyone had come to hear Dad, and now everyone was cheering him. No wonder he shone like a waxed apple. What would old Coatsy make of it, knowing as he should have that history was shaped by back-room meetings like this, with the likes of Dad stamping on wooden stages, beating the crowd's blood up? That's how great rebellions started. But the sort of pitchfork history old Coatsy taught – Wat Tyler, The Tolpuddle Martyrs, Captain Swing – might have been fine for the old days, but not now. At least Dad was dealing with actual happenings. That's why he held the meeting, why he drew up the petition. You won't change the world from your armchair, you've got to get out there and grab hold of it. Coatsy and his mob were wrong: history wasn't just the big stuff, it was all the little stuff too, like darning nets, laying fences, bagging grouse. But at the Anchor that night, we weren't pages in a history book that no one reads. We hadn't been written up and left to dry. We were history in the making.

"I'm sorry, ladies and gentlemen," said Dad, his voice soft now, apologetic, as though ashamed of getting carried away. "But what you're seeing tonight isn't the good old Stan Bowen who wouldn't say boo to a goose—" (this confused me. I hadn't met that Stan Bowen). "What you're hearing is the Voice of Conscience, the voice of someone who's sick and tired of having his life hijacked by foreigners."

He said he felt duty-bound to speak up, like he'd heard a calling. Similar, he said, to the way some are chosen to receive the word of God – which confused me again. Dad always said God was an invention, something for old dears to gripe about over a glass of Mackeson.

Holding aloft his petition designed to force the Bhargavas to sell the Sunnyside and leave us all in peace, Dad bathed in the applause and stood for all the world like he'd just been made king. He called for silence, and invited Judge Gavin up to accept the petition on behalf of every loyal participating sole proprietor in our community, to ensure that what was ours remained ours and what didn't belong to anyone else would under no circumstances be permitted to pass into the hands of foreigners who were neither entitled nor welcome.

I'll never forget the way his smile wilted when the small, round, white-bearded judge took the mic, nodded curtly, and delivered his own shorter, calmer speech.

"Ladies and gentlemen," Gavin said, in his thick Scottish brogue. "I'm honoured to be invited here this evening to hear your concerns. But I must say that while I was back there listening, my heart sank. In all my years on the bench – of which there have been more than a few – I don't recall a time when I felt more disappointed, nay ashamed, of my fellow man than I do here tonight. (A low groan moved through the crowd.) I mean, what in God's name are you thinking? What's the meaning of this nasty little rag?" He waved Dad's petition at all of us. "I'll take it home and put it to some use in my fireplace, where it might at least provide a modicum of war-mth." (He said the last word very Scottish.)

He might've wanted to carry on for longer – he looked the sort who'd be hard to stop once he got going – but the crowd made no bones about what they thought of his summing up. The same people who'd cheered and hooted for Dad now jeered and hissed at Gavin. He tried to rise above it, act dignified, but to no avail.

An insult and a disgrace was what Dad called Gavin. Besides, as one of Dad's cronies said afterwards, what did the judge know anyway, being a Jock? No wonder he'd sided with the Bhargavas. Uncle Norm said we should've kicked Gavin's lot out when we had the chance, and got some proper brickies in to redo Hadrian's Wall.

"But the Scots invented the telly," I said.

Dad gave me a clip round the ear and told me to go home with Uncle Norm while he and his cabinet talked tactics.

Before we left, Judge Gavin walked past us on his way out of the hall. I still had my eyes out for Cindy, but she wasn't there. Not that I would've plucked up the nerve to say anything if she was with her mum and dad. Everyone standing with Dad went silent. I watched the judge coming. For some reason, maybe because I felt bad about how unpopular he'd made himself, maybe out of embarrassment for Dad, I mouthed a quick Sorry as he went by, which I know he heard because he gave me a quick dip of his chin before he left.

* * *

"He's passionate, your dad," said Uncle Norm, as we drove home along the seafront.

"So was Hitler."

"Yeah, and so was whoever invented Gripperrods. It's not always a bad thing."

"It is with him."

"Your dad's a Taurus. He's headstrong."

"Is that another word for pillock?"

"You know what he's like. Once he gets a bee in his bonnet there's no stopping him."

"He's always trying to put me right, make me run properly. I feel like a traction engine. How'd he like it if someone kept fiddling with him?"

It went quiet. I thought of Shoreham harbour, of all the Russian-sounding ships that came in there, and the mountains of scrap metal and ballast along the dock. All that loading and unloading. Besides, weren't the Russians supposed to be the enemy? Why wasn't Dad outside the town hall with his sandwich board ranting about them?

I said, "Why don't you get him a punch bag for Christmas? He could take his whatever drives him mad out on that."

"He's got angina. He'd keel over."

"So? He could shout at it. Anything's better than those pills he's on. Even he says they mess him up. You should hear him in the mornings."

"Just because a man talks a lot doesn't mean he's right. Some people don't need to talk."

"I'm not made of nuts and bolts."

In silence we passed nine identical, evenly spaced lampposts. We passed the turntable for the miniature railway, and the crazy golf. "He's got a lot of sadness," said Norm. "And when you're not happy in yourself, you're not likely to find much to smile about."

"I do everything he says but he still hates me."

Norm laughed, gave my head a light shove. "Don't be daft. It's not you. You're his lad."

"Try telling him that."

We pulled up outside the house.

I said, "Mum might be home."

"What happened to her tonight?" He pulled out his Golden Virginia tin, with the lettuce leaf inside to keep his backy moist.

"She's learning," I said. "Tuesdays might be French."

"French now, is it?" He tucked his chin to his chest and smiled, like he didn't believe me, like it probably wasn't French but something else. Then, drawing the backy out in his Rizla, he added, "P'raps she could do with a bit less of the old French."

I opened the car door to get out. "Well, p'raps it's none of your bloody business." I slammed the door and ran to the house. Scared he'd come after me, I jabbed the key at the lock without even looking. My hand wouldn't stop shaking. But when it finally went in, and I opened the door and stepped into the house, Norm wasn't tapping me on the shoulder. He was still in the car. He bibbed and drove off.

13

The Bhargavas might've been his main target, but Dad wasn't exactly smitten with the Greeks from the kebab shop next to the Bradford and Bingley, or the Poles who worked at the brickyard and who sent their wives in for beetroot to make their funny-sounding soup. But at least they weren't cocky like the Greeks. Dad called them Little and Large, after the comedians, who did a stint at the Pavilion most summers, and who Dad said were about as funny as hemorrhoids. There was a third Greek, medium-sized, who lived in the kebab shop window. Whenever I went by, he'd be fiddling with some spit-like contraption attached to a mini gas fire. Other times he'd be carving scorched meat from a block. Sometimes I stood and watched the fat as it dripped into the tray. Anyway, Little and Large took turns to come in for their salad. Dad tried his best to offend them so they'd leave us in peace. But his plan backfired. Instead, whenever one of them came in they treated Dad like a friend from the old country – Large even hugged Dad once just to niggle him – and acted as though their black-and-white world exploded into colour the second they saw him.

The day Olive's bronchitis made her cough so hard she twisted her back and had to be sent home in a taxi, was the same day Dad's wish came true. I was clearing dead onion skins from the display when Large came in. Most customers were in and out of the shop in a flash. As far as they were concerned, I didn't exist. The only ones who ever said hello were the crumblies, but then they'd chat to a lamppost. But Large actually spoke to me, asked how I liked my job. Not bad, I said. My hatred instantly withered. Clearly he was very decent. I filled a paper bag with onions and gave them to him. He smiled, thanked me, then put a few back. "Just couple," he said, and winked.

Dad held Large's note up to the fluorescent tube above the till that was supposed to spot forgeries.

"Turn over," said Large, shoving his hands at Dad in protest: "It say fake on other side."

"I don't do this for fun," said Dad.

"So why you do? Every time you same. Not just me, my brother. You think Greek money what, slippy?"

"It's all the same to me, Fred. I don't care if it's Greek or Timbuktu-ly. A con's a con."

"What? Me, con? Give it."

He reached across the counter for his money. Dad warned him to get back. When he wouldn't, Dad tried to fox him by standing on tip-toe. Large snatched at the air. "I show you who con, preek." My adren-aline was going. I grabbed some Maris Pipers. I didn't want to hurt Large, but I wasn't having him hurt Dad.

When Dad brought his arm down, Large whipped the note from his hand, left his salad stuff on the counter, and went. Dad's hands were trembling.

"That's what you get," Dad shouted after him.

We both stood by the window and watched Large go up the road as though battling a blizzard. For the next week or so, Dad got as much mileage as he could out of the row. He'd turn a short story into an epic without blinking. "Wasn't it, Matthew?" he'd say, roping me in to add weight to the story, which changed from one day to the next. I waited for it to get completely out of hand, till he came up with a ver-sion featuring me as Kid Cod, the seaside superhero, and the nemesis of all evil, though specialising in the foreign sort.

Large was well up the road before I felt the weight of the spuds in my hands. I couldn't remember even thinking about picking them up let alone doing it. I felt bad for Large. He was always laughing. Trust Dad to put the mockers on that.

14

After Dad's speech at the Anchor, I went into the kitchen for a night-cap. Mum's keys were on the hook by the swing door, her bag on the table. She must've come in and gone straight to bed. Sometimes she left a note saying which leftovers I could have if I was peckish, but that night there was no note, and nothing in the fridge worth eating. I made a jam sandwich and poured some Tizer, then sat at the table wondering if what I could smell was marzipan, which I could eat a whole block of. Then I went through her bag. Along with the usual purse, eyebrow pencil, receipts, palm-sized mirror in a leather pouch, hairbrush and bank book, and then more receipts, there was a glossy colour pamphlet. On the front it said *Château d'Estaing: Le Première Ecole de la Cuisine Française*. Wrought-iron gates framed the cover. From there a long gravel drive lined with mottle-barked trees led to the mansion. Beyond the stone fountain, a wide flight of steps led to double doors. The house's symmetry was brilliant. You just knew that if you laid a ruler from the middle of the door to the right-end wing, and then did the same with the other wing, the distances would tally (about an inch and a quarter). The pamphlet opened into eight photos, showing a bunch of activities. In one a group of women watched a white-hatted chef run a big knife through an even bigger fish. Another showed a line of people on horseback, with rocky hills in the distance. Another was of a shady bedroom with shutters on the windows and a single sunflower in a jug.

The photos were similar to Mum's calendar next to the window that she was always jotting things down on – lard, light bulbs, Domestos. Blades of mace. Whatever she was out of. And she always chose calendars with French paintings made of dots and dashes, like Morse code in pictures. I didn't bother asking why all French painters had bad eyesight. It was just another one of those annoying things that was true, even though no one would explain why. You were left to come up with your own explanations, which suited me.

For the past four years, Mum had waited till the peak season was over to go off on her own holiday to France, normally with Ruth, who worked part time at the Co-op and did a spot for us when we were stretched, or with her painting group. Although Ruth didn't paint, she went along for the company. She was Mum's best friend.

Nice as it looked, a week or two in a hotel like that would be worse than solitary. But even that didn't matter. I'd happily suffer the boredom and the language if Mum would say yes for once and take me with her. Every year I begged; every year she gave the same answer: "You'll have your turn when you're older." Plus Dad wouldn't let me go. "Just because your mother does something doesn't mean you have to." What he meant was he needed my help to run the house, which wasn't true because Mrs. Hodges did the kitchen and he knew it. Mrs. Hodges used words like scullery and buff. Put the copper on. She'd stepped out of an old book. The house was better with her in it.

In the run-up to Mum's trip, the air in our house would be thick enough to slice and fry. During dinner one night, Dad said she was a traitor for going abroad. "Think of the message it sends the neighbours."

"Sod the neighbours," said Mum. "You and your going abroad. Bloody tightwad. That's what all this is about, Matthew: your father being too tight to shell out for a holiday. 'Why spend your hard-earned money when you can let it sit in the building society doing nothing?' That's him for you. See the world? What's the point? Save yourself the trouble. Read about it in the paper. If you can be bothered, that is."

She was looking at me as though waiting to hear what I thought about it, which she wasn't.

"He hasn't got a passport," she said. "Won't."

"It's not my fault," I said.

"It's a wonder you don't still ride around in a horse and cart," she said to Dad.

"What's she on about now?" he said. "I've never had a horse and cart."

"It'd be safer. That car's a joke."

"It's a Vanden Plas."

"It's a bloody death trap," Mum said. "I nearly hit a wall the other day."

"You know what they say about bad workmen."

"I know what they say about turning the wheel one way and going the other."

On it went.

Mum poked her food with her fork as if to provoke it. I mixed my peas into my mash. Dad sipped his jungle juice and fell into a trance, staring dead-eyed at the cupboard handle directly across from him, behind which stood Tupperware boxes full of every conceivable flour. I looked at the cupboard, then at him, then back at the cupboard. Was he planning on making a cake?

When she'd finished, Mum left the plates on the table in a sign of protest, grabbed her coat and bag, and went out. Or tried to. A few seconds later she was back.

"Can you deal with these people?" she said in a huff.

"What people?" he said.

"They can't get in their room."

"Tell them to put the key in the lock and turn it."

"Stanley, all I'm asking you to do is talk to them."

Mum left. Dad wiped his mouth and got up. I stayed where I was.

Seeing the brochure that night brought back the same yearly dread of Mum's next holiday, knowing that the second she got on the subject Dad would be dead against it, sparking another almighty row, followed by a week of deaf-and-dumb breakfasts. Mum's last holiday, to Provence, had been with her watercolour group – a mix of young and old, couples and singles. Even Bill Turret went. He was the man with the fish. Mum had been sending me down to his stall on the prom week in week out for years. He was a nosy sod.

"Whoever heard of a fisherman painter?" said Dad, in the run-up to her last trip. "He'll be learning bloody French next."

"Funny you should say that," said Mum. "He already is."

15

Turret's stall was a couple of hundred yards past the pier. It looked like a jumbo chest freezer made from bits of wood he'd scavenged. The weather had turned the stall's thick blue paint to crispy peel. On the prom end of the stall was a blackboard with a cartoon fish singing *Catch of the Day* into a bubble. Beneath that was a list of the day's specials – skate, sole, huss...Next to the stall was a pile of green fishing nets held down by gas bottles. At the top of the beach stood one of those flat-roofed, round-ended Deco buildings you see all over the coast, along with the cruise-ship hotels. If you weren't all at sea on dry land, you could float in a timeless chamber of gin and sequins and fast-forward dances. Lots of crumblies did.

As usual, Turret had our order wrapped and ready by the time I got there. Sometimes I wondered how he knew what we wanted before I'd even asked for it, but then we only ever bought cod or haddock, so it wasn't hard. I wasn't likely to trip him up with an order for octopus. But not only was our order always ready, it never needed paying for, which again seemed odd until I asked Mum about it. She explained that she'd let him off the commission he owed her for selling his paintings, so had plenty of credit. It made sense. Why wouldn't a fisherman pay off his debts in fish?

For someone who'd spent his life at sea, Turret had tiny hands. But he wouldn't put up with my moods. One time he picked up a whole fish from his counter and held its face level with mine, like a reflection. When I said that it looked more like him than me, he chased me down the prom with it. He'd won again: I'd stopped wanting to be miserable.

"Get a grip," he said. "Some people have it really hard."

"What's that got to do with anything?"

"You're young, lad. There's all this." He waved his arm at the town, the sea. "Moping about won't get you anywhere."

I was glad when a customer showed up. I'd had enough of his finger-wagging. She wore a long beige coat and a headscarf. The wind had got inside her.

"Breezy enough for you, is it?" said Turret.

"How's your cod?" she said.

"Back in the sea. It got fed up with waiting." He pointed to a flat thing on the slab. "I saved you this gorgeous bit of plaice."

The woman looked like she'd caught a whiff of the drains.

Gazing at the Channel, I tried to imagine going out there every night in the pitch-black, over the horizon in all weathers, getting tossed about like a toy. What did he have to smile about?

When the woman peered closer at his display, Turret gave me a knowing wink that reminded me a bit of Dad on one of his cheerful days – rare as they were – when he actually had fun with a customer. But Turret was the same every time. A permanent happy chappy. Sometimes I thought he might be a bit simple. How else could he smile for no reason? Maybe he had a headful of Tom and Jerry, or he'd memorized some Morecambe and Wise. God knows how he did it, but he did.

Draping the fish over the scales, he stood back to see the needle.

"Just over four pound. Tell you what, love. You look hungry. Take him home for a tenner. But you come to see me for your cod, all right?" Without waiting for an answer, he took the fish off the scales and started wrapping it. "Sold to the young darlin' on my right."

The woman pulled her lapels to her neck as though smartening herself. Then she got her purse out. I pulled myself out of my sulk in case Turret wouldn't want to talk to me when she'd gone.

Taking her tenner, Turret turned to me and said, "A lesson for you youngsters: always listen to your elders. Old is wise, isn't that right, love?"

She wasn't interested. She'd got her fish, which she was working into her string bag. When it was safely stowed, she ducked as though the sky had just dropped to within a foot of her head, then left.

Turret laid our fish on my bike rack and strapped the bungee across it. He rubbed some dirt from the frame, revealing the Reynolds 531 double-butted sticker. When he rubbed the sticker clean and read it, I was as proud as when I'd first wheeled the bike out of the shop.

"What's it mean?" he said.

"It's the tubing they make the frame out of," I said, "and the way they weld it. Reynolds 531 double butted's the best." Actually, the next model up had an even better frame, but Turret didn't need to know. Besides, that sticker was a mark of quality, a guarantee. It was good enough that anyone who was into bikes would admire it. Even though he didn't know anything about bikes, he stuck his bottom lip out in respect.

I slipped my leg over the crossbar and wiggled myself square on the saddle. "See you next week," I said.

He nodded, then pointed to my feet. "Where's your bike clips?"

I looked down. The inside right leg of my jeans had dashes of grease. "I haven't got any."

"I bet your old mum'll have a word or two to say about that."

Beaky, I thought. Who asked you?

"I think Mr. Turret likes you," I said to Mum later as I polished my shoes by the back door. She was icing a cake with a piping gun.

"Don't be daft," she said, leaning closer to the cake and following the nozzle, concentrating on a tricky bit. "Mr. Turret's a gentleman."

"Is Dad a gentleman?"

"Your father's many things."

"Don't you wish he could paint and then you could go on your holidays together?"

She stood up, licked a drop of icing from her finger. "No."

"I do. Then we could all go." I threaded a lace back through the eyelets. "Don't you wish you'd married a painter?"

"People wish for all sorts of things, Matthew. That's life. I married your father."

I never could tell what Dad had against Turret. They were both independents, and Dad always went on about how independent traders were the salt of the earth, even though Turret was more like the salt of the sea. Even if mates was too strong a word for them, they should've at least been on speaking terms. Mutual respect. Maybe that was the problem: land versus sea. Not of the same pod. Still, even though I'd been getting our fish from Turret ever since I could remember, his reputation had soured in our house over the past few years. I put it down to money. Dad was always threatening to take down Turret's paintings in reception if he didn't settle up with us. Mum said that was rich coming from him. "Since when were you a stickler for settling up? You've got thousands in uncollected." Dad concentrated on slicing the top from his boiled egg and then covering it with salt.

Whether it was a new thing or just something I'd started to notice, I don't know, but it seemed that whenever the subject of Mum's holidays came up, Turret's name came up with it, as though the two were attached by strings – a pair of black balloons, tied at the tail. Like everything else in life, it made no sense, just another blip out of nowhere that suddenly became a fixture. Whatever the reason, Turret rubbed Dad up the wrong way. I made a note not to mention him, at least not when Dad was around. Why add more grief to the pot?

16

Instead of a dad, Lance had an Uncle Harry, who acted just as dimly as a dad, which made up for it. He worked in Yemen. The Romans called it Happy Arabia. Lawrence was *of* Arabia but not Arabian, though he probably rode one of their horses, which are called Arabians, but that's another story. Anyway, Harry had rented his house out and so had nowhere to stay when he came home. He was Lance's mum's big brother. They were as close as egg and chips. He helped her out on the cash front, and she gave him a room when he came home, which was I'm not sure how many times a year. All I know is that once in a while the words Harry and Yemen would fill Lance's sentences, and then he'd be telling me how he and Harry had been fishing off the pier at the weekend, or watching hang gliders at Devil's Dyke, neither of which I'd ever done with an uncle or dad. The next time I went round to Lance's for tea, there'd be Harry laughing on the phone at the kitchen table, or watching snooker on the sofa with his feet up. Sometimes he watched snooker while he was on the phone, sometimes he smoked while he ate. He also walked in his sleep.

Lance worshipped him.

That year it transpired that Harry would be home early November. Because he wouldn't be able to have Christmas at Christmastime, he'd celebrate it a month early, which was nice for everyone who knew him: they'd get two Christmases instead of one. As a diver who welded – or was it a welder who dived? – Harry had lots of money. He couldn't keep it to himself, both the money and having plenty of it. He also didn't have a wife or kids to spend it on, so he was stuck. Well, not that stuck. His answer was to throw his cash around as loudly as he did everything else. Because he couldn't get many luxuries in Yemen, he said, he liked to go to town when he was, well, in town. Lance said that the previous Christmas, which Harry had come home for, they had a turkey, a goose, a lump of ham, and six locally shot pheasants, plus all the add-ons you could think of. So much food they had to line it up on the kitchen counters like a cruise ship buffet. Just for the three of them, except for when they picked up Lance's nan from her nursing home and brought her round for some mince pies and cream, Mr. Kipling's, her favourite. Harry fell asleep watching *The Alamo*.

(We, on the other hand, had a duck, courtesy of Uncle Norm. It turned out to be one mouthful of orangey fat after another.)

This year, Harry wanted a fireworks/barbecue/disco for anyone who didn't fancy the annual neighbourhood Guy Fawkes bonfire on the common, which he said was always an embarrassment, even though it was one of the biggest every year and sort of famous. There was talk about who they could get to do the disco. They had to do some ringing around on account of it being late notice. Finally they got someone. When I asked Lance the name of it, he shrugged and said the first thing that popped into his head, which that time was "Barry Manilow's hankie." All he cared about was the fireworks.

The only time I liked Harry was when he gave Lance and I a fiver each for delivering a wad of party flyers. After hearing for the hundredth time exactly what fireworks Lance was going to buy when Harry took him to Goodacres, I said it made more sense if we split the flyers and delivered to different roads, then met for a smoke at the back of the cricket club when we were done. Lance agreed. We went off in different directions. I dumped half my flyers under some out-of-date cakes behind the Co-op. No one would want to go to Harry's stupid party anyway. Even I didn't want to go, and Lance was my best mate. Lorraine told me to bring Mum and Dad along, but they never went anywhere together, except to the cash and carry once every blue moon. (Dad liked to do the shopping himself, even though he complained about not having the time.) I decided not to tell them they'd been invited, and prayed that Lorraine didn't phone to invite them.

Which she didn't. She probably had enough to worry about getting everything the way Harry wanted it, down to the festive serviettes, and his favourite floury baps for the burgers.

At the party, I hung around wishing they'd let me join in, give me something to do. While Lance and Harry nailed the fireworks to the fence posts, which I also wasn't allowed to help with, I went inside to see Lorraine. But she'd brought her friend in to help with the food, especially the slicing and dicing. Between them they had it covered.

"Please let me help," I said.

"Relax, Matthew, you're our guest."

"No, please. There must be something I can do."

"Nope" she said, all jolly, like she was doing me a favour. She looked at her hands to make sure they hadn't been hurt.

"Can't I just—"

"Matthew! You're not at home now."

The table and countertops were crammed with plates of nibbles. I couldn't see any vol-au-vents, but there were lots of picky bits, mostly cheese – cheese-and-pineapple sticks, cheese straws, a jug of celery with different cheeses. Things needed moving outside. A tug in my stomach told me I wasn't being useful. I hated that feeling. It was my inner alarm bell telling me I'd passed the point where there was no excuse for not helping, for still waiting to be told.

"Don't make me do nothing," I said, going over to the sink. They were very busy. Maybe they were too shy to ask.

Lorraine veered around me like I was an unsteady statue that might topple at the slightest breath. She was doing the same headless quick-step as Mum (another thing they had in common). That meant that if I stood there long enough, she was in the sort of mood where she could turn on me and be a real cow. And then she was.

"Matthew," she said, wagging her investments at me, "would you mind being an absolute love and just *go away?*"

"It's not easy not being at home," I said, and left the kitchen.

Lance was too busy adding the finishing touches to the firework display to worry about the bonfire over the common. "But you love fires," I said. He didn't answer, so rather than hang around being useless I went out the front gate and over to the common, where the bonfire was about to start, and where lots of wholesome-looking families were rubbing their hands, adjusting their hats, shrugging their shoulders around inside their coats to stay warm. I had a smoke on a bench by the phone box and watched how the bonfire seemed to shrink as the crowd got bigger. Across the road, I noticed for the first time that there was a flat above the off licence. I'd gone in there often enough. Why hadn't I seen what was above it? Next to it was only the Co-op, which hardly stole your eye, so it wasn't that. The flat was small and cosy, sort of Dutch, and handy for your bread and milk. I'd bear it in mind when I was older.

The crowd was loud and annoying, so I left the fire before the flames took hold and swallowed the Guy, who was already slumped at the top in his wooden chair, and went back to Lance's. I was meant to be staying the night, which I'd already decided I wasn't going to do, so I had to come up with a good reason to leave the party, especially with having no lights on my bike, which the law always pulled you up for in Farthing. It was their one chance to push someone else's kids around and get paid for doing it. I'd wait for the right moment and then make up some old flannel about having to leave. Hopefully they'd all be too sloshed to care.

There was a van parked outside Lance's when I got back. Something about it rang a bell. When I got closer I saw the gold *Hot Magic Mobile Disco* logo down the side. It was Sid's brother's van. Hopefully he wouldn't recognise me. Still, I don't know what was weirder that night, seeing the flat above the off licence for the first time or having Gary turn up to do the disco. Bet your life Harry's face sank when he opened the front door and saw Gary on the doorstep saying he was the entertainment for the night. Harry might've worked in Yemen, but it didn't mean he liked them, any of them. And it definitely didn't mean he would've wanted them choosing his music. God knows what sort of jangly din they listened to.

As the bonfire on the common got higher and brighter, you could see its shadow dancing in the trees around it. Apparently Harry wasn't so unpopular after all. There must've been fifty people in the garden by the time Lorraine called out to him that the charcoal had died down enough to start grilling. Harry put on the apron she handed him – a glow-in-the-dark skeleton. Knowing Harry, you'd expect him to wear one of those saucy French maid jobs with stockings and suspenders, and then cavort around like a ponce. The skeleton was probably Lorraine's choice. It looked spooky, but it was a better choice than anything Harry might've chosen.

After not scaring the life out of people as The Hilarious Fluorescent Skeleton, he got on with the barbecue, loading the grill with burgers and sausages. That's as far as he went. He waved smoke from his eyes and handed the tongs to Lorraine's helper, even though I told him I knew all about cooking and that I was more than happy to take charge. "Kids can't cook," he said, out of the side of his mouth, so that no one else heard. If I'd had a garden fork in my hand, I'd've rammed the prongs through his foot.

Gary must've seen Harry's apron, 'cause the next tune he put on was "Thriller." Harry naturally took the song as his theme tune and moved out to the middle of the garden to show everyone what he could do. Expecting us to follow his lead, he picked up the rhythm and ran with it. Well, he did something with it. After all, wasn't it the host's job to take the lead? And weren't parties for dancing? His belly had come out for the night, and from the side his skeleton looked blobby, like one half of a pear.

"Don't make me look daft at me own do," he shouted, trying to get people to join his fun. Then he decided to be really funny by doing a full-frontal skeleton belly dance to Vincent Price's voice-over.

Gradually people joined in, and it wasn't long before the patch of grass in front of the left speaker was full of people jigging about with their drinks. By then I'd gone to the table for a burger and a sausage in a bun. Before loading my plate, I slid on a splat of potato salad or coleslaw. I bent down to wipe my shoe with some napkins. While I was down there I picked up a load of crisps, bits of burger, and scooped up some pasta salad with a paper plate. Still annoyed about the barbecue, I felt a bit better for being useful. During that time we'd had "Dancing Queen," "Karma Chameleon," "Una Paloma Blanca," and then a song that sounded like a wheelchair crashing down the stairs in a block of flats. Harry lost his rhythm, got caught up in his feet. He'd led everyone in the dance and now didn't know where it was going. Someone had a word with Gary, who seemed hurt by the complaint. He got his own back by playing "The Birdie Song," which everyone danced to, except Harry. After all, you couldn't go making a fool of yourself to just anything. You had to draw a line somewhere.

Harry announced that it was time for fireworks.

"Where's my boy?" he called, looking around for Lance, who was beside me, crunching a handful of Polos to cover the smell of fags. He stuck his hand up. "Over here."

"There's sparklers for everyone," Lorraine said. She was lighting some square red candles on the buffet table. The sparklers were standing in a jug. "Just mind where you wave them."

People drifted to the table as though they'd just snapped out of hypnosis.

"You wait," Lance said. "It's gonna be mental."

"Can I help?" I said.

"No."

"Why won't you lot let me do anything!" I said.

Rockets went off. Roman candles flared. Kids nearly poked each others' eyes out with sparklers. Lance ducked around, following Harry's instructions. The idea seemed to be to set off many fireworks at once, to turn the sky over their house into a kaleidoscope. What went through my mind as my eyes slid in and out of focus the longer I looked up at the sky, was that a bag of sugar and a bag of weedkiller would've been a lot more value for money than all the fireworks in Goodacres.

Gary cranked the volume and put on an oldie but goldie – "Devil Gate Drive" by Suzi Quatro, which I'd heard once when I was four. The dancing picked up, the sky popped and banged. For a split second, I almost wished I could dance. About a minute after that, when everyone had their eyes on the sky to see Harry's next stunning effect, the Catherine wheel blew up in Lance's face.

No thanks to Harry, who told Lance to re-light the touch-paper when it didn't catch. Lorraine was dancing with her hands in her shoes when it happened. I was standing about ten feet away, not really thinking how stupid Lance was to try lighting the firework again. No alarm bells went off when he bent towards it to make sure the touch-paper had caught. No flashing lights. It was just something he was doing. Besides, disasters like that only happened in the papers, or on the evening news, in parts of the world you hadn't heard of and/or couldn't pronounce. They didn't happen down our way. And they definitely didn't happen to your best mate.

His face was barely a foot from the firework when it went off. No wonder he screamed his way around the garden as though the grass was on fire. His hands were shaking in front of his face.

There was probably lots of other screaming, but all I remember was how silent everything went, especially the fireworks in the sky, like the world had been unplugged. I saw Lorraine's face looking like it was screaming, which was so ugly with no sound, just a gaping mouth and eyes so wide they might never be normal. Not even Harry looked the same. He actually looked better, his belly in, his body not slumped, his eyes tracking Lance's course around the garden. I half expected him to pull out a stopwatch.

I didn't move. It seemed better to wait for things to become whatever they'd become when everything died down.

Then the sound came back on. Suzi Quatro was still playing. (After the accident, I ordered the single from W H Smith's to remember the old Lance by. I got it in picture cover.) There was actual screaming again. Harry had caught up with Lance. Lorraine came steaming in and shoved Harry away. Her face was uglier with sound. Her hands didn't know what to do with Lance, and his hands didn't know what to do with himself. All those hands being useless.

I didn't go to the hospital in the ambulance. Either no one thought I'd want to, or they were too worried about getting in there themselves. Ambulances aren't made for taking passengers. They're not buses. You can't hold your hand out and catch one. I think it was just Harry and Lorraine who went in it. There was so much fuss that my hearing shut down again. I couldn't look. My heart curled up at the edges, like in the first stage of grilling. My chest felt crisp.

After the party stopped, I went over to see Gary.

"Need any help packing up?"

"Did you see what happened?" he said. "I missed it."

"He got a firework in the face," I said. "The kid. He's my best mate."

He sucked air through his teeth to let me know that he knew how painful something like that probably was.

Then I said, "My dad taught me how to coil a hose round my elbow." I bent my arm vertical, elbow down, palm up. "I could do the lights if you want."

I don't know why that was so confusing to him, but he seemed unsure how to take it.

"I'll just…let me get organised," he said. "I'll give you a shout."

He pulled the leads out of the speakers. I stood and watched to see if he was going to coil them around his hand and elbow. I could save him a lot of time. I waited in case he needed me. He was doing things quickly, like he wasn't comfortable. Neither was I. The ambulance had taken all the fun away. All the guests had gone. Even Harry, the dancing skeleton, whose glowing form filled my eyes when I stared into the dark.

17

On my ride to the hospital, I didn't even think about having no bike
lights, about getting pulled over by some small-minded copper with
nothing better to do. I pumped my knees like a maniac, till my feet
slid from the pedals. The wind seemed to come towards me no matter which way I went, and although the roads to the hospital were flat,
my thighs were burning when I reached Casualty. I was sure I'd col-
lapse if I got off my bike. It took me a while to brave it.

I was in the right place. Half the town had collapsed, in one way or
another, for the time being. It felt odd to be the only one with nothing wrong with him.

"My friend just came in here," I said to the nurse at the check-in window. "Lance Cornish. He's burnt."

The nurse looked at the other nurse. Something got said without
words. They both nodded in agreement.

"They're treating him now," said the nurse in the window.

"Is it serious?" I said.

"Are you his brother?"

"Sort of." Then I said, "Yeah. I just got here on my bike. They
wouldn't let me in the ambulance. You should've seen the wind. My
legs are killing me."

"Why don't you take a seat and catch your breath?" she said. "I'll
see what I can do."

"But I've got to see him. He was running everywhere. Like this." I
put my hands to my face. Instead of running around the room like
Lance had done around the garden, I ran in a tiny circle. More of a
slow spin.

"Take a seat," she said. "I'll tell someone you're here."

I sat in one of the plastic Ryvita chairs and looked around the busy
waiting area. People clutched their arms or ribs or jaws, wherever the
pain was killing them. One girl had her head tipped back to stop her
nose from gushing. Across from me were a mum and three kids, one
of who had a clump of gauze stuck to his ear and his head wrapped
in a bandage, up and under his chin, war-style. You could tell he was

more worried about looking a prat than about how much his ear hurt. To kill some time, I counted how many people were visibly maimed and how many weren't. The tally was ten visible to seven not, but the numbers kept changing, plus you had to take into account how many were family and friends, not victims, which made the whole exercise crap. As far as types of injuries went, leg trouble was big, as usual – lots of limping and crutches. Even the young fell down in our town. Either that or they got hit by things. People might've laughed at Farthing for being slow and sleepy, but you could get just as hurt there as in any town.

Somewhere in the middle of all that emergency noise, I crashed out. It was either that or go mad. I didn't sleep for long, but I had a good dream while I was out. I was on stage at the London Palladium in front of a sold-out crowd, herding sheep. I had a crook and everything. The problem was the sheep kept dropping off the stage, straight into the orchestra pit. Not only was I struggling to keep them away from the edge, I kept having to calm the band members, who weren't at all happy. At the same time, I had to talk them into handing back the sheep that had fallen. As if that wasn't enough, the stage manager and other staff were on the sidelines yelling for me to get my fucking sheep off the stage so that Liberace could come on.

My shoulder was being rocked. I awoke to Lorraine's teary, bloodshot eyes peering into mine. She was crouching. She rested her investments on my arms. She looked like a confused member of the Palladium audience who'd just stepped out of my dream.

"What happened?" I said.

"It's all right, Matthew. He's in good hands."

"What hands? Where?"

"They're arranging for him to go to another hospital, in Chichester. They specialise in this sort of thing."

"I've got to see him," I said. I stood up.

Lorraine stood up too. "I'm afraid no one's allowed to see him for the time being. They need to keep him away from people because of the high risk of infection. I promise I'll take you to see him just as soon as they give the all clear." She stroked my hair, but it didn't mean anything.

I didn't know what to say so I started crying. And once I started, it grew in no time to a big, embarrassing, blubbery cry, with a power supply of its own. Lorraine held me to her chest. That didn't matter either; she was only being nice, only doing what anyone with half a heart would. All I remember is the tickle of tears rolling down my cheeks and onto her rough white shirt, a Levi's, which was probably Harry's – she usually wore softer things than that. Her shirt was hot from my breathing, and now the left pocket and the red tab were wet. I pulled away for air. She handed me tissues. I'd started her off too. Together we blew our noses and didn't even try to talk with our useless, croaky throats.

When we were back to normal, I wadded my tissues and asked Lorraine if she was going to the new hospital. She said she was. "What about Harry?" I said. She said that he would be going too. "You shouldn't let him," I said. "It was his fault. If he hadn't made Lance go back to the firework, we wouldn't be here now. I'll kill him when I see him."

"Accidents happen," she said. "Fireworks are dangerous. That's the risk we take."

"No it's not. That's the risk Harry made Lance take for no reason, except that he was too busy being a wanker to do it himself." Things were rushing inside me. "He's a fat pig and I hate him. And he's a welder. He should've known."

"Grown-ups make mistakes, the same as anyone," she said.

"Grown-ups ruin everything," I said. "They should be banned."

She said I was overly emotional and that I needed to get some sleep. Did I want to sleep at their house or go home? I told her not to worry about me, that I'd make my own way home on my bike. When I said that, she looked at me suspiciously, like she didn't trust me to be by myself.

"Are you sure you're all right?" she said. "You're not going to do anything silly, are you?"

"No," I said, looking around for a bin to throw my tissues in. "I'll leave that to Harry."

When I came down for breakfast later that morning, after not sleeping a wink, Mum was busy making individual cottage pies in little oval clay dishes, ready for freezing. The kitchen smelled of celery, carrots, and mince. The back half of it, by the cooker and window, was full of steam. For a second I felt like an extra in *The Railway Children*.

Mum tasted a bit of carrot to see if it was done.

"I thought you were going to phone to say what time you'd be back," she said. "They drop you off?"

I tried to tell her the whole story, but her cooking was at the crucial stage so she worked and listened, took the potatoes off the boil and drained the water, disappearing in a cloud of steam at the sink. By the time I got to the accident she'd added butter and milk to the potatoes and was mashing them in the pot. She sort of was listening and wasn't. Could I get the pepper? I saw it on the counter by the fridge and gave it to her. She tapped it into the spuds. "What firework was it?" she said.

"Who cares what firework?" I said. "It burnt his face. He's in hospital."

"I told you before he was no good."

"It wasn't his fault. That's what I'm trying to tell you."

"Kids," she said. "Eyes in the back of your head." She banged the masher on the side of the saucepan and took the spuds to the table, where her little dishes were set out. "He's old enough to know better."

"That's what I'm saying! It was his uncle's fault."

"Go back to a firework once it's been lit..." Her mumbling trailed off as she dolloped mash into the first little dish of meat.

I gave up. When she was in cooking mode, there was no point trying to tell her anything. She wouldn't hear if I told her she'd won a boob job.

It was too busy to have my breakfast, so I went back upstairs, wondering who else I could tell about what had happened. The only person I could think of was Vi, but she was very anti us at that time. Her rift with Mum was still going. Not that she had anything against me, mind. But it always paid to be careful. Not that any of us ever were.

18

On our trips to market, my half-asleep mind kept churning over the business with Lance, the new Lance, the Lance I didn't recognise, in more ways than one. He was so stupid. Only someone that stupid would've done whatever his Uncle Harry said, when anyone with a crumb of sense could see that Harry was an utter twat. If Lance hadn't been such a soft-centred weed, he'd have told Harry to re-light the touch-paper himself. Harry might not have been his official dad, but he proved he deserved the title by acting as dumbly as one. But another part of me knew that Lance couldn't help it. He needed an Uncle Harry, or an Uncle Brian, or an Uncle Frank. An Uncle Anyone. It wasn't his fault he'd drawn the short straw.

Even though some of his old ways were annoying, we'd known each other so long that I was used to him. I didn't think twice about sticking up for him after his accident, even though he was happy enough fighting his own battles. But then after the accident, he went soft and wimpy, like in his mind he wasn't worth sticking up for. Soon everything was different. It wasn't only his world that had changed. Mine had too. The more angry and miserable he got, the more those changes worked on me. I hated seeing him with his skin-quilt face, fiddling with his mask, avoiding going places. He'd even stopped going to the shops. The only reason he kept going to school was because Lorraine wouldn't let him mope around the house feeling sorry for himself. So he moped around me at school. And even though we'd had plenty of ups and downs, I'd've given anything to be racing over parked cars with him at night the way we used to. That had been our favourite game. He'd take one side of the street, me the other. After a three-two-one, we'd race to the other end by running over every boot, roof, and bonnet. First person to touch the ground was the loser. One time he dislocated his shoulder when he slid on a wet bonnet. He was lucky he came away with just that. He could've easily landed head first on the road. What I'm saying is that we fitted each other. We didn't have to pretend we weren't weird. But since the accident he'd got weirder, in an ugly way.

Not long after that, Lorraine phoned to say he wouldn't be going to the Globetrotters. I thought I was hearing things. Even if he had to hop all the way from Land's End, he wouldn't have missed them. I said I didn't believe it.

"He's just not ready to go out in public yet," she said in the same drippy voice she always used to over-explain the obvious, like what would happen if we went to the rec without our coats and it started to rain, which it might, there was no way of knowing, seeing as we lived in the grip of two weather systems. And then we'd get wet when there was no need to. Genius. Her worried whine made me feel like I was three and a quarter.

"But he goes to school easy enough," I said.

"I know," she said, "but I'm afraid that if he's in a crowd it might trigger an attack."

"He won't attack anyone. I'll make sure."

"Not *attack* attack. I mean his *asthma*." Why she whispered asthma I don't know. They didn't have another phone for him to listen in on. And if she was worried that he might hear her, why didn't she wait till he was at school and phone Mum?

"That's a lie," I said. "He's never had an asthma attack. He hasn't got asthma."

"He had it as a child, Matthew. It can flare up any time."

"What's his face got to do with asthma?"

"We need to be careful."

"We who?" I said. There was hot liquid in my throat. I tried swallowing it, but it wouldn't go. "You're not helping him," I said, my voice a raspy burn. "You might think you are but you're not."

"I just want him to be as comfortable as he can be, in the circumstances."

"You don't know how mad he is on the Globetrotters."

"I do know, Matthew." Even though she switched to her sad voice, I could tell she wasn't listening, at least not so she'd have a rethink and maybe change her mind. "Look," she said, "I don't think we're going to see eye to eye on this, but trust me. I'm doing what's best for Lance. You do understand that, don't you?"

Patronising cow.

"It won't work," I said, "trying to run his life. It's not fair."

"That's not very nice, Matthew."

"You don't need to tell me that."

The last thing she said was that she'd like to take me to the Globe-trotters herself, except it wouldn't go down too well with Lance.

"He wouldn't have to know," I said. She said of course he would. And then I said, "We're best mates. He'd understand."

She thought he probably wouldn't. "What about your mum or dad?" she said. "Wouldn't one of them take you?"

I told her that was the unfunniest joke in years. Then she said that if I found someone else who wanted to go she'd give me Lance's ticket for nothing, to make up for the disappointment. I thought, Don't talk to me about disappointment. Talk to Lance.

19

I kept my holiday brochures in a secret compartment in my chest of drawers. Under the bottom drawer was a removable shelf that slid into a couple of grooves. If you took the drawer and then the shelf out, there was a shallow space – a couple of inches at most – the full length and width of the unit, in which I hid things, like Lance's lockknife, which he let me keep because his Uncle Daz had given him a much better flick-knife, which didn't exactly flick but shot out the end when you pushed a button and then shot in again. Really it was a tortoise knife, but no one called it that. I also hid my fags in the cubbyhole, and anything I'd nicked, like my Pritt sticks. Oh, and when I wasn't wearing them, Mum's tights, which held me together. At least that way she was always close.

After school was the best time to go to Thomas Cook. If I stuck to a couple of brochures at a time, I could slip them in my folder without Dad seeing their covers when I went to the shop. Depending on his mood, I sometimes put my bag in the shop's toilet or behind the bin, where it wouldn't catch his eye. Not that he went through my things for no reason; you just never knew with him. I might be sitting at his desk logging payments in the ledger while he sorted through old papers, and then out of the blue he'd say, "What rubbish are they teaching you now?" and he'd hand me my bag and expect me to talk him through whatever I'd written in my exercise books, careful to skip past my doodles of tits and minge – bird wings with nipple dots over a hairy V. (Lance taught me how to do them. He left his Vs bald.) Most of the time, Dad couldn't have cared less what I'd been learning as long as I listened to him.

The Thomas Cook uniforms made you think you'd just boarded a plane rather than stepped in off the High Street. Zap! There you were, on holiday. They had exchange rates and package deals in the window. Disneyworld specials. Stunning Madeira. A week's self-catering on Kos. Every time I went in there I smiled at whichever air hostess look-alike was at the desk closest to the brochure stand, and then went about my business, picking brochures with the sort of faces you never saw by the seaside, unless some Russian Orthodox church group came down from Chiswick for the day on a charter coach. American and European brochures were boring, unless you chanced upon a flamenco dancer or a Romanian gypsy, which wasn't often. The best you could hope for was an across-the-square shot of a shawled woman holding a knackered basket of flowers. Lost between the pages of all the Hotel Eurekas might be a stray photo of a peasant taking a quick leak behind a lemon tree. But that was about it.

It was Lance who got me thinking about Identikit pictures, the ones the police put together when they chased criminals. I loved the idea of making people exactly how you wanted them. That way, they'd only ever change if you let them, unlike Lance, whose new face was fast turning him into someone I didn't know, and didn't want to know. Life had been empty since the accident. The old Lance had gone away. I needed something to replace him.

Mum always had a stack of Good Housekeeping and Woman's Own lying about the place, plus there'd be the newspaper and the Radio Times, some of which had better photos than others. Source-wise, second to Thomas Cook was the school library. At lunchtimes I'd leaf through Amateur Photographer, slicing out portraits, cutting them close to the spine to cover my tracks. National Geographic was a godsend, but the library only stocked it once in a while, or they got it three months in a row and then stopped. I don't know who else ever looked at it, or why they got it at all. But that was the place for flamenco and belly-dancers, and gypsies. Eskimos too. Kalahari tribesmen. Indian brides. But not all of them were close-ups.

In order to mix and match eyes, chins, noses, etc., I had to find the same-sized features in different photos, which was virtually impossible. I spent long evenings going through newspapers and magazines, carving out promising new portraits on my cutting board, trying to remember ones I'd already seen to match with any new ones I came across. I decided there needed to be a law made, Standardised Portraits, like the strips of photographs from passport booths, so that everyone's eyes and nose would be of identical proportions, making them easier to cut and paste. If they could standardise passports, why not do the same with all portrait photos? It made no sense. Still, there wasn't a law, and no likelihood of getting one made, so I adapted.

Hair, ears, lips, dimples – you name it, I had a big yellow envelope for it, all of which were stored in an empty satsuma crate that lived at the bottom of the wardrobe. The vanilla-and-caramel swirl on my carpet was identical to the pattern of my favourite ice cream, which was great except that I couldn't keep track of my cuttings. Once I'd tipped my features from their envelopes, they got lost in the swirl, especially the black-and-white ones. So I spread a white bed sheet from the airing cupboard over the floor before each session. Cutting board beside me, I'd set about carefully carving my saved features so they'd fit the new face I was making. That way, the new face would look as real as any of the donor originals.

I started creating supermodels to my own personal spec. Not that I didn't fancy the real ones. I just wanted to make my own.

Which was where my scrapbooks came in. To begin with, I couldn't get the hang of matching one feature with another. The first thing I'd set out on the page were the eyes. For my first umpteen tries I glued my chosen features straight into the scrapbook before making sure I'd found any others to match. But then just when I thought I'd found, say, the eyes, mouth, and ears – ears helped me frame a face, helped me see where it was heading – I'd lose my rag sifting through piles of other features trying to create what I saw in my mind. I filled six scrapbooks that first month. All of my pocket money went on buying them. Pritt sticks were best for gluing the features in, and were easy to pinch. I got through a ton of those too. If I hadn't gotten the photos for free, I'd never have been able to keep going. But once I started, there was no turning back.

The off season in our house was like a five-hour documentary of Hull, in German. For the bleakest half of each year I was tortured by the ticking of clocks. It never dawned on anything to happen. Ordinarily, I would've happily swapped places with the kid in *The Shining*. But for the first time in my life, that winter gave me all the time in the world to master my hobby. I had until Easter, which was when trade started up again, even though the weather was usually naff, and the sea breeze was so strong it would blow you halfway up the Downs. But being the first Bank Holiday weekend of the year, it gave the punters a reason to come out of hibernation, to blow off their cobwebs with a dose of sea air. Until they started knocking at our door, I could hide upstairs and bury myself in my creations. I'd have enough time to make a whole new world, if I wanted.

Seeing as our school was all boys, the closest I ever got to girls was during breakfast or dinner at home during the peak season, and even then I'd be serving and wasn't allowed to talk, not unless they wanted beans instead of tomatoes, or chips instead of mash. Or if one of them choked on a fish bone. Otherwise, silence. I'd see guests' daughters drift through the house and cadge glimpses when they weren't looking, secretly plotting to raid their drawers the next time they were out. Apart from that, girls existed only at a distance, through our shop window, in magazines, or on the beach. All a world away.

Except for Zoë Trimble and Monica Sprake, of course, who I saw in the window of Bonetti's every Saturday sharing a Knickerbocker Glory. Bonetti's was on the other side of the road from our greengrocer's, a couple of doors down. When I came out to stock the front display, Zoë and Monica would start hammering on the café window. They'd be giggling when I looked over. Sooner or later, Zoë would stick her head in the shop door. "I like the look of your cucumbers," she'd say, or, "Could you spare two poor girls a banana?" The same joke every week. It took nothing to make me blush, which was all they were after. As soon as they'd succeeded, they'd go off somewhere else, leaving their saucy cackling behind.

All anyone talked about at school was girls or sports, which amounted to the same thing. What kept me wondering about Zoë and Monica wasn't anything they actually did or said – they always livened up a dull Saturday, so I never minded their ribbing – but more the stories I heard about them in the playground, where much uglier kids than me bragged about shagging some make-believe bird in the shower, or about getting their ends away under the pier, which was where I used to find all the used Durex wrappers. I hated that they made me think twice. If it wasn't them who'd put them there, how else could they know about the pier?

"I had three fingers up Zoë at the pictures," said Saul Quek.

"Monny let me rub her clit with a KitKat," said Troy Mallow.

"Zoë sucked me off in the Wimpy," said Orson Pike.

How everyone knew Zoë and Monica was beyond me. Other girls put it about more than they did. They weren't half as bad as some of the slappers you'd see waiting at the gates after school, the same way our lot waited outside Millais. Zoë and Monica were all right. And besides, the only person likely to get within a pier's length of sucking Orson off was Orson, or his dog, which was a dachshund, and loyal enough to do it. But probably not in the Wimpy.

20

Tuesday's were definitely French. My school might've been all boys, but in the evenings it changed from a crap comprehensive to an award-winning community school, on a mission to teach the town how to make doilies and fudge. There were classes in everything: pottery, guitar making, metalwork; French, basket weaving, maths. You could learn climbing on the purpose-built wall up the side of the gym that looked like a bunch of giant concrete dominos stacked end to end. You could learn to paint or sing. Seeing as she already painted, and had nothing much to sing about, Mum did French.

They met in a hut. If the school had used even a portion of the evening class profits to buy equipment that had been invented even a year after the Ark, we might've had such things as language labs. But as the French classrooms were no different to the geography or economics ones, except for whatever posters or charts or class projects had been Blu-Tacked to the walls, it made no difference where the class met as long as it had a teacher, which it did, Miss Zostic, who was from somewhere foreign, but not France.

The huts were at the back of the school and looked out onto the lower field, the opposite side to the one that rubbed shoulders with Old Francis's land. This would have made spying a lot easier had Mum's group met in one of the normal classrooms, say my old tutor room in Tyler, which was on the ground floor at the back, and perfect. But the huts were too high to see in to from the field unless you were in a cherry picker or on stilts. So during school time I did some detective work. This entailed standing different distances away from the hut and seeing how high I'd need to jump to be able to see inside. The answer was, not high enough. I worked on alternatives. Space hoppers and pogo sticks were out. What about boring a peephole in the floor? But then I thought of Mum and her class going through their *écoutez et répétez* drill while I grunted and shuffled beneath them.

There was no way around it. I'd have to get closer.

It was dark by the time the class started at half seven. I'd never seen so many cars at school. The playgrounds, which doubled as car parks, were both full. Jenkins Lane ran along the front of the school and was packed on both sides. So that's where everyone went at night. Judging by the turn-out, Farthing must've been the cleverest town around. Before long we'd have someone on *Mastermind*.

The conditions couldn't have been worse. The night was wet, the field soft and trudgy. Crossing it from the far end was like riding with my brakes on. In no time my legs were dead. I got off and pushed. The huts stood in a line. All were lit. They cast a thick band of light across the grass. From a safe dark distance, I could only make out a bright rectangle with Miss Zostic at one end of it, in front of the blackboard, pushing up her sleeves, and addressing, from what I could make out, an empty room.

I wheeled my bike wide of the light and came at the hut from the blind side. After leaning my bike against the hut, I ducked around the front to the main entrance, where the steps were. But that was no better: the hut had an outside light, and the steps were as bright as the grass at the back. Instead of standing on the steps and looking in, I crouched against the hut at the low corner of the window, used the handrail as a lever, and pulled myself high enough till I was eye level with the window.

There were a dozen or more in the class, some young, some old. Mostly women. Mum was in the second row, chin up, straight as a nail, like she was posing for a portrait. The seats on either side of her were empty. It was obvious one of them was Turret's. Where was he? I looked to see if he was sitting at the back. Maybe they'd fallen out. Maybe they were having a difficult time, giving each other some space. That's how it was in our class: if you hated someone, you moved to another chair. It wasn't hard.

Miss Zostic crossed that floor like Nijinsky. The racehorse.

The hut door burst open. She was standing over me on the steps.

"Would you mind explaining yourself?"

"What?"

I let go of the rail and dropped to the ground.

"What you're doing out here. There are people in here trying to learn."

"It's my mum," I said, looking up at her. "I've got a message."

"And who is your mother?"

I told her. She held the door open. "In," she said.

"No, it's all right. I'll wait out here."

"Jean?" she called into the main room. "In, in." She was determined to get me inside, but I wasn't going. The trouble was, now that she'd announced me, I couldn't run and pretend later when Mum quizzed me that I'd never been there, the way Lance would. I was a pretty good liar, but not a patch on him. Then and there, for the only time in my life, I wished I was him.

"What are you doing?" said Mum.

"He has a message," said Miss Zostic.

"Oh?" Mum looked worried. "What's wrong?"

I didn't know what to say. There wasn't anything to say. But there had to be something.

I said, "Is *he* in there?"

Mum looked at Miss Zostic. Miss Zostic looked at Mum.

"He who?" said Mum.

"You know."

"Matthew, I haven't got time for games. Either tell me what you're talking about or go home."

"Turret."

"For God's sake, Matthew. What's this about?"

I jumped up for a peek into the classroom. Several students had turned around to see what was going on. I saw most of them clearly. None were remotely like Turret. He must've had a cold. Not done his homework. Any other night...

"This not fair on the others," said Miss Zostic to Mum. "Maybe you go now and come back next week?"

"Oh no," said Mum. "I'm staying right here." Then she told me to get home before she phoned Dad and told him what a nuisance I'd made of myself. She turned, as if heading inside. I stepped down and stood on the path.

"Wait till Dad finds out," I shouted, then went and got my bike.

This time I rode from one end of the bright strip of grass to the other, as though on a prison break, my hands tight on the grips in case the mud locked my wheels and sent me flying. As I sped from the range of the floodlights, I didn't feel even the slightest bit like Steve McQueen.

21

Dad said it would've been fair enough if the Raffertys had gone back to Ireland to see their relatives, but no, they'd taken their three daughters to Torremolinos on a fortnight package. They hadn't said a word about squaring up with us before they went, just gave Dad a date when they'd be back. He was livid, told me to put two OVERDUE stamps on their bill, top and bottom, before I posted it. For three whole days he was narked. I couldn't put a foot right. So I just kept quiet and did whatever he said, which I'd had plenty of training in. Even then he found reasons to pull me up: my shoes needed polishing, or I'd let my shirt collar get tucked up in my V-neck. He tugged me about, put whatever he didn't like straight, unless it was my shoes, which he made me polish and leave on the doormat before I went to bed.

Not that I didn't side with him on the Raffertys. I might've been sick to death of hearing about how every holiday-maker boarding a plane for some exotic destination amounted to another nail in our coffin, but we were a team. I knew what it did to him. Life wasn't fair. It wasn't fair to him, to me, and most of all to Lance, who to all intents and purposes was fucked. The minute that Catherine wheel went off in his face, both our worlds changed. The few times I went to see him at the hospital were horrible. At first he was wrapped in bandages to keep any infections out. That was bad enough. But when they decided it was time for the skin to get some air in order to start healing, it was much, much worse. He had no eyelids. He was like Simon the Welsh bloke on *Wogan*, who'd been burnt to a crisp in the Falkland's. Except that Lance wasn't a war hero, and he wasn't on the telly. He was just a burnt kid in a bed.

I did a lot of quiet crying in my own bed, without telling Mum or Dad. I didn't want to have to listen to their empty wisdom, like they knew anything about anything. 'It'll work out for the best' or 'Everything happens for a reason' or 'You never know what He's got in mind for us.' It was a bit late for God to be waving his magic hand. Why hadn't it come down to light the touch-paper that night instead of leaving it to Lance? I knew that if anyone said another wise word about Lance, I'd flip. Which meant there was no one to talk to about him, or about how I was feeling about him. Lorraine was probably in a basket. If I didn't soon do something to take me out of my life, I'd be joining her.

Dad's customers had no idea what an opportunity they'd handed me. On top of everything to do with Life After Lance, I was bored of breaking into guests' rooms. I was convinced that if a bog-standard kid like me had plenty of secrets, other people must have them too. I needed to get out in the world and find them. At the same time, I'd make Dad's customers pay for shafting us. And while I was at it, they'd pay for Lance, too.

One night after Mum had gone out, I found Dad in the kitchen, kneeling behind the fridge, which he'd pulled out almost to the middle. The flex was taut. He was replacing some rotten bits of lino and gluing down edges. (He liked edges: sealing them, painting them, scrubbing them...) I told him I was off to the library to research my project. Not knowing what project I was talking about, he didn't say anything, except don't be late. So that he wouldn't ask what I was doing with his masking tape and gardening gloves, I went out the front door, left them on the doorstep, then got my bike from the back. It was a strange sight through the kitchen window. Everything was washed up and put away, in its usual order, except for the fridge. It threw the whole room out, divided it into new chunks of big and small, fat and narrow, square and sloped. All those rooms within a room. Topping it all off was Dad, arse-up behind the fridge, half hidden.

The fair was in town for its yearly visit. After rounding the corner by the bus station, I saw its miniature city of lights flashing in the distance beside the pier, twined as always around every ride, kiosk, and railing. Just the sight of the Big Wheel was enough to put the wind up me. Every year I'd queue to ride it, take my place and shuffle forward as the queue grew behind me, and watch kids half my age rush aboard without a care. But every year, no matter how much I tried convincing myself, I'd bottle out at the ticket gate, leaving Lance to go on his own. He didn't care; all he wanted to do was get to the top and swing the car till he was upside down. Hating myself for being a chicken, I wandered off till the ride was over and waited for Lance, who always moaned about the ride being too short or too slow. But I couldn't get away quick enough.

As I reached the fair, the blur of noise settled into solid, distinct sounds – The Teardrop Explodes over the PA; robot voices from the arcades; generator drone – just as the distant moving shapes became real kids and adults, flocking from all over. A dad, faced by his pleading daughters, dug in his pockets for change. Two skinheads in matching green Harrington's shared a fag by the railings. One was shouting at a group of girls on the Merry Mixer while his mate kicked a litter-bin. They had matching bulges in the backs of their heads. Maybe that's why they were mates: they shared the same buckled brain.

A mile later I ditched my bike in the hedge down the street from the Raffertys'. By then it was dark, with a half-drawn curtain of cloud in the sky, covering the moon. I walked head down, studying the pavement, only looking up to check house numbers. The houses were dull and identical: brick on the first floor, black wood on the second; four blocks of white plastic windows, two up two down. Twice I passed the Raffertys' door before finally ducking up the drive, then through the tall wooden gate to the back.

I slid my strip of plastic up between the door and frame till I caught the latch. But when the strip slipped the latch and freed the lock, the door still wouldn't budge. It was deadlocked. No amount of jabbing away would help. In the neighbouring house, a woman was at her kitchen sink. Watching from beyond the light of her kitchen, knowing that she could stare straight at me without seeing me, was unlike anything I'd felt in any of the rooms I'd sneaked into at home. Maybe it had to do with being out in the night and hearing it alive around me – it was faint, but I could still make out the sounds of the fair – without needing to be a part of it, without getting involved, the same way I'd felt round Lance's that day with the weedkiller. That might've been it: the relief of not having to join in with things you'd give your right arm to avoid. That's what mums and dads did, interrupted your happiness by taking you with them to places you knew you'd hate, like choosing curtain fabric in a department store, or shopping for table lamps, or trying to decide on a set of patio chairs. Why would you go in those places by choice? They should all be fitted with suicide rooms.

I stuck three strips of gaffer tape along the bottom of the kitchen window then taped a big cross from corner to corner in case the whole pane gave in, a trick I'd practiced on a greenhouse up the allotments. It had worked perfectly there, after a few goes. To make sure no chunks of glass fell and smashed, I plastered the rest of the window. For the first few goes at the allotment I'd been tight with the tape. Glass went everywhere. By the time I finished with the Raffertys' window, you couldn't see anything but tape.

When the light went out in the neighbour's kitchen, I pulled on the gloves and punched the bottom of the window as fast as I could. The trick worked; none of the glass smashed. I slipped my hand through and lifted the latch. My foot caught a plant on the windowsill as I pulled myself through. It fell into the sink. The pot was plastic, but the saucer it had been sitting on wasn't. Scrambling at the noise, I hit the floor shoulder first, one leg trailing, like a dog had it. When I got up and checked the side window, the neighbour's house was still dark. No one had heard.

High swivel stools lined the breakfast bar. Walking through, I imagined the Raffertys first thing in the morning, sharing their plans for the day between gulps of cereal, the daughters giggling, shoving each other off their stools. Imagine having a sister? Opposite the door into the front room stood a tall cabinet stuffed with trophies and cups. It was too dark to read what they were for. My hand found a big wooden ball on the top of the stair post. I wondered how many swings of a bat it would take to knock it for six. If the Raffertys had a son, he was bound to be a genius at some sport or other – cricket, rugby, golf. Even more cups to cram on the shelves.

The only light on the landing came from the last room on the left. Upon entering, a weak strip of yellow cast by a streetlight picked out posters of Spandau Ballet and Culture Club, and a framed picture of the Three Little Pigs, whose heads had been replaced by those of three girls. When I looked closer, I saw names under each: Megan, Katrina, and Shannon, from left to right.

In the framed photographs on the dressing table stood a smiling family of five, arms around each other at some kind of celebration. Another was just of the daughters, the Three Little Pigs. I held it to the light, peered closely, guessing how old they were. The prettiest looked a bit older than me, with straight black shiny hair and a clingy black dress that showed the top inch of her tits. In another she looked more like a model posing for a magazine, staring at the camera as if giving her boyfriend the come-on. The name along the bottom was Katrina. Katrina Rafferty. She was staring straight at me, through me. Her eyes followed me no matter what angle I held the photo.

I went through the drawers of her dressing table, found a pair of white knickers. They smelled of Persil, the same as Mum used, and felt cool and light against my cheek. I took her photo to the bed, laid back till my head found her pillow. A buzz ran through me, the way an electric shock keeps you pinned to the spot so you can't move. I pulled my jeans to my ankles. As I wanked I pictured Katrina coming back into the room from a shower, closing the door, then standing over me, telling me to dry her. She shook out her wet hair as she straddled me, leaned forward as I pulled her down, and gasped as I slid deeper. Her wet hair whipped my face. She moaned into my shoulder. The world shot out of me in seconds. I caught it in her knickers. Drained, I stared at the ceiling, wondering if she stared at the ceiling at night conjuring shapes from the swirly Artex.

Eventually forcing myself up, I fastened my jeans, took the photo of Katrina out of the frame, and put the empty frame back on the dressing table. I took a red pen from her jar by the bed. On her notepad I wrote, *I'm sorry, I just wanted to know you.* Leaving the pad on the bed, I threw her knickers in the bin beneath the study desk and paused in the doorway for a last look at her bed. Then I folded her photo neatly, tucked it into my back pocket, and left.

After the pale light of Katrina's room, the landing seemed darker than before. I took a few steps, stopped, glanced back at the glow from her doorway. When I looked forward again, my vision shrank. Dark rushed in at the edges. My hand found the wall, knocked a picture. The frame slid up; I steadied it from falling. The handrail led me down the open landing until the hall narrowed again, and the air grew cooler. Even though it was dark, I could sense the new space around me.

The next bedroom was brighter. There was a white portable telly on a wheelie table at the end of the bed. You could tell they were rich. They probably spent their Saturday nights in bed watching *The Generation Game* and sipping bubbly out of foot-high glasses. Not a care. A motorbike went by. The noise startled me, reminded me where I was. I took a quick look around. On what must've been the woman's bedside table was a round porcelain dish with birds on it. In the dish was a pair of diamond-like earrings. By the phone was a stylish watch with a thin brown-leather strap. The woman wasn't daft: why take your watch on holiday? You go to forget time not to keep track of it. I took the watch and the earrings and went downstairs. That was enough.

Outside, the road was quiet. The wind had picked up and the air felt rainy. I fought the urge to run until I was far enough away from the house. In time I sped to a jog, my feet light, treading air. It felt so good to run that I almost forgot my bike.

The fair was in full swing now – music louder, lights brighter, the crowd bigger and noisier. It was like arriving too late at a party to find someone to cling to – everyone had already paired off. All you could do was loiter and smile with the others. But it didn't matter. I'd just lost my cherry: company was the last thing on my mind. It was me and Katrina. There was nothing else in the world.

After padlocking my bike to the railings in case those two skinheads were still about, I went to join the queue for the Big Wheel. On the way I heard my name being shouted, and looked to see where it was coming from. Massimo the Scrounger was waving me over from the Dodgems, his two older brothers beside him, chatting up some girls. He must've said something about me to the girls because when I waved back, even though he was the last person I wanted to see, they all fell about laughing. But this time I wasn't bothered, didn't feel myself blush or shrink with embarrassment at being the butt of their jokes. They were just as stupid as ever. I, on the other hand, was cherry-less. A real man. They could laugh all they wanted.

I joined the queue for the Big Wheel, shuffled forward, swelling inside with my secret. Fingering the watch in my pocket, rubbing my finger against the grooved knob of the winder, I followed the wheel as it climbed another notch and each car filled with riders. I pulled Katrina's photo from my back pocket, unfolded it and snuck a glimpse, imagined her there beside me, on our first date. I had to be brave for her.

When the fair worker slammed down my safety bar, I yanked it to make sure it was locked. Next thing I knew I was rising backwards as the wheel shunted up to let the next car fill, and then the next, until I was stranded at the top, my toes pressed to the floor, the coast lights weaving before me like a nightmarish eel, fat, long, electric. In the next car along, kids rocked and howled as if wanting to turn the thing over, exactly what Lance would've done if I'd been with him. Trying to forget that only a few nuts and bolts were holding me fifty feet in the air, and with the wind whistling through the girders, I shoved Katrina's photo in my shirt and gripped the safety bar.

Convinced the bar would work loose and catapult me half way to Brighton, I prayed for each new turn to be the last. On the downswing, the MC's promise of Long Rides Tonight made me wish I'd never left home that evening, let alone set foot in the Raffertys'. The wheel went up; my chair tilted forward and snatched my feet from under me. As the rain came down, I prayed that if He'd just blow the fuses and bring the wheel to a stop, I'd be a saint forever. But the wheel kept turning.

I opened my eyes as my chair crested the top and then swung over – eleven, ten, nine on a clock-face – my legs high out in front of me, my face skyward, the rain needling my eyes. Then something happened. Whether as the rain fell harder I forgot my fear, or whether the thought of Katrina beside me triggered some deep, untapped courage, I don't know. All I know is that the next time I crested the top and my chair tipped back as I flew over, it felt in that lightning moment as though I'd been fired from a cannon and was hurtling through nothing, high and free, towards some safe celestial net.

22

Lance and I were at the top of the school field by the stile. It was lunchtime. Instead of helping me build my ant city like he said he would, he
was sitting on the low plank of the stile, moaning. "At least you've got
a face," he said, for the ten-millionth time, as if the only reason I still
had one was because I'd pushed him in front of the firework at the last
minute to save myself. His skin grafts were only healing slower than
the doctors predicted because he kept not wearing his mask. I had to
bite my tongue from saying that if he wore it like he was supposed to,
like every doctor and consultant had told him to, like me, his mum,
and all the teachers had told him to, his face would heal perfectly, and
he'd get enough confidence back to go to the Globetrotters. I felt bad
for him and all that, but his moaning drove me loopy. He wouldn't
stop going on about what it felt like to have the whole school call you
Bernie, about how girls checked their blouse buttons when they saw
him, about how townies were so frightened that they fled into charity shops when they saw him. Then it was my turn. Apparently, all
the times I'd stood up for him in the playground didn't count: I was
as bad as the rest of them. He had a knack for making you feel like
you'd betrayed him. And when he made himself cry – which he could
at will – it was hard not to believe him, not to hate what you'd done.
Plenty of times I walked home from school a Judas, until at some point
I'd realise that he was just doing a Lance, and that there was no reason to feel bad.

When he gave me the Globetrotters tickets earlier that day, I didn't
want to take them. "I'm not going if you're not going," I said, and I
meant it. With his lying record, it was hard to know whether Loraine
really had stopped him from going or whether he'd whined so much
about having the piss taken out of him that she made the decision herself, for his benefit, which he'd naturally resent, and take as another
example of the world turning against him. He shrugged. "I don't care."
"Yes you do," I said: "what're you talking about?" He didn't answer. I
knew he was hoping I'd see just how wounded he was, and then beg
him to go with me. Nothing would make him happier than to have me

spend the day telling him how mean Lorraine and Harry were, how the world didn't care, and what a rotten hand he'd been dealt. But not being in the mood for Lance the Martyr, I took the tickets. They fitted just right in my blazer.

I was kneeling by the fence, excavating. The ant bridge was nearly finished. I liked having dirt on my hands, how it clogged my nails. It stayed there for days.

Suddenly Lance snapped out of his sulk and did his submarine-dive noise.

"Pak attack, Pak attack."

He always said that about Sid, who he hated as much as my dad hated Sid's family (or the idea of them, more like).

I stuck my digging stick into the ground and turned. It was Sid all right, mooching along with his head down, acting like he hadn't seen us. Knowing him, he probably hadn't.

"What's he doing up here?" said Lance.

"How should I know?" I said.

He veered towards the other corner of the field and sat under the lime tree, the way he often did during break.

"Weirdo," said Lance.

Next thing we knew, Sid was standing on his head, as steady and straight as the trees behind him. He'd gone on about the benefits of headstands in biology, but I'd never actually seen him do any, though other people had, hence his being famous for them. All my attempts at them were against the wall; he just crouched and raised his legs till they were a perfect ninety degrees to the ground. Lance had no idea how hard that was, not that he cared. With his white shirt offset by the bark, Sid looked like a door in the tree, opening to a long ladder all the way down to Australia, or some other world. It was incredible for about a minute. Then Lance cupped his hands to his mouth and shouted "What're you doing?" He looked at me and laughed. I didn't. I said, "Spastic. How's he going to answer?"

"Come over here and do that," Lance shouted.

After a minute or so, Sid brought his legs down and rolled back and up all in one go, so that you couldn't tell where he started and where he stopped, and where he started again. Lance kept shouting. Eventually Sid came over.

"What are you doing?" I said. He had symmetrical bristles. Half his face was a man's.

"My gran used to stand on her head for twenty minutes every day," he said. "Guess how old she lived to?"

"Eight hundred and forty-two," I said.

Lance had his arms crossed, unimpressed. "Ten thousand."

"A hundred and six," said Sid. "You should tell your dad," he said to me. "It might help his heart."

"What do you know about his heart?"

"Everyone knows about his heart."

Then he went back to standing on his head.

"He won't even listen to his doctor," I said. "I can't see him taking up headstands."

Lance walked a few yards over to the fence dividing the school field from Old Man Francis's land, and started yanking on a post. "Oy, guess what I said to Mrs. Pike?"

"What?"

"Told her I was dyslexic. 'I need help with my homework,' I said."

"What did she say?"

" 'Of course, Lance,' " he said, mimicking her voice. " 'Anything for you. Come to my office after school.' "

"Dreamer," I said. Then to Sid, "He reckons he's gonna blackmail her into shagging him."

"A tenner says I do it before we break up."

"She's married, isn't she?" said Sid. He was still upside down. His voiced sounded strangled and flat.

" 'She's married, isn't she?' " said Lance all girly, mimicking Sid.

"Ignore him," I said to Sid. "It's his burns. They fried his head."

"I ain't stupid," said Lance, kicking the post before coming towards us, all piss and wind. "Watch me. You'll be gutted when I do."

Sid climbed down and dusted his hands off on his trousers. "Your dad put another thing through our door."

Shortly before he organised the petition to get the Bhargavas out, Dad posted a string of complaints through their door about their rubbish. They'd been leaving the lids off their dustbins and letting their rubbish blow up the street. He reckoned it landed in other people's gardens, including ours (which it didn't), not to mention the welcome mat it laid out for the rats.

"He's an arse," I said. "I can't help it. I can't stop him. I would if I could."

I got my digging stick and went back to work.

"My dad's going to call the police if he doesn't stop."

"Boo hoo," said Lance. The fart he let out was like a bear dying. When I looked up, Sid was fiddling with something in his hand. I asked what it was. He played with whatever it was like he wanted you to see it but he didn't. Then he opened his hand and showed me.

"A cow. My dad made it out of papier mâché."

I said, "Give us a look then." He handed it over reluctantly, like it was heavy or precious. A miniature painted cow. I turned it in my hand, felt the soft bits on the sides, the ridge along the spine. It was perfect in a small, strange way. Even the teats and eyeballs were painted.

"He can make any animal you want," said Sid proudly, watching to see my reaction. "Monkeys, snakes, chickens—"

"Where were you born, Bullshit Hill?" said Lance.

"What's the point of that?" I said, handing the cow back.

Sid dropped it gently in his blazer pocket. "All animals are sacred in India."

Lance was kicking the fence post now, pretending he wasn't interested. But he couldn't help from poking his nose in. "If it's so great there, why's he come to this dump?"

I said, "Watch your mask doesn't come off." That always made Lance nervous. Sid smiled. He didn't have a bad word to say about anyone. I, on the other hand, could name a hundred people I hated, like that.

"What about frogs?" I said to Sid, feeling guilty about the one I'd squished on my ride home from the shop, even though I didn't think it was sacred because it was already flat in the road.

"Them too."

"Frogs are shit," said Lance, adjusting his mask again before going back to kicking the post.

Sid had the idea of extending the ant city by building a subway under the stile and into Francis's field – littered with doodlebug craters, the teachers said, therefore forbidden. But we all knew that Old Francis, with his wellies and unzipped trousers, and his head that kept jerking back so far he could see yesterday, was the real problem. He owned the land, and sometimes we'd see him watching us from outside his dilapidated barn or his sloping shanty house. There were all sorts of rumours about Francis inviting kids into his house for cake or biscuits, and then not letting them go. No one had the nerve to play knock and run on his door. I thought I'd give Sid a dare, just for a lark, so while Lance was busy with the fence post I said, "I'm going over old Francis's tomorrow. You coming?"

The fear on Sid's face was a picture. "We'll get murdered if they find out."

A loud cheer came from the bottom of the field where some kids were having a kick-about. I turned, saw a goalie on his knees, the ball miles behind him. The scorer was running around with his arm in the air till some kid leapt on his back and bundled him over. More cheering. I was crap at football, and envied them.

"Chicken," shouted Lance. "I'll do it. I ain't scared of that perv."

"They won't know," I said to Sid. "We'll be back before the bell. Bet you a quid you won't knock on his door."

Sid stood looking across Francis's field, mulling it over, the fear still plain on his face, eased by the promise of a prize. He didn't say a word. Lance grunted and yanked at the fence post.

"Two quid then."

Sid still hadn't answered when the bell went for end of break.

23

When I saw the report of the Raffertys' burglary in the *Argus*, I bought an extra copy and cut out the article for my scrapbook. After years of trying to get in the paper for doing such good deeds as cutting Miss Jinny's grass with her blunt push mower that bent the grass one way and then the other, forcing me to fuck about on my hands and knees with her prewar shears, which were as crap as her mower, and all for a glass of Robinson's Barley Water, orange not lemon, I couldn't seem to keep out of it. Suddenly I was a star.

Lance stopped by the shop with some envelopes. Hawaii and Poland. I showed him the clipping. He snatched it and read it to himself. I watched as the doubt crept over his Budgie-jacket face until finally, after swallowing his envy, he said, "Was this you?"

"Yep."

"On your own?"

I snatched the clipping back. "No, with me dad, spackhead." I folded it neatly, tucked it in my pocket.

"Prove it."

I told him about the watch and the earrings.

"If you had them you'd show me," he said.

"Oh right," I said, "like I'd wear them to work."

He was more worried about whether or not we were still partners in his plan to shag Mrs. Pike. I'd only gone along with it in the first place 'cause we were mates, but the more I thought about his plan, the stupider it sounded. I didn't want to know.

"You promised," he said. "You can't back out now."

"She'll call the law."

"What, and let her bloke find out she's shagging Basher?"

"You're off your nut. She's not gonna let you shag her."

He'd been planning it so long there was no talking him out of it. "It's up to her. Either she lets us or she's in the shit."

"You'll get murdered," I said. "Besides, what are you gonna do if she says no?"

"Make her."

Before walking out the door he said, "Don't think you're the only one who'll do things on your own, 'cause you ain't."

It turned out that the Raffertys' neighbour had checked the house the day after I'd been in there and had seen the broken window. They couldn't tell if anything was taken, and the neighbour had no luck getting through to the Raffertys' hotel. The report went on to say that apart from the window there was no other damage. A note had been found, but they weren't at liberty to divulge its contents. The last part read *a terrible invasion of privacy. Police are urging the public to be more vigilant about home security. "Don't send criminals invitations,"* *said a police spokesman.*

Dad said it served the Raffertys right. If they chose to go off for a fortnight, the first thing they should've done was pay their bills, and the second thing was to make sure they put their valuables in a safe place rather than leave them on a plate in the kitchen along with a welcome note for the robbers. Olive, on the other hand, took it personally. "It's awful," she said, "strangers coming into your house like that. There's no such thing as safe." She said it could just as easily happen to the poor defenceless likes of her, because that's how cruel the world was. It was all well and good for the police to warn the public about securing their homes. What about making ends meet? "We can't all afford to go putting locks on our windows," she said. "And then we'll be the ones who'll get robbed."

Once the Raffertys came back, another report appeared, this time about the jewellery. According to Mrs. Ann Rafferty – "It's a good job we were insured," she said – they weren't only missing a pair of diamond earrings and a treasured anniversary watch, with the combined valued of a grand, but also a diamond engagement ring, an emerald necklace, and Mr. Rafferty's Rolex, valued at nearly six grand. When I saw that they were fiddling the insurance, I stopped feeling bad about what I'd pinched. I'd done them a favour. They must've loved me.

I took Mrs. Rafferty's watch to school, put it on in the toilets at lunchtime, and then took it off again when afternoon lessons started, hiding it in my geometry set till I got back home to my bedroom, where I kept it in the secret compartment under my chest of drawers.

It was thin and plain and ladyish, and always ran fast. Maybe that's why Mrs. Rafferty left it behind. The last thing you'd want on holiday was a watch that gobbled time. And for a kid with barely enough free time in the day to eat his Weetabix, a watch that gobbled time was a curse. For a month after the break-in, I panicked every morning, thinking I was late for school, late to the shop, late for tea . . . After a while I stopped taking it to school and left it hidden in my compartment. One day I'd have a girlfriend, I told myself, and when I did I'd give her the watch for her birthday and the earrings for Christmas, and probably a tortoise for Valentine's Day.

Olive's friends always came in the shop for a grizzle. You name it, they'd had enough of it: too hot, too busy, too noisy, too many kids (and all with no respect for their elders), too much seaweed, too few buses, and too long a queue at the post office. The shop was the miserablest place in the world when one of her lot came in, so I just made excuses and went in the back and punched boxes or hid outside by the bins till she called for me. She was easy to boss about, though. She needed the money.

"You know," she said as she buffed the scales, "I'd be lost without this little job." She was an automatic talker. I sat at the till flicking through the paper. "You'll find out one of these days. Living on your own's not easy."

"Don't s'pose it is," I said.

"The way prices are going. Guess what my water rates are now?"

"No idea." Pretending to be deaf or half asleep made no difference. Her audience was in her head.

"No, my boy, you haven't," she snapped, as if my answer proved her point. "You youngsters don't appreciate having your bums wiped for you. Just you wait till you have to do it yourself."

I said, "I already wipe me own bum." Then I said, "By the way, Dad wants you to do the windows after that." I tried wearing her out by making up jobs, but there was still no stopping her. While she kept busy, I read the paper and took all the credit for keeping the shop tidy when Dad came back later to close.

The best thing about those afternoons in the shop was watching all the girls go by in their shorts and T-shirts. Standing in the doorway was like having a gang of mates backing me up: on home turf I could say or do anything. Now and again I'd imagine that I owned the shop and that all the girls thought me well set up, and worth going for.

Everyone had a job of some sort. I'd wander in and out of their shops during one of my escapes from Olive. Pete Ritson worked in the newsagents across the road and gave me free cans of Irn-Bru. Sandra Dawlish worked in her mum's old-fashioned teashop on the corner and gave me free flapjacks, which I only usually ate part of because they were burnt.

Greg Chubb's dad had the butchers. We traded fruit and veg for meat. Whenever he came over for a break there'd be dark oxtaily smears on his apron, and dried blood under his fingernails from all the chopping and slicing he did behind the counter, in full view of the public. He also fed brains and eyes and lips, and any other part that hadn't already been sold for lunch, through the mincer to make the filling for their prize-winning sausages, pork and sage, which were so popular with the crumblies that come Saturday morning when a new batch was made, there'd be a queue as far as the pier.

I spent most of my breaks listening to Greg's stories about his dad, Horace, who'd supposedly won the A.B.A. light-middleweight title in Camber Sands the same week that Ali and Foreman had rumbled in the jungle. (No matter how I tried to wangle it, I could never get Greg to say Horace.) He'd light a fag before his story, and smoke it like he was trying to suck a lid off a bottle. And every time he took a drag, there they were again, those blood-caked fingers. If that wasn't bad enough, in summer he stank of warm mince. Naturally, he thought all the girls loved him. Whenever girls approached he'd make himself beautiful by combing his quiff and then stand with his legs apart. "Watch and learn, mate," he'd say. Blocking their path, he'd wiggle his legs like Elvis and try chatting them up, sucking his fag even harder, baring his teeth when he inhaled. The girls would always try to go round him, tell him to get lost. Once when I was there a girl noticed his fingers. "Wash your hands, you dirty git," she said, trying to get away. "Wash yourself, no arse," he shouted back.

No arse?

24

My next four break-ins were the Morris's, the Clennell's, the Belton's, and the Fortino's, in that order, and all in the space of a month – May – before the season really took off. All of them had gone abroad without squaring up first with Dad. The Morris's owned a few greasy spoons along the coast. They were famous for their all-day breakfasts. You didn't go there for wilted spinach. Well, you might, but you wouldn't get any. Stewed tea, more likely. The Clennells owned the Atlantis, Farthing's top fish restaurant. They'd been at the Anchor that night, supporting Dad's petition. I know for a fact they used spinach 'cause we delivered it. The Beltons had a caravan park, plus they owned the old airfield. I don't know how you come to own an airfield, or why, but they did, and they'd turned it into a gold mine. Its weekly car boot sale was the biggest for miles. You could buy any amount of crap there for a quid. The Fortinos owned what they called a *trattoria* on Dent Street, which was just a posh word for a pizza place. Actually, it was *the* pizza place in Farthing. Everyone went there, except us. Plus they had an Italian bakery-cum-grocer's in Goring, which stood out along the high street because of its apron-striped canopy. It looked like they'd piped the name with an icing gun.

Those four customers had one thing in common: they didn't use their loaves. If Dad had decided to put a stop on their unpaid accounts while they were away, they'd be stuffed. They thought they could pay old soft-touch Bowen when it suited them. And Dad, good as he was at managing his stock, making sure he could meet every order, wouldn't lower himself, as he called it, to go cap in hand. He'd send out reminder after reminder in the hope that they'd keep their end of the bargain. Then, as a last resort, he'd phone them up and explain politely that they were just as familiar with running a business as he was, and that the same basic principles applied. You made sure you paid your suppliers, because no suppliers meant no business, and no business meant no foreign holidays, no fun in the sun. And most of the time they'd be decent, and cough up. But as he said, some liked taking the money so much they couldn't bear to part with it. Which is where I came in.

The Clennells lived in a stone-chimneyed bungalow off Marine Drive, which hugged the coast. Mrs. Clennell's undies drawer was full of once-coloured knickers and nylon bras that had been washed so much they were covered with bobbles. Their lives revolved around outdoor bowls. I counted fourteen caught-in-the-act pictures of them on the walls, the mantelpiece, and on the pine dresser in the sitting room, whose centrepiece was a string art steam engine over the fireplace. Wherever I pointed my torch, the beam landed on another picture of Mrs. Clennell trotting down the lake-flat green, neck and neck with her ball, or her hubby sizing up the small white jack at the far end. Then there were the posed shots of them in their club uniforms, all very proper, with blazers and medals for things they hadn't done. They were decades younger than the others.

I found some brochures of the Channel Islands. All I ever seemed to find were details of holidays I wouldn't be going on. There was nothing worth pinching – a cheque book with no cheques, a pair of pewter tankards, some LPs by King Oliver, who was probably the king of Sark. By the time I left the Clennells', I hated them more than I had when I went in there, not because of how they'd treated Dad, but because they were so dull. Bowls my arse. I bet they played croquet too. They didn't even have a settee, but they had a nice set of kitchen knives. The stuffing came out of those armchairs like a dream.

The Beltons were another wash-out. If I'd wanted one of his sets of golf clubs in one of his three flashy bags, great. If I'd wanted to drain one of his colourful aquariums, each of which had enough little buildings in them for a whole village of fish, great. If I'd wanted a brass coal scuttle and a matching brass-handled poker and hearth brush, great. Other than that, nothing. Whatever they did with their valuables, they were too careful to leave them lying around. The only thing Dad said about them was that they'd gone on a cruise to the Baltic, hence the pile of Scandinavian brochures on the coffee table, which had a glass panel in the middle and what looked like a reindeer etched into it.

They also had a Bang & Olufsen stereo that looked like it had been made about thirty years in the future and then beamed back to the display shelf at Curry's. It was slim and strange and probably made a nice sound before I killed it with Belton's putter, which was dense and blunt and made for precision hits. Whatever metal they used in the future might've looked pretty, but it buckled like tin. It was no match for our golf club metal of today. The speakers were light to throw but sturdy enough not to break on impact, just to leave deep dents in the walls. Plus they rebounded well. If the Beltons had any sense they'd think twice before going back to the fjords.

Then came the Fortinos.

Even though Mr. Fortino had taken his family to Italy for some sort of reunion, by that time I'd got the bug for sneaking into other people's houses and wasn't about to give anyone the benefit of the doubt. Relatives or no relatives, he should've paid up before he went. There were no exceptions.

They lived by the railway on the outskirts of town in the old stationmaster's house, a square, solid block made of local stone. The front and back walls were whitewashed; the sides hadn't been touched. Mr. Fortino was too cheap to buy the paint just like he was too tight to settle up with us. The house sat alone, below the road and beside the bridge that Dad and I always crossed on our way back from deliveries. Before the railway was built it would've been a lovely little number, with the grazing peace of a water meadow out the front and climbing fields at the back, dotted with oaks thick enough to have been waving their arms and cheering when Sir Francis Drake – the patron saint of greengrocers – came back across the Atlantic and presented old electric hair with The Spud.

On my three-mile ride to the Fortinos' it was so dark that even the wind and clouds seemed black. After hiding my bike under the bridge, I took my torch and masking tape and edged through the apple orchard with my arms in front of me to keep from knocking myself out. It seemed to take forever before I emerged at the back of the cottage. When I did, the looming, wide-open silence gave me the chills. I was this close to going home.

The sash window slid up as though it had been freshly greased just for me. I clamped the torch between my teeth and climbed in. And even if the silence amplified every sound I made, no one would hear me. There wasn't another heartbeat for miles.

All houses have a smell, but the Fortinos' didn't smell of anything, not books or onions or furniture polish, not cat food nor dried flowers. Walking through the lounge, I had the weirdest sense that something was missing. Maybe it was just that they'd gone away. Even the air felt old, like it hadn't been stirred in years.

I kept the torch beam to the carpet and went upstairs. The first door had a plaque on it – *Tony's Room*. Its hinges squeaked when I opened it. The room was tidy and sparse, with just a bed, a desk, and some shelves. Photos in heart-shaped frames were lined up at identical angles, as though he'd used a protractor. Each photo had a picture of what must've been Tony, but in most of them you couldn't see his face for his hair. I ran the torch along the bookshelf. A collection of *Eagle* annuals and *Commando* comics. Some metal knights. At the wall end of the shelf was a collection of paperbacks by Dennis Wheatley. I pulled one down. *The Dennis Wheatley Library of the Occult* it said above the title. Propping the paperbacks up was an atlas-sized *History of Witchcraft*. Goose-pimples burst all over me. That was enough Tony for me.

The next room was the daughter's. She had kiddy photos all over her room: feeding sugar lumps to a horse, riding in a gymkhana, playing the violin, holding a frog by a pond...The odd one out was a photo of someone in fancy dress, at what appeared to be a kids' party, judging by all the costumed dancers in the foreground – Big Ben, Frankenstein, Kermit...Behind the main group was a row of chairs along the wall. Only one was occupied, by a giant carrot topped with a fringe of shredded green loo roll. In the photo you could just make out a couple of eyeholes and a mouth slit, but that was all.

There was nothing of interest in her drawers, just good little girl stuff – school report cards, birthday and Christmas cards, a locket with nothing in it. Her school uniform was hanging in the wardrobe: the green and white of Millais, just up the road from ours, and the allboys equivalent. Unlike Katrina Rafferty's crammed wardrobe, this one was mostly empty, except for a long burgundy-velvet dress that looked like it used to belong to a witch. What else? A Spalding tennis racket in a wooden press, a riding hat that someone had sat on, and a blue acrylic toy that must've been half her size. Apart from that, the wardrobe looked more like it belonged to someone who'd just moved in and hadn't finished unpacking, unlike her brother's room, which looked more like someone had just moved out.

But when I pulled out the bottom drawer all the way, I saw a shelf similar to mine. It had the same hollow sound when I tapped it. I lift-

ed it up. Tucked in the back corner were a bunch of books. I reached
in and took them.

On the front of each book she'd written *The Private Property of Miss
Lucy Anna Fortino*. They turned out to be diaries. Lucy wanted to live
in a tree in the middle of nowhere and spend all her time swimming in
the river and learning to sing like the birds. She dreaded going camp-
ing with her uncle and auntie, who weren't real relatives but her parents' friends, the Manvilles. Her number one favourite thing in the
world was Nutmeg, her horse. Her least favourite thing was people.
Then, skipping through another of the diaries from a few years ago,
I found this:

> The big red rock in Australia is alive and you can sit on it and then
> when the sun goes down the voices start talking and you can ask them
> things and thayll answer you whatever you ask them about. I'd ask
> them how to stop it but that's rubbish becose then I'd be their and
> not here and safe so I wouldn't need to ask the voices, would I stupid!
> I don't want to ask. I hate asking. Asking is what gets you in trouble
> and then not asking gets you in trouble and then he'll do it again. If I
> did ask the voices anything I'd ask them to tell someone like Mrs Bee-
> cham so she could make it stop...

Another diary started with the heading *My Perfect Family* underlined
three times. The pages were filled with pencil sketches of what I took
to be imaginary people, unless they were her friends. But somehow I
didn't think so: none of her photos had friends in them. Besides, from
the shutdown look on her face, she didn't seem like she had lots of
friends. Her sketches were very odd. Instead of mouths she'd drawn
lengthwise daggers in red pen. I flicked through all the drawings.
Every face had a dagger mouth, and every drawing had the same dagger, long and thin, with a skull on the handle. Otherwise the drawings
were perfect – the way she'd shadowed their faces, the sharp realness
of the eyes, even the way the hair grew and fell, curling around the
ear or over the shoulders. I took a photo from the bedside table and
studied her face, then the daggers, then her face again, trying to find
a clue. Before I went I wanted to leave her a note, not like the one I'd
written Katrina, but something kind, something to make her feel like
she wasn't alone. But if she hated people already, knowing that some-

one had been through her room might send her over the edge. As I left her room, my torch beam caught the big poster on the inside of her door. The Jam. They didn't look very happy.

Riding home, I couldn't get her out of my mind. Her face was so vivid she could have been perched on my handlebars facing me. Instead of being out in the gusty night, I felt an invisible protection from the boxed-in warmth of her room. I thought so hard about her that the blood supply rushed from my legs to my brain. My legs went to jelly; my pedalling slowed. I freewheeled till I lost balance. It could've been any time of night – everything was quiet. I wheeled my bike into a bus shelter and sat inside. My mind was like my bike's dynamo lights: the harder I thought of her, the brighter her face glowed, only to dim again when I thought of something else. Trying to work out what had happened to her, and what she'd meant in those diaries, I lost track. Keeping her face bright was tiring. At some point it must've got too much because I nodded off.

"Shouldn't you be in bed?"

I opened my eyes. It was the milkman. It was cold and getting light.

"Yeah," I said, feeling the ache in my back and shoulders. My knees cracked when I got up. I lowered myself slowly, touched my toes. It felt like every part of me needed oiling. I watched the sunrise on the ride home.

25

When the buzzer blasted, I thought for a millisecond that I was still in my room, and that my night at the Globetrotters had just been a dream. Was it Mum or Dad calling me down for duty? But then a woman came over the PA telling people to take their seats – the show would be starting in five minutes. As soon as she said that, I got the same case of chronic butterflies I'd felt before, but only rarely. Once was when I snuck into a guest's room for the first time. Another was when I pulled Mum's tights on for the first time. And then recently, when I climbed through the Raffertys' kitchen window. Something life-changing was about to happen, I knew it. All of a sudden I was in a bright white anteroom, waiting to be called through to meet the next stage of my life. The houselights dimmed. People rushed to their seats. I kept my hand on the seat next to me in case someone tried to take it. Where was he? How long did it take to go to the loo? He'd miss the start if he didn't hurry. I panned the rest of the Centre, which was like a giant gym – a polished wood basketball court enclosed by tiered seating. What if he'd gone out one exit and couldn't find his way back? But then, just when I'd given up on him, there he was, hands aloft, trying to balance whatever he was carrying as he squeezed along the row.

"What's that?" I said.

"A hot dog," he said, handing it to me.

"Oh." I felt awkward, embarrassed. I hadn't asked for one. "Where's yours?" I said.

"I don't eat them," he said, sitting down. "We're vegetarian."

*Ve're wege*tarian, he said. I hated it when people pronounced things wrong. But I couldn't really correct him after he'd bought me the hot dog. So I made a mental note to tell him another time. Instead I just said, "Why would you wanna be *ve*getarian?"

Sid shrugged. "There are very few animals that aren't sacred. Sacred things are not for eating."

"You said that before."

"So I repeat it. Anyway, it's good that you can't eat many animals there because the human gastrointestinal system is not good for breaking down meat."

He took his right shoe off and shook it. It was too dark to see if anything had come out. The smell from his one shoe reminded me how ripe mine would be if I copied him. Mondays were fresh sock day.

"It sticks in the colon and makes cancer," he said. "This was John Wayne. He had forty pounds of meat in his large intestine when he died."

"That's nearly an elephant's heart," I said.

"No good. Fruits and vegetables are very healthy. Eat plenty." He clasped his hands on his lap. He sat straight and eager, as though awaiting a procession. I suppose all of us were, really.

I ignored the mix of v's and w's and was about to talk about fruit and veg, about how Dad ran a greengrocer's, but then stopped myself again. It was hard work slamming on the brakes every time I wanted to talk, but you had to be careful what you said to him, to anyone. Every word had a price tag dangling from it. I bit off a mouthful of sausage. "So you've never had toad-in-the-hole?"

"Toads in the hole? Hot dogs?" He smiled and shook his head.

"Give me John Wayne any day," I said, then slurped some fried onions from my hot dog. They were as good as toad-in-the-hole onions, or liver-and-bacon onions. It was better than being at the fair. I told Sid I'd pay him back when we got out.

"Don't worry," he said. "I've never bought a hot dog before. Tonight is new."

Something about the way I ate seemed to amaze him. Either that or he was horrified. But he kept watching, studying even, as if planning to write a report.

We had great seats, in the second tier, just up from the halfway line. Lorraine must've been feeling generous when she gave Lance the money for the tickets. I didn't feel bad. It was his fault for letting Lorraine dictate whether or not he could go to the game. He always did whatever he wanted. If he'd really wanted to go, he would've. Knowing how crafty he was, I tried to work out what he had to gain by not going, what he hadn't admitted to. Maybe Harry had offered to pay his airfare over to Yemen. Who knows. What really mattered after the initial shock wore off was that his ticket hadn't been wasted. Sid might not have heard of the Globetrotters, but he seemed glad he'd come. I was too. At least he didn't moan. He was happy to be doing something he'd never done before. And he wasn't about to let what people thought of his face stop him from going anywhere.

The band was making its way off the court. Judging by the musicians' outfits – red tunics, white belts, and gold egg boxes on their shoulders decorated with curtain braid – it looked like their next stop was the Crimea.

And then the whole place went black. Spotlights swept the audience, crisscrossed the court. A different announcer, a man with an American accent, boomed over the PA:

"Ladies and gentlemen, introducing to you, all the way from Hinckley, Illinois, in the U S of A, the amazing, the brilliant, the most dazzling entertainers in the history of the world...the Har-lem Globetrotters!"

The crowd went ballistic. One by one the players ran onto the court, waving and bouncing balls, all wearing their famous stars-and-stripes outfits, so big they looked like three football kits stitched together. There was Curly, then Geese, then the rest of the team. Meadowlark Lemon pretended to be shy, keeping his head covered with his tracksuit top till he was fully on the court. When he revealed himself, the rumble of foot-stamping was so loud I thought the stands would give.

Then the MC announced the other team, the Seajets, who weren't from anywhere near Hinckley or Harlem. They looked more like a darts team from the pub up the road. Or deckchair attendants. Some of them were as old as Dad. And about as fashion-conscious. (Their shorts were more like golf trousers from the thirties.) A few tried bouncing their balls like the Globetrotters, which was embarrassing. They fluffed it every time, and then had to chase their balls down before one of the Globetrotters beat them to it.

Funny as it was to see the larger-than-life Globetrotters on the same court as a bunch of dustmen, I couldn't help thinking something fishy was going on. No one in England played basketball. And if they did, I couldn't imagine the Seajets competed for anything other than who could down the most pints after a game. What were the promoters thinking? What about value for money? Putting on a show? Admittedly the crowd had only come for the Globetrotters, but still. They might as well have rolled a dozen cabbages onto the court and let the celebrities kick them around.

But then as soon as the game started, the joke was on us. The team of darts players, deckchair attendants, or dustmen turned out to be circus performers and ex-gymnasts, brought in to give the Globetrotters the runaround, and to act as their foil. At one point there were six or seven balls in play, each being spun on one finger by members of each team. It was a letdown: I thought only the Globetrotters could do that. Other times it was hard to tell whether Meadowlark Lemon really was too slow to stop one of the Seajets from stealing his ball, or why Geese kept playing to the gallery so much that the Seajets stormed ahead. Didn't they care about winning? We cheered their theatrics, but booed each time they fell further behind. Talk about emotional yo-yos. We were at breaking point. This wasn't the Globetrotters we knew. I shook my head, baffled by why the men-who-could-do-anything were acting like goons, as though it was their job to let the Seajets run rings around them.

Trust our luck that the one night in our lives we got to see the legendary Globetrotters was the same night they ran out of steam, ending their however-many-year reign as the greatest whatever-they-weres in history. Thank God Lance *was* at home. If he'd braved the public and come to see his heroes, he'd be so knock-down devastated that his life wouldn't be worth living. And if that didn't make him top himself, he'd probably turn into a hermit, weird and overgrown, with Howard Hughes fingernails. At least Lorraine could give him tips on how to protect them, on how to make them look their best. I don't know what advice she'd have for his hair.

Sid was leaning forward, his chin propped with a fist. He might've been shaking his head. When I nudged him to make sure he was all right, he leaned across and shouted in my ear. "Basketball is not Pareto efficient. This is the problem. Sport is economically unfair."

To be honest, at the time I didn't catch what he said. It was only when we walked to the bus stop after the show that he explained what he meant, but after the first couple of sentences he'd lost me, and I stopped listening. My mind was reliving the match, and the Globetrotters' comeback. Life didn't have to be grim, after all. You could buy miracles for a tenner.

The timing was perfect. By the time the Globetrotters finally slipped into gear for their comeback, the crowd was on the verge of a riot. It was a bit like Dad's speech at the Anchor, when the men cheered and waved their caps and newspapers in the air. But not that part. What I sensed in the air at the Globetrotters was the same tense static that hung in that hall after Judge Gavin slammed Dad's petition. I thought of Lance's Uncle Harry, and his welder's arc. It was that sort of a crackle. If Sid had grabbed my sleeve at that moment and told me he was leaving, I'd have followed like a shot. So when the Globetrotters eventually flicked the switch and went to work on the Seajets, all that built-up tension, even the leftover anticipation from the beginning, leaked out of me, as though a huge gate valve had wheeled open. And by the time the game was over, with the Seajets dizzy and staggering, and with Meadowlark Lemon offering their players consolation piggyback rides to their dressing room, I had no fear of exploding. I'd deflated. It felt good to be back to size.

In bed that night, my mind roamed over the evening. But whenever I landed on a feel-good moment that I wanted to stick with, like when Sid gave me the hot dog, I kept getting pulled back to a different moment, one I wanted to forget. It was as though my memory was snagged on a doorknob and wouldn't unhook.

The moment I wanted to forget was when Sid and I got the last bus home. Not that a bunch of skinheads had beaten us up or anything. I wasn't lying in bed with a bag of frozen peas on my eye. No, the bus was full of normal people making their way home after a night out. Some of them got on at the same bus stop as us. Some of them had Globetrotters' programmes. We'd shared the same show, the same experience. For a couple of hours, our lives had come together under that one arena roof. At any moment you could've turned to one of them and said, "What about when so and so did such and such?" and immediately you'd have something to talk about.

Most of the seats were taken, except for a few at the front. Sid and I sat behind the driver, facing each other on opposite benches. Despite my yawning, Sid was determined to teach me about Pareto efficiency. He was like that. In the queue at the paper shop, say, he'd tell you about the buildup of silt deposits in some Orinoco tributary, or he'd paint a day in the life of a research biologist on Spitzbergen while you were trying to scrape dog poo from your trainers. He was always odd and interesting, but it was late and we were going home. So finally I said, "I really want to be quiet." I don't know if he minded. I was so glad for the silence that I didn't care.

Mulling things over, I couldn't decide if it had been as life-changing a night as Lance and I were sure it would be when we first bought the tickets. When would I know? What would that life-changing feeling feel like? What if my being unsure about it meant it couldn't have been as great as I'd hoped? I pondered, and looked around. The bus was nearly all young blokes, and couples. At some point, without being fully conscious of it happening, I sort of came to. It was then that it hit me, just how people on the bus were looking at Sid, or at me, or at him and then me. What really got me was how none of them made even the slightest effort to be sneaky, to pretend that they weren't looking, the way any normal person would. No wonder Lance decided not to come. And no wonder Sid kept to himself. Oddly enough, he didn't seem to notice. If he did, he didn't say anything about it after we got off the bus. Maybe he'd had it happen so often that he no longer cared.

Anyway, that's what I drifted off to sleep thinking about – being stared at. You couldn't pretend to be invisible even if you wanted to; people would always stare. Same with being a mongol, or anything like that. I couldn't stand having people look at me everywhere I went, specially when you knew they weren't looking because they envied you, or wanted to be like you, or anything good. No, there was nothing good about it. They were only weighing up how much better they were than you.

26

I split my foreskin over Katrina. Luckily there was a tube of Bonjela in Mum's bathroom, which soothed the cracks and eventually put me right. After a weekend of marathon wanking, I threw Katrina out. I had to. But by then I didn't mind. I was bored of her. The more I took her photo out for another session, the plainer she seemed. There was nothing new. That's when it hit me. I'd been barking up the wrong tree. Even though I had envelopes full of different-sized features, I'd pulled my hair out hunting for features that looked identical to the ones in the real photos. *National Geographic's* lepers and beggars became my new models. Life was all about the lumps and bumps, not the smooth bits. I came of age. Mixing all sorts of shapes and sizes, I set about jumbling up my new women so that none of their features matched. Sometimes I'd leave off an eye or an ear, or give them sharp chins and tashes. When I'd got each one as close as I wanted, I spent ages gluing her parts together in the scrapbook and then left her to dry overnight. The next day I'd think up a name for her and then imagine her life. My favourites were Lightheaded Holly, whose hair fell out when she was ten and never re-grew, and who'd patented hair implants using corn silk. I was also fond of one-eyed Pippa Tompkins, who'd overcome her orphanage upbringing to become the first lady in space.

These new creations seemed ten times realer than any I'd done before. For the first time they felt like pieces of me, like they'd been inside me all along, waiting for the right form to inhabit, to come out and live. They were my family. My job was to make them whole and send them out into the world.

Time passed. I picked my five favourites and expanded their bios. The one for Davina the jug-eared barrister went something like:

> Although Davina had the misfortune as a child to have her nose bitten off by a donkey, she is too stubborn and determined to let her visage stop her from realising her goals. She is a successful barrister, and for the last five years has been the Torbay rumba queen. She is a keen snorkeller and enjoys taking novices under the pier.

In red capitals at the bottom of each portrait I wrote *This lady wants you. In the next few days she'll contact you. Open your heart.* From the phonebook I jotted a list of men's names and sent out batches of five envelopes at a time, each to a different stranger, with no note as to where they'd come from.

Paranoid about getting caught, I cycled around town dropping one envelope in each letter-box. I was almost tempted to send a couple to myself. The only post I ever got were the tourist information packs I sent off for from around the world, and even they had to go to Lance's so that Dad didn't find out. My chosen recipients had no idea how lucky they were.

After sending out thirty, I came across my Anastasia Bulimia Iden-tikit on the CrimeWave page of the *Argus*, heading a column warning the public against accepting offers from female strangers, and urging them to come forward should they receive a copycat envelope in the post. Dad was right: people are stupid. I took the clipping and stuck it in my scrapbook. If that was the thanks I got for sending my fam-ily out to add light to people's lives, then those miserable gits didn't deserve them. Let them spend the rest of their days in the dark.

27

If Norm hadn't mentioned how much mess his new loo and conserve-a-tree were going to make at the back of his house, we would've been none the wiser. But all that DIY on his assistant-manager-of-a-carpet-shop's wage? Not likely. The rumours started. Some said he'd been left a packet by some rich spinster he'd been knocking off and who'd recently pegged out. Others said he'd hit the jackpot on the Premium Bonds. Dad plumped for Spot the Ball, which he and Norm filled out on their regular weekly snooker nights down the Legion. "He can see what's not there better than what is," said Dad, who fleeced Norm so often at snooker that anyone else would have called it quits. Others took Norm's win as a lucky sign. If the tide could turn for him, it could just as well turn for them. Which, funnily enough, it didn't. And even though he did his best to cheer everyone up by standing a whole night of drinks at the Legion, plus a buffet headed by crab-and-cucumber triangles, it wasn't enough. It couldn't be. He'd struck lucky, and there was no getting away with it.

Word of a free drink and nosh-up got everyone going, even Vi, who almost never set foot in the Legion. She knew that Mum wouldn't be seen dead in there, no matter what the occasion, so there was no danger of a scene. Not that Vi minded: hanging her dirty washing out was second nature to her. I kept trying to get Dad to teach me bar billiards, but he said it wasn't the time for it, so I went and stood by the vol-au-vents, which were prawn, my favourite. I was scoffing my fifth when Vi came over with her paper plate and started another what-she-thought-of-Mum speech. Dad cut her off by saying I'd been bending his ear about bar billiards and why didn't she give me a game? After loading her plate with half an asparagus quiche, she agreed. Over we went. She put her plate down and picked up her quiche. It went floppy. She rescued it with the other hand and ate it like that, one hand supporting it, the other feeding it in.

"Got any change?" I said. She shook her head. Looking around, she saw Dad, who was listening to a lady with high hair and pearls. Vi swallowed something the size of a pebble and called him over. He didn't look happy, but he came. He even put his own change in the slot. When he pulled the lever out, the ticking started. That was the timer, he said. The balls we potted would keep coming back until the timer stopped. The game ended when there were no more balls to pot. Then he explained the pegs, which were miniature wood-and-wire crosses that stood directly in front of the holes. You couldn't pot a ball with a direct hit, only with a crafty rebound off the cushion. If you knocked one of the white pegs down you lost whatever you'd scored on that go; if you knocked the only black peg down at the front of the table, you lost your entire score, and probably the game.

We started. It was tricky to get the hang of, hitting the balls with just the right pace as well as working out the angles. I only scored three hundred on my first two turns. Vi was a natural, and steamed ahead. I felt a sulk coming on. The cues were crap, the timer annoying, the table sloped.

Bored of the game, I knocked the black peg down on my third shot to see what Dad would do. His reaction was classic.

He was about to wipe my score from the board when Vi stopped him. "What are you playing at?" she said.

"Doing the score," he said, innocently.

"I've hardly got going," I said.

"He who has nothing can't be punished," said Vi.

"He knocked the black down," said Dad, enunciating each word. "He loses automatically."

"Why didn't you say this was the Olympics?" said Vi. "I'd've worn a nice frock."

"All right," he said. "Do it your way."

"I'm the one winning," Vi said, "and I say my opponent gets another try."

"I just—"

"What?"

Dad sounded sad, like we'd got him all wrong. "How can you play the game if you . . . by making it up as you go?"

"Oh, Stanley," said Vi. "Get some Ex-Lax, will you? Give us all a break."

Dad kept going on about how Norm didn't have to tell him about his winnings if he didn't want to. After all, it was no one else's business but his. Then he said something about a man and his castle. Still, they *were* mates, and in-laws, and they *did* play snooker every Thursday. You'd think he'd say something. It got to Dad. He did his best to keep his nose out of it, but he wasn't made that way. So when Norm came in the shop one afternoon to ask if he could borrow me at the weekend to help with some demolition, Dad's face beamed like a fruit machine. "Demolition?" he said. "Demolish what?"

I didn't mind. The plan meant not only a weekend at Norm's house but also a Saturday away from the shop.

"You're my eyes and ears," said Dad. "Find out what he's got."

When Norm picked me up from home that Saturday morning, who should be in his van but Vi's Roy. Roy was like ten master craftsmen in one. Hawthorn hedges were his favourite. Vi said he'd learnt how to lay them in Devon after his breakdown, which was before they met. All that threading and weaving kept his brain straight. But there wasn't much call for hedges by the seaside, so he took whatever he could find. He'd rebuilt a section of Vi's garden wall using pebbles and flint to give it a local feel – they built everything with them down our way. Vi's wisteria climbed a trellis Roy had made and fixed to the back wall next to the kitchen window. He changed the brake cables and cotter pins on my push-bike. His shed was full of bombproof army radios, their guts spread across his workbench. Mum would've fallen over backwards for him all those years ago when she was doing up the Remora. Who knows, he and Mum might've been made for each other. We might've had a house without all the picking and digging, all the tit for tat. We might've had something to smile about.

Norm wanted to sell his flint cottage and buy something with a bigger garden. He had a mind full of teepees and runner beans. But when the surveyor came round, Norm soon learned that the downstairs bathroom extension he'd inherited was craply built and needed to come down before it did him or anyone else some damage. So Norm had second thoughts. He put his beans on hold. He decided he liked his cosy cottage more than he thought he did, so he took it off the market. There was room enough out the back for an extension. And if he was as keen on gardening in a couple of months as he was then, he could get an allotment. A tenner a year? Say no more. That way it could be an occasion, somewhere to trudge off to of an evening to do the watering. Chances were you wouldn't bother so much if it was in your garden. Too easy. An allotment was a project. That's what he needed. He'd learn to be happy where he was.

Roy climbed onto the sloped roof while I stood near the top of the ladder, gripping the gutter for dear life, petrified, dreading the ladder sliding from under me as my feet tried to hook it back. It might've only been eight feet off the ground, but it felt like I was swinging in a cradle, ten stories up, cleaning windows. The bone in my arse ached. The sooner Roy got those tiles lifted, the better. He handed them down a few at a time. I clutched them to my chest with one arm while the other clung to the ladder, then trembled my way down. If Roy had been my dad, I would've been born braver, without my chicken gene, plus I'd have huge fat paddle hands and arms bulging with veins. Even when he had his feet up in the garden, which, like Dad, wasn't often, Roy's arms looked like they'd spent the morning lifting cars. It wasn't fair. But after loading the barrow at market and then slinging the fifty-pound sacks of spuds onto the lorry, mine still only looked like they'd been playing fiddlesticks.

Norm was in the cellar with his demijohns, setting them up on a not very steady bench made from bandstands and scaffold planks, which he'd shown us when we got round there. The base of each bandstand was covered in dried pug, which made them uneven. Roy rocked the bench with one finger. His face said it all. Norm said he'd thought about cleaning them up but then changed his mind. They'd be fine. Maybe if I got done with chipping the pug off of the bricks so they could be used again for the dwarf wall on the conserve-a-tree, I could chip away at the bandstands? Roy pointed to the row of full demijohns, then looked down to where I'd be kneeling beneath them if I were down there chipping.

"Hardly," he said.

When Norm came up for elevenses, he was pulling some webby cack from his hair. He had two corks on his hand.

"It's like rocket fuel that last batch," he said. "The speed they come out those bottles. Catch one of them in the back of the head you'd know it."

If Roy hadn't been so nervous of words he might've said something like, "Yeah, and catch a row of demijohns in the back of the head when you're under the bench and you'd know it too." But he didn't. After making the teas Norm sat against the wall and rolled a fag. I was dying for one but couldn't let him see me smoke. If he was as crafty as Dad reckoned, he wouldn't think twice of grassing me up. You can't find room for every secret. Keeping your winnings close to your chest was one thing; not telling anyone I smoked was another.

There was a slug at the edge of the path. I pointed to it. As soon as Roy saw it, he got up and looked for a stick. When he'd found one, he crouched down and started bothering it.

"It's not hurting anyone," I said.

He prodded it a couple more times then got up. His knee cracked. He came over and sat down again.

"So where'd you get the money for all this?" I said.

Norm grinned and tapped his nose. If anything happened to Mum and Dad and I had to go and live with him, I'd kill him in a week. He did that to you.

"What's the big deal?" I said.

"My thoughts exactly."

"No, with you, I meant."

"There isn't one," he said. "Since when did they make a law saying a man's not entitled to a stroke of luck now and again?"

I looked at Roy, hoping he'd help me dig the news out of Norm. Cross-legged opposite me, he seemed to flit between listening and drifting off, his eyes glazed over, his whatever he called it floating up and watching us from above. His not being bothered made things worse. "You're my eyes and ears, remember." I felt like I couldn't come away from there without knowing, without hearing it from the horse's mouth. Where was Norm hiding it? You can't win a fortune and not tell anyone. If it *was* a win, that is. I understood why Dad and everyone else wanted to wring Norm's neck.

"Got yourself a girlfriend yet, Matthew?" asked Norm.

"Yep."

"What's her name?"

"What's it to you?"

"I knew it."

"Knew what?" I said.

He sniffed. "Pinocchio."

"Where's yours then?"

He moved his tea about, wiped his Rizla papers against his leg. "Trunky want a bun?"

"Given her one, have you?"

"Little boys should be seen and not heard." Pleased by his own cheek, Norm smiled at Roy, as if hoping for a gold star. But Roy was picking at the stitching on his boot.

"Tell us," I said. "Who is she? That old tramp bird on the roundabout with the kitten?"

Norm looked at where the sun was, then at his watch. Like he knew anything.

Roy yawned loudly. The sun came and went on the wall.

"What's your IQ?" Norm said.

"A million," I said.

"Can't be. It only goes up to . . . nowhere near that. I got a book from Oxfam the other day, all different tests. One of them, you tick the boxes that apply to you and then you add it all up – different boxes get different points, and then some get none and then others you take away and – anyway, you turn to the back and it tells you what your perfect job is, your ideal, like, what you'd exceed at. Not just that. You can work out what the best place to live is for someone with your qualities and temperature."

"Heat-wise, you mean?"

"Go on then," he said, folding his arms. "Job."

"What?"

"My perfect one. Guess."

"Helen? Sylvia?"

"Don't be funny. Go on."

"I asked first. Fair's fair."

"A hundred and seven," he said.

"Who is?"

"My IQ. That's well above average. Roy? Not bad that, is it?"

"Mercurial," said Roy, with a yank at his stitching.

Later that day, while I was chipping pug from the old bricks, a sharp flake flew into my eye, my right one, which luckily wasn't my best one – it always went blurry when I looked through my telescope. Talk about agony. My eye streamed. I couldn't open it. Cornea, said Roy. Norm phoned Mum. Twenty minutes later, as I sat on the ground with a balled-up tea towel pressed against my eye, Mum arrived. Off to Casualty we went. As we were leaving, I looked at the pathetic stack of bricks I'd cleaned. I'd have to make up for it the next day. What Dad said about a change being as good as a rest wasn't true. Only a rest was a rest; a change could be anything, including a trip to Casualty and life with one eye.

Coming round the long sloping curve of Salmon Street, past the new space-age church on the right where the old arts centre used to be, we stopped at the traffic lights. A bride with her puffy peach dress bunched in her hands scurried across the road. Other wedding people followed. My good eye was on the small group of kids standing about twenty yards past the church. They obviously weren't there for the wedding. And then I twigged: it was Massimo. He was one of three kids on the pavement, two standing side by side in front of a third, blocking his way. It looked as though Massimo was up to his usual, hassling someone for fags or change. Couldn't he take the weekend off from being a wanker? It must've been tiring. Massimo's older brothers, Frank and Gino, were on the low wall beside the pavement, along with their little brother Marco, who slept in the bath 'cause his parents were too poor to buy him a bed.

It took me a while to realise that the kid Massimo was blocking was Sid, who had his arms at his side as he tried to pass them, first on the left, then on the right, then on the left . . . When the kid standing beside Massimo moved closer to Sid as if to grab hold of him, I nearly had a seizure. That kid was Lance.

"What's wrong?" said Mum.

"Nothing," I said.

"What was that sound for?"

"What sound?"

She mimicked a sharp intake of breath. I shrugged and stared at the kids. I couldn't believe it, couldn't trust my one good eye to be telling the truth. Lance was prodding Sid while Massimo just stood there. Then, as Lance began circling Sid, Sid followed him round warily, like he was on a revolving dish that Lance was turning. When he'd turned enough that I could see more than his back, it was obvious that Sid was trying to get away, trying to appeal to Lance and Massimo's better natures, which he should've known was a waste of time, especially with Massimo, who often went through Sid's pockets at school to nick his dinner money, even though Sid never had any.

Then I saw Lance spit at Sid. I wiped my good eye and looked at the church to see if it was blurred. It wasn't. Sid looked down at what had landed on his chest. Rather than look up again, he kept his head down to avoid eye contact, in the hope that Lance would stop. It was a good idea, but it didn't work.

"Isn't that the boy from up the road?" said Mum. I'd almost forgotten she was there. "Your friend?"

"Whose friend?"

"You know. The dark boy?"

"Looks like it."

"Shame. Fallen in with the wrong crowd..."

"That kid's gobbing at him."

"What's 'gob' when it's at home?"

Lance closed in on Sid. If Sid hadn't been looking at the ground, arms at his side, concentrating on being invisible, on transforming his own bodily matter to gas, they would've been face to face.

Then Mum said, *"Le poisson est sur la mer."*

The last thing I saw as we drove off was Massimo and Lance stepping aside to let Sid by, and Lance landing one last gob on his back, which Sid had no choice but to ignore. Even if Sid had it in him to fight, the feeblest excuse would be enough for Massimo's brothers to jump down from the wall and pummel him. But rather than turn around and go home, Sid carried on walking in the direction he'd been heading, into town. It would he heaving on a Saturday. Everyone would see he was covered in gob. I felt like winding my window down and shouting out at him to go home, jump in the shower, and throw his clothes in the wash. But knowing how deaf to the world he was, it seemed pointless. Besides, I didn't want Lance to know I'd seen what he'd done, even though I couldn't believe how cuntish he'd been, or how no one had lifted a finger to stop him. Before we changed lanes and got buried in traffic, I caught a last juddering glimpse of Sid in my wing mirror. Rather than slumping along with his head down, he looked proud and determined, like he was on his way to an interview.

28

There were many drawbacks to the Schlieffen Plan. Perhaps the most impor-
tant was that it called for seven-eighths of the entire German army to be sent
against France on what would become known as the Western Front. It made
no provision for protecting Germany in the east. Although Schlieffen wasn't
interested in naval warfare, the piers along the south-east coast of England
were rigged to explode in case the Germans invaded. They thought about it
but they couldn't get enough boats. Piers are an institution. Our seaside would
have been ruined forever if they'd blown them up.

29

"How long for?" I said, checking the booking register. It was my night for reception duty.

"Sunday," said the kid, who was Japanese, and in his early twenties. So was the girl. I'd never seen anyone from Japan before. They had flat plastic faces. I made a mental note: no lines, no eyelashes.

I ran my finger across the booking grid. "All we've got are en-suites." I waited. Then I said, "Own bathroom. No share."

For a moment they conferred in silence. Then there was a quick burst of chat.

"Very nice," I said to persuade them.

They both smiled, pleased, apparently, that their stay was about to turn luxurious, or at least nicer than they thought. They nodded a lot. How much? he asked. If Mum had been dealing with them, she would've thrown them out there and then, said she'd made a mistake, there weren't any rooms after all, and sent them off to Pea Lane, by the cement plant, where all the prostitutes stood. I told them the difference in price to a normal room. More nodding. OK, he said. I got their key and offered to help them with their cases, but they only had rucksacks, which were ten times too big for them, and which they'd kept on their backs. Once they'd embarked on the stairs, I went over and watched.

The next morning, I was eating my Weetabix in the kitchen when Dad charged in. He looked like he'd been in a crash.

"What's going on?" he said to me.

"What?"

"The Nips. Who let them in?"

I told him that they came late last night and I'd sorted them out a room. Five was vacant so I'd given them that. I thought he might get a bit excited about having some non-Anglo-Saxons under his roof, and what were probably our first ever Japs, but not like that.

"Come with me," he said.

"He's eating his breakfast, Stanley," said Mum.

"I'll give him breakfast. You. Now."

I got up and followed him into the breakfast room, to the Japanese couple's table. They looked scared. With good reason. Other guests noticed, and looked up. Dad didn't care.

"Listen," he said to the Japanese kid. "My boy here, he double booky. Room no more." He drew a line across the air. "After breakfast, you go. No stay. Understand?"

The bloke might've understood, but the girl didn't know what was going on.

"You can't," I said. "The room's free."

"Your mouth's done enough damage as it is. You two, hop it."

Whether they translated Dad's speech word for word didn't matter, they got the gist. They weren't welcome. And twenty minutes later, without so much as a peep, and with Dad refusing to take their money, which was totally unheard of, they were gone.

"Enjoy your march," Dad shouted after them.

The last thing he said to me about it was that he didn't want their sort anywhere near us. And woe betide me if I let any of them in again.

I told Mum how much I hated Dad not just for treating the Japs like that but also for dragging me into his nasty little world in front of the other guests, and that until he said sorry I wasn't going to talk to him or go to market with him or help him in the shop, and if that meant he had another heart attack then so be it. That's what he deserved. She told me to calm down and listen. She had something to say. She wiped her hands and sat down with me at the table. She was using her funeral voice. I'd only heard it twice.

"You know your father, Matthew. He keeps a lot inside. But I don't want the two of you falling out. That business earlier."

"It wasn't fair," I said. "They didn't do anything."

"All right, all right. Now, what I'm about to tell you goes no further than these four walls, you hear?"

"Yeah."

"I mean it."

"Double yeah."

"All right. This is something you should know. He won't tell you. He almost didn't tell me. Now, do you remember any mention of your granddad, your dad's dad?"

"Not really. Oh, not Uncle Rex's brother?"

"Right. Alf. Well, he was in the war. In Burma. Fighting the Japanese. When the Japanese won, they took prisoners. It was a terrible business. Thousands died. A lot of your granddad's mates didn't come back. He was…well, not lucky, but—"

She was having trouble. She went to the counter and got some tissues from the box, came back blowing her nose.

"He never told a soul. Then, about three years after that, he walked into the sea. Out by Angmering. The last anyone saw of him. Your poor dad. He was six."

"Didn't he say anything?"

She reached under the table. "They found this." She put a folded piece of paper on the table. It was thick and creased, ancient-looking. She slid it to me. We both looked at it. "Read it then."

I opened it on the table. It looked too fragile to pick up. Knowing my luck it would fall apart in my hands. Try explaining that.

> My Dearest Stanley. This world isn't for everyone. I tried my best, but it kept on being not enough. Be a good boy for your Mum. Forgive me. Love, Dad.

And then Mum burst into tears, which started me off. Considering she never cried, she was pretty good at it. I didn't know what to do except wipe my eyes. I thought about getting up and putting my arm around her, but we weren't like that. We didn't cry, or hug: we shook hands. I asked if she was all right. She nodded. While I waited for her to clear her tubes, I thought of Lucy, and wondered when she'd phone.

"Honestly, Matthew," Mum said, her voice jumpy and strange. "I didn't know. I really didn't."

"Didn't know what?"

Whatever she meant to say made her cry so hard she couldn't. She folded the note and put it away. Then, shaking her head as though I'd just asked for a new bike, she waved me away.

30

Lance was suspended from school for setting fire to the lockers. Instead of being tamed by his accident, his pyromania had got worse, as though he wanted revenge for being scarred for life. That the accident was his own stupid fault didn't come into it; he was a victim, and victims deserved justice. So he squirted lighter fluid over his PE kit in his locker, then emptied the rest of the can over some coats and bags hanging on the racks opposite. The fire spread in no time. He said it was a conspiracy, that Massimo had done it. But by then the powers that be had put up with so much of his lying that they were as sick of him as I was.

After his suspension, and while his psychiatric report was being done, he showed up at the shop with some of my newly arrived tourist envelopes. Fiji and Turkey. I was still waiting on Zanzibar.

"What do you take me for?" I said, checking the envelopes to see if they'd been stamped or franked. They almost always franked them. Fancy a tourist office not using its country's stamps. What sort of a message did that send?

"You're smart," he said, "that's why I'm telling you. You know what Massimo's like."

"I know what you're like. You'd tell the truth just to lie."

Confused, he picked off a branch of red grapes and walked to the door.

"I *was* gonna show you the rubbings I did at that graveyard in Durrington," he said.

"What a tease," I said.

"Fuck off," he said, and threw a grape at me. "D'you know what you should've been?"

"Here we go," I said.

"A seagull."

"Why?"

"Cause you shit on everything."

"Me?"

"Yeah, you."

"That's strange," I said. "I was reading the *Guinness Book of Records* the other night. They had you down as the world record holder for Shitting on Things. There was a photo of you, too. The old you. You looked much better."

He thought for a second. A second was his limit. Then he let out a sly smile. "I saw your mate the other day."

"What mate's that?" I said.

"Your Paki mate. Yeah. 'pparently he's a mad Globetrotters fan." He popped a grape into his mouth, chewed it. "Funny that."

"Is it?"

He nodded. "As a matter of interest, would you say my mum's a liar?"

"No. Why would I? I've always fancied her."

"That's disgusting," he said. "Trouble is, she told me that you told her that you were going to the Globetrotters with your old man."

"And?"

"We both know old Stanley never goes anywhere, specially with you. Which wouldn't've mattered really, if I hadn't seen him the other day. You'd be surprised who I see. So I says to him, 'Did you enjoy the Harlem Globetrotters, Mr. Bowen?' D'you know what he said?"

"Obviously not," I said.

"'Trotters? We don't sell trotters, lad. Try the butcher's over the road.' How 'bout that?"

"So?" I knew what was coming, but I didn't know how to get out of it. Lance could smell a lie from a mile off. I could tell by his voice that he'd decided the same thing that I had a while back: that our friendship was nothing like it used to be. I'd heard him use that same slow cocky tone with other kids when he knew they were lying. But knowing what's happening is easy; knowing what to do about it isn't. I knew he definitely wasn't expecting me to look him in the eye and tell him the truth. So that's just what I did.

"So why'd you lie to my mum? She paid for the tickets."

"I knew you'd go up the wall," I said. "I felt bad about it."

"Not that bad."

I stopped myself from saying that if he hadn't wanted to make everyone feel even more sorry for him by denying himself the pleasure of seeing the Globetrotters, his heroes, the heroes he'd dreamed for years of seeing, then he would have gone with me. But no, he had to squeeze every last drop of pity he could get.

I said, "We were chatting on the way home from school. Sid asked me if I was going. His brother tried to get tickets but it was sold out. I told him I could only go if I had someone to go with."

"Does your old man know you went with a Paki?"

"For fuck's sake! Does it matter? You weren't using your ticket. You didn't wanna go. You could've easily—"

"What?" he said. "Could've easily what?"

I stopped and swallowed. Outside, a quick gust caught our sign for cheap marrows, making it spin. I saw a steeple in my mind, and a weather cock. N, E, S, W.

"How d'you think I feel?" I said. "It's not exactly been a laugh a minute for me either."

"Yeah? Well poor fucking you," he said. He dropped the rest of the grapes and walked out.

The sign kept spinning.

31

The next day, when Sid and I went over to Old Francis's place, Sid tried ducking out by using Lance as an excuse. I'd gone over the stile and was looking across the overgrown field trying to suss out the best way to the house, less than a hundred yards away.

Sid kept turning to look at the playground. "I'm waiting for Lance."

"They chucked him out. Didn't you hear?"

He hadn't.

When I told him about the locker fire, he wasn't surprised, even though I was, and I'd known Lance since Cubs, which we both went to only twice. Nor did Sid say anything about Lance's suspension. There was silence. Then he twigged. "So who's going with me?"

"No one. That's what I said. Two quid if you go up and bang on his door."

Crouching through the long grass, we angled our way towards the tatty barn with its square gaping doorway and its sides full of rotten slats. It looked derelict, but then so did the half-collapsed house to the side of it. And, come to think of it, so did Old Francis. From the barn it was only a quick dash to the house and then a longer sprint back to the stile. Halfway there, I stopped.

"I'll wait here," I said. "Follow the side of the barn. And remember: you get the two quid only if you bang on his door."

Sid stared at the barn. When he moved off alone he looked like a sleepwalker, or as if he were being controlled by remote, stumbling in and out of potholes like a Meccano man. At the back of my mind I wanted him to bottle out. I didn't have the two quid on me.

All he had to do was skirt along the barn and then sprint to the house, but he froze at the barn door, and stood there looking in. Eventually he shifted round and eyed the house, planning his final move.

Then, just as he was about to make his final dash, I shouted: "Francis! Quick! Run!"

He was off like a shot, bolting back towards me through the tall grass like he was on the last leg of a relay. I felt the wind from him when he passed me. If he could run like that on sports days, he'd hold the school record for centuries, and probably the county one too. He was over that stile like a hurdler. I followed.

"Christ," I said, clutching my ribs like him. "I thought you were a goner."

As we stood there, his eyes didn't leave Francis's field. I had to tell him he was safe, that Old Francis could hardly walk straight let alone sprint.

"You knew that would happen," he said.

"No I didn't! Swear on my mother's life."

He sulked off towards the playground.

Again I followed.

He said, "I don't believe you."

"Don't then," I said, thinking he was as childish as Lance. We walked for a bit. When I got bored of the silence I said, "I bet he's killed tons of people. Bet he chops them up and boils them in acid and uses them for fertiliser. That's why the grass is so long."

"Shut up."

More silence. Then, "You could be the next Allan Wells."

He wouldn't let on that he was proud.

I waited for Sid after school that day and made him walk home with me. Well, I didn't make him, but I did everything I could to get him talking, including telling him again how fast he was. (I didn't say that I'd seen him getting spat on by Massimo.) At first he was quiet. Then he gave the odd grunt. As we walked by the gasometer, which was only about a third high, with its round iron frame poking into the sky, he finally piped up. "I bet his house is full of skellingtons," he said. He said other words funny too, like sword, which he pronounced as it was spelt, but then so did kids from up the road who'd never been to India, or to Margate even, and who had no excuse. And even though he was every teacher's pet and never shut up in lessons, that didn't mean you had to nick his bag, run off to the field, tip everything out of it, and then sling it high into a tree the way Saul Quek did one break time. In order to get it down, the caretaker lugged round one uselessly short ladder after another until he finally recruited a couple of kids to help him carry a three-section job, which did the trick. Quek got a thousand lines for it – *I will not throw other people's bags into trees*. He said he got so bored of repeating himself that by the end he'd whittled the line down to *I will throw trees*, which earned him a week's worth of detention and another thousand lines.

When they bullied kids like that, I sometimes told them how stupid it was and tried getting them to stop, but unless you were prepared to push your point further than you really wanted to, even as far as a punch-up, it was a waste of breath. I'd had enough of sticking up for Lance without starting all over again with Sid, who was tons more unpopular, and a losing battle from the start. I'd probably end up with a kicking.

Once you got Sid talking, he wouldn't stop. Still, I liked being quiet. I could listen. That day he told me about the Koh-i-noor diamond, how it was found in a tin box in a tool shed and given to Queen Victoria ("and your lot still won't give it back," he said). Another day he told me about his mum's beard and why she drank ten cans of Coke a day – it was good for the squits – and how he was worried about inheriting her problem, which he hadn't yet. Then I learned about his granddad who, when he was dying in India, swallowed his secret collection of rubies so that his greedy brothers wouldn't get them. When his granddad died, the hospital nurse opened the windows to release his spirit. If they didn't, he said, his granddad would be forever roaming the corridors looking for a way out.

It made me think. After I'd thought I said, "I doubt they'd do that on the NHS."

What I liked most about his talking was how his hands worked overtime with his mouth, like a double act, a ventriloquist and his dummy. The more he talked, the more his hands flew about, as though frantically keeping up. I wanted to get good at it, so I practiced in my room, but every time I made myself move my hands when I spoke, it felt weird, wrong, like I was trying too hard to copy him instead of getting better at being me.

More often than not, and without ever really agreeing to, we started walking home from school together. Mostly this involved one of us catching up with the other. On our walks, Sid told me about going out with his brother to do discos, but only in the daytime. His mum wouldn't let him go to the sorts of places his brother worked in at night. Hard as I tried, I couldn't think of any reason to have a disco in the middle of the day, but Sid reckoned there was a lot of call for them along the seaside, with kids' birthdays and stuff. In summer, companies set up beach parties to promote their new drinks. Sid said it was like the *Radio One* roadshow, which came to Farthing once when I was seven. I didn't go.

"Gary's got more records than anyone," he said. "That's why he's always out. He's buying a Transit soon. The Escort isn't big enough for all his new dry ice machines. I'm his top roadie."

"Who's second?"

"You ask lots of questions," he said. "Normally questions are good. At school people get very annoyed with me for asking so many questions, but how else can you learn? Where are their questions? Do they know so much?"

I nodded. "So who's second?"

"My sister, but she doesn't know anything. That's why I'm top."

A week or so later we were standing in his front garden. I was teaching him the throw-the-cat-in-the-air game to see if it landed on its feet. "What if your dad sees us?" I said, imagining him running out and rescuing the probably sacred cat, and then complaining to my dad about me, which would set off a huge row and make Dad hate the Bhargavas even more, and make him flog me for fraternising with the enemy. But he didn't, and the cat soon got tired of our game. It ran off and disappeared for weeks, which Sid blamed on me, saying it wouldn't have happened if I wasn't so cruel and hadn't come up with the game in the first place, which I hadn't. Lance had taught me the game at his house. Eventually it came back, but Sid wasn't so keen on it since the top of its ear had been bitten off and one of its back legs dragged.

It got more and more awkward coming up with reasons why I wouldn't go in his house, which was stupid because I wanted to. But Dad would know I'd been round there by the smell on my clothes. After coming up with a plan, I waited for Sid to ask me again, and for him to moan about why I always said no, and how he'd run out of reasons to explain to his mum and dad, who really wanted to meet me.

Their house didn't smell of tea and toast, more like the Indian equivalent, a concentrated version of what clung to Sid's clothes. If I'd combed a dictionary for the next ten years I wouldn't find names for those smells. God knows where they got them. In all my poking about town, I'd never seen a shop sell anything close to the sort of spices the Bhargavas must've used to make food like that. Where did you start? I looked at the coving, the skirting, the carpets – all the edges needed doing. If only I could tell Dad that when he ran out of things to do at home, there was a whole houseful of jobs waiting for him there.

They used the same room for meals as we did. I counted six sets of tables and chairs. That wouldn't get them very far in summer. The main thing they had was a giant gold elephant's head in the fireplace, which seemed a bit daft. How could they use the fire? I don't know whose idea it was to hang flowers around the elephant's neck, but it cheered things up a bit, made the room more friendly. Around the elephant were little dishes of petals and some fresh-looking oranges and bananas. Did they sing songs to it? Stand on their heads for it? Chant with their hands on it? I didn't want to ask.

Sid went off to see his mum. I counted nineteen gold bowls, most of them in a big glass cabinet in the same corner as our bar. Instead of the Taj Mahal photos I'd seen in magazines, theirs was made out of different-coloured velvet, like a collage, only more careful, probably done by someone who had at least a B in 'O' level art. There was a snake light around the frame. Waiting for Sid, I watched the light move along the top, down the side, along the bottom, and change from green to white to purple...

He bought in two tall glasses, handed me one.

"It's jaggery," he said. "Do you like it?"

"Love it."

"Liar. You don't know what it is."

"So? What did you ask me for?"

"I knew you'd lie," he said.

"I don't lie."

"You always lie."

"I was agreeing. That's not lying."

He sipped his drink. "It's ayurvedic. Jaggery-treated rats showed enhanced translocation of coal particles from the lungs to the tracheobronchial lymph nodes. It's a natural remedy to pollution. And it cleans your blood."

I was thinking that their house was probably about the same temperature as Sarawak.

"Trees are the lungs of the world," I said. "In Sarawak, which is the world's second largest rainforest after the Amazon, which is in Brazil, which is easily the biggest country in South America, they've cut down so many mahogany trees that it's an endangered species. Like tigers. They make tables out of it." I sipped my drink. It was chilled and tasted sweet and sherryish. It wasn't horrible. "I think we've got one."

"My mum and dad want to meet you," said Sid.

We took our drinks and went through to their personal front room, which was the same one that Mum used for her studio. (Layout-wise, their house was identical.)

With the curtains drawn and the chandelier on, it was hotter than the dining room. Sid's mum and dad both got up from the table at the same time, as though someone had blown a whistle. They were very smiley. Mr. Bhargava was thin and short. (As a family, they were nearly as short as us.) He put his hand out. I shook it, then put my hand out to Sid's mum. She kept hers down, which made for an awkward few seconds until she smiled at my hand as if to say, "Thanks, but no thanks," which was what Sid then said to me. She was the first person I'd ever met who didn't want to shake hands. Well, apart from Roy. I liked her. Across the room, an old grey-haired woman sat on a low stool, mixing something in a bowl with her fingers. That bowl wasn't gold. She carried on mixing when she looked up. I smiled, she smiled, then she went back to her mixing. I looked at all the chairs. They had enough for a convention.

"So you are Siddharth's friend, no?" Mr. Bhargava said, rolling his Rs. He also chewed his words.

"Who?" I said.

He nodded to Sid. "Siddharth."

"Oh. Yes. I thought it was short for Sidney."

"Oh, Sidderney," he said, catching on. "No. Tell me, how is your father?"

"All right. I mean, he's my dad. He's, you know . . . him."

"I see."

Sid's mum listened, expecting me to say something funny or nice. At least, that what her face said. I felt dim when my words dribbled out.

"Well, we are very honoured to make your acquaintance," Mr. Bhargava said. "Please enjoy our home."

"Thank you for your hospitality," I said.

"Don't be stupid," said Sid. "Come on."

His mum pointed to a small pile of clothes on the ironing board. "Put those on Sangeet's bed." Sid tutted before scooping them up and walking out. For a second it was just his mum and dad and me standing by the table, and his nan in the corner. There was something full of arms on the wall. It was a weird moment. For a split second I was Indian, or as good as. Then I shook Mr. Bhargava's soft, limp hand and went after Sid.

He was already halfway up the stairs.

"What did you say that for?" I shouted.

"Say what?"

"You know."

"No I don't."

"About being stupid."

He didn't answer.

We got to the first landing. The hall was so dark you could only see the end of it by the light through the toilet window. Ours would've been just as dark if we didn't have Dad's ingenious wall-mounted carriage lamps spaced at two-yard intervals. As we climbed the last flight of stairs to my floor, it occurred to me that their house was empty – at least, it felt empty. I couldn't imagine that house having the same peak season madness as ours. And even though Sid talked like the clappers, he never said a word about anything guest-related, about any of the things that for half the year made me want to stick my head in the oven – the kids, the noise, the endless doing what I was told. The having no say. He seemed oblivious.

They had a toilet in exactly the same place. He opened the second door along. A totally different smell came out, a girl-getting-ready smell, the same as I'd find when I took soap or towels to one of our guest's rooms. I breathed it in and waited. He dumped the clothes on the bed and came out. "Don't ever have a sister," he said.

"I thought her name was Sandy."

"It is," he said.

"Well how many names have you lot got?"

We walked down the hall to the exact same attic room as mine. It even had the same set of steps leading up to it. But in the alcove, where our hot water tank sat, they had a mini-bathroom, with a sink, toilet, and shower stall. I wasn't jealous.

"Is this your room?" I said.

"No, Gary's."

The room was full of speakers and records and turntables, and spot-lights with all sorts of coloured gels, aimed at the middle of the con-sole, or stage. Not that there was a platform or anything in the middle; he just stood in the square behind his turntables and selected whatev-er records he wanted to play.

In a frame on the wall was a signed photo of Bobby Moore. He was in typical footballer's pose, down on one knee, ball in front. "Is that real?" I said.

Sid looked at it. "Yes."

"What's it doing there?"

He shrugged, then ducked under the console and came up in the middle. "Do you like Devo?"

I was still looking at the photo. "I don't know. What is it?"

The music he put on sounded like hammers and factories, which was all right, but not what I imagined blasting out on the beach during some fizzy drink promotion, or some kids' birthday party. It might've been by the same band that Gary had played at Harry's party, when he was told to take it off. Sid turned the volume up and started doing a weird robotic dance – well, not so much a dance as a chopping his hands up and down and staring at the wall without blinking or moving his head. All I could think was, I wish you wouldn't . . . please don't . . . I'm a guest. But he didn't care. And after a little while, embar-rassing as it was to watch him not being remotely embarrassed, the music and the undance-like dance actually suited him. He'd found music that matched what went on in his head, which might not have worked like a production line, but it wasn't far off. In a way, it made sense of him.

I shouted that I needed the loo. He nodded and carried on.

I closed the door behind me and went down the corridor. Even though the music was still loud, the buzzing in my head was deafen-ing. Devo had gone.

I went into Sandy Sangeet's room.

My dick was harder than *kanji*. The world stopped. Every other woman kept her undies in a top drawer, but not her. Hers were in the bottom. I opened and closed three drawers before finding them. In a blind fumble, I pulled out a tangle of three or four pairs of knickers. They fell on the floor. I chose the lilac ones and threw the others back in the drawer. I stuffed the lilac pair into my pocket and left the room. For all I knew there was another old woman sitting on a stool in the corner.

If I hadn't been wearing Mum's tights, I would've put Sandy Sangeet's knickers on there and then in the loo, but it was too complicated, plus I couldn't rely on my hands, which were shaking like mad. Sid might wonder where I'd been. Approaching Gary's room, I heard Devo blaring. When I went in, Sid was still doing his dance. Everything was the same, except for the knickers. I couldn't wait to wave to Sandy Sangeet when I was wearing them.

32

Zoë was at the same window table in Macari's that she always sat at with Monica, only that day she was alone, with her cheek propped on one hand. She was picking at a scone. I ordered a tea at the counter and pretended I hadn't seen her so that she wouldn't think I'd gone in there because of her, which I had. But she saw me. "Oy, banana boy," she shouted. I looked round. She was doing a slow wide wave over her head.

"You must keep this place going," I said, putting my tea down on her table. I sat opposite her. She licked her finger and dabbed crumbs off her plate. "No Knickerbocker Glory?"

She pointed across the road. "Guess how many seagulls were on that letter-box?" The only one I could see was in front of the Oxfam shop, which had a dummy in the window wearing a spangly *Titanic*-style evening dress. In Farthing the *Titanic* was still news.

"Fifty?"

"On that? Don't be stupid. Seven."

I slurped my tea. "I was gonna ask you something. Do you know Lucy Fortino?"

"I might," she said.

"Right. It's not a trick question."

"What's it worth?"

"A poke in the eye. Do you or don't you?"

"Why, should I?"

"Christ almighty," I said. "Hard work, aren't you?"

"You ever been to Madame Tussauds?"

"Why, should I?"

"Don't be stupid. I'm asking."

"I asked first. Lucy Fortino."

"I said, 'What's it worth?'"

Lucy definitely went to the same school as Zoë: I saw her green-and-white Millais uniform in her wardrobe. So that narrowed things down. I described her brown-blonde hair, centre-parted and a bit hangy. Something about horses and frogs.

Zoë went cross-eyed. "Who's Paul Harding?"

"I don't know. Why?"

She pulled her hair up into a pineapple and fixed it with a scrunchy. "I heard he fancies me."

"Doesn't everyone?"

"Do you?"

"Lucy Fortino," I said. "I've got a really important message for her. Could you give it to her?"

"Nah. Well, I might for a quid."

"Wait a sec."

I went to the counter and asked the girl for a pen and paper. As she searched under the counter, I asked for an envelope too. She rooted some more. "Here," she said, looking hassled, and gave me what I'd asked for. A bloke was waiting to be served, so I went to the end of the counter and wrote *Dear Lucy. I have serious news about your brother. He might be in big trouble. Please phone 816571 and ask for Matt.* I folded the note neatly and sealed it in the envelope.

Back at the table, I handed Zoë the envelope. "Here's what I need you to give her. Promise me you will."

"Where's my quid?" she said.

I got a pound coin from my pocket and slid it to her.

"I'll see what I can do," she said, and winked.

33

After parking my bike outside the kitchen, I peeked through the window and saw Mel, Ruth's daughter, who was further down on the Another Pair of Hands list. She helped when Ruth couldn't make it when Mrs. Hodges couldn't make it when Dad couldn't be bothered and when Mum was having one of her the-world's-too-big days. Mel was dancing in front of the full-length mirror that Dad had put there to make sure the staff, me included, was neatly turned out. Mel was in a world of her own, studying her own moves as she danced to some song in her head. (It definitely wasn't coming from the radio that Mum hid behind the pressure cookers.) After a while I tapped the window and ducked. Nothing. I waited, then tapped again. The back door opened. Mel stuck her head out.

"Nosy sod."

She was sweating. There were small silver crocodiles in her ears.

"Where's Mum and Dad?" I said, arms folded to hide the envelopes down my shirt.

"They had a row. Something about fish. Your dad was behind the bar last I saw."

"What about Mum?"

"Out. She left me with all the cutlery."

"Tough titty."

I ran past her. She put her foot out but missed me. I ran through the kitchen. It smelled of baked beans. Must've been Mel's BO.

Reception was quiet; all I could hear was the telly in the lounge. I crept through, thinking I was in the clear, and that Mum and Dad must've called it a night. But when I reached the third or fourth stair I heard, "Cat got your tongue, has he?" I turned to see Dad holding a wineglass and a polishing cloth.

"No."

"Come on. I'll teach you how to play poker."

I clutched my gut and groaned. "I've had a turn," I said. "I need the loo." Before he could say anything, I ran upstairs.

When the buzzer went a few minutes later, I stuffed the embassy

tourist brochures back into their envelopes and paced the room, trying to decide where to hide them. My secret compartment would take
too long. The buzzer went again – two long, irritated blasts.

"Hello?"

"You all right?" said Dad.

"Yeah."

"Coming down then?"

"Hang on."

"Good lad. Oh, and bring that boot of yours."

"Boot?"

"Your piggy bank. You can't play poker with no chips."

The intercom clicked off. I put the envelopes under my pillow till
later. Then, grabbing the boot, I thought, What does he know about
poker?

Dad was pouring himself a whisky at the bar when I walked in. He
brought it over with a pack of playing cards and his pipe in an ashtray.
I put my boot on the table. "Sit your arse down," he said. I did. "Have
you ever tasted beer?" I shook my head, lying. Round Lance's once
we found an open Party Seven that must've been in the cupboard for
weeks. Lance poured two pint glasses and challenged me to a race.
His didn't touch the sides. I got three quarters of mine down before
throwing it up in the sink.

"'Bout time then," said Dad. He went to the bar and came back with
half a pint of bitter the same colour as the Party Seven. I cringed. The
lounge was empty. "Put hairs on your chest, that." He sat the glass
in front of me.

"Where's Mum?"

He shrugged. "Swimming the Channel for all I know."

Mel poked her head round the door and said she was off. Night, I
said, but Dad was concentrating on doing some fancy shuffle, halving
the pack and edging the corners of each so that they locked into one
another, then arching them in his hands so they'd spring together into
a tidy pile. I waited till he wasn't looking to sip the top inch of my beer,
which tasted so warm and beery, so much like that flat Party Seven
that I had to pretend it was cream soda just to get it down, and still
shuddered as it went. Dad spilt his cards, tried covering the mistake
by scooping them up and giving them a normal amateur's shuffle.

"How come your hands are so big?" I said, spreading mine on the table. They looked stupid, girly, not a vein in sight. Lance had old hands like his uncle and thick veins up his forearms. Each night I checked my arms, convinced I was born veinless, except for the pale blue spidery ones at the sides of my ribs which only stood out when I stretched my arms high over my head.

"Hard graft," he said. "Yours'll be like that one day." As I watched him deal, the pack seemed to shrink in his hands like they were kiddy cards. I looked down at my own hands, hating that they'd never grow anywhere near as big, unless they swelled by miracle. Maybe it was time to talk to God again. "Your Uncle Rex used to say, Small hands, small heart. Can't trust 'em."

I picked up the boot and poured change onto the table. Dad swept a load of coins towards him and started sorting them into piles. I'd never seen him play cards before, and couldn't work out what he was up to. He seemed happy though, as if he'd hit on the idea that my manly future depended on how well I played poker, and that it was his job to teach me.

"Count yours," he said. "Make sure we're even Stevens. A couple of quid should do her."

"Mum's got tiny hands and *she* works. I must have hers."

I put the boot down and wondered where Mum was and when she'd be back, picturing her disapproval when she saw me with a glass of beer. She hated drunks. Refused to work in the bar.

"Don't you trust us?" I said.

"Don't be daft," he said.

Then, counting my change I said, "D'you think there's enough in there for a camera?"

"Could be."

Dad carried on counting aloud for a minute before stopping and looking up. "Tell you what. You guess how much there is. I'll take the boot tonight and count it. If you guess to within a fiver either side, I'll match it. How's that?"

"What if I'm way off?"

"Then I'll come up with a forfeit."

I didn't know what he meant, and said so. He explained it as being like poker, gambling your stake on what was in your hand versus what cards you were dealt next. Bad cards meant you lost your stake. Good ones meant you were quids in. My forfeit would be to clean the car inside and out every Sunday for a month, which was strange seeing as that's how I earned part of my pocket money anyway. Not much of a gamble. Still, I didn't argue. But before I had a chance to guess, the doorbell went.

"Must be Mum."

"Where's her bloody key?" said Dad. He got up from the table and went out to the door. I reached over and took a quick peek at his hand, even though I had no idea what to look for. He might've had a four and a two. Some eights. Nothing to write home about. Saying that, I wouldn't have known if he'd had a full house or a flush.

My ears pricked. Whoever's voice was out in the hall, it definitely wasn't Mum's. I went over to the door, heard a man's voice, murmury and deep. By the time they came in I was standing by the table, about to sit. It was Sid's dad, of all people, wearing a brown pinstriped jacket and a white button-up shirt, and holding a pot covered with a tea towel.

"This is my boy, Matthew," said Dad.

Mr. B switched the pot to his left hand and put out his right. "Yes, yes," he said, smiling. "I know him." When I shook his hand we locked perfectly, a brown and white pair. Dad always said that a firm handshake meant everything, but Mr. B's was again like warm Plasticine, and friendlier. Besides, why would you want to crush someone's hand if you were glad to meet them?

I said, "You make animals, don't you?"

"Just little, you know," said Mr. B.

"Sid showed me your cow. It was excellent."

"You are very kind."

Dad closed an eye as if I was up to something, but I was too intrigued by Mr. B and his pot to worry. Mr. B held the pot with both hands again, out slightly, like an offering. He didn't seem to mind holding it, but I was itching for Dad to put him at ease instead of making him stand there like a lemon.

Finally Mr. B said, "My wife is sending deserts."

I waited for Dad to correct him, but he didn't. Mum would've sat Mr. B down, written the two words out, and educated him on their respective etymologies. He was lucky she was out.

"I'll take it," I said, which I did, nudging my boot aside on the table and setting the pot beside it. The table reminded me of a party game I'd played at Lance's where someone shows you a tray of bits – key, comb, corkscrew, etc. – for a minute and then takes it away. You have to write down all the bits you can remember. I was crap at it. Looking at our table, I thought: beer, boot, saucepan, pipe, coins, cards, ashtray. And whisky, which Mr. B eyed suspiciously, hands behind his back, as we all stared at the table, as if at any moment it would glow or hover or give us the winner of the next Derby.

"You have party, no?" said Mr. B.

"No. I'm teaching Matthew to play poker," said Dad.

"I see," said Mr. B. "Very good."

Mr. B continued to find something funny. From the moment he walked in he had a half-smile on his face which the pot in his hands somehow justified, the pride of a gift waiting to be given, or the aware-ness that taking pans full of pudding as a gift to your enemy wasn't a very normal thing to do. Had it been his idea? And although the pot was now on the table, his smile hadn't changed. I wondered what he was thinking. It was obvious that Sid got his smile and wide-open face – the sort you can't help smiling at even if you're laid up with flu – from his dad. Mr. B's face was an invitation, Dad's a warning. As we stood there quietly, I wished for a split second that Mr. B were my dad too.

Dad said, "Can I get you a drink?"

"Oh, thank you, no," said Mr. B.

Dad sipped his whisky.

"So," said Dad, motioning for Mr. B to sit. Mr. B eagerly acknowl-edged the offer, as if it was a huge relief, a gesture to break the ice. We all smiled. But when Dad pulled his own chair out and went to sit, Mr. B didn't move, didn't seem to register Dad's offer as being an actual offer. Dad looked baffled. "So," he said, "what do we ... How can we help?"

Mr. B stayed where he was, hands still behind his back. Dad didn't move either. The silence got bigger. Whatever Mr. B had come for – maybe a showdown with Dad over the leaflets or the petition? – he was in no rush. His delay was obviously making Dad squirm. I'd nev-er seen Dad like this, awkward and lost for words. After a moment

Mr. B said, "Very special deserts."

The front door slammed.

"Anyone home?" Mum's voice floated through reception and into the lounge like a life jacket, saving us – well, Dad at least – from drowning in silence.

"In here!" I called.

When Mum came in, Mr. B's presence stopped her so fast, like she'd caught her handbag strap in the door. "Oh," she said. Then she put out her hand and, with her fake polite smile, said, "Jean Bowen. A pleasure."

Mr. B smiled, dipped slightly, and took her hand. I watched him give her the same soft shake he'd given me. Their hands fitted too. "No, no. It is my pleasure." He touched the pot on the table. "My wife..."

"Oh," said Mum, glancing at Dad, whose blank face told her nothing. "Well, thank you. There's pork in the fridge if you're hungry."

"Mr. Bhargava just got here," said Dad.

"Thank you," said Mr. B. "Now I go."

"Not on my account," said Mum.

He paused for a moment as if to gather his thoughts. Then he spoke. Something told me that we were at last going to learn why he'd visited us. "My uncle is coming from Kashmir," he said. "With family. Veeery big. Beautiful cookings. Please, you must eat with us before we go."

Dad's ears flicked to attention. "Go? Where?"

"Bry-ton," said Mr. B. "We buy restaurant and shop, here and here." "When?"

"Hmm, perhaps one month. Bed and breakfast not so good, you know? Restaurant veeery good."

Dad said, "We do very nicely, thank you."

"Yes, yes. Good night. Thank you." Mr. Bhargava smiled and made to leave. After Dad followed him out to reception, Mum looked at the pudding pot and then at me. "What was that all about?" she said.

"He was just being nice, I s'pose."

Mum was looking at the table when Dad came back in. Judging by the smile on his face, you'd have thought we'd just won the Ashes.

"It worked! I knew it would."

"What worked?" said Mum.

"The petition," he said. "I got them out."

"Don't flatter yourself. What's this?"

Dad looked at the table. "What?"

"Beer," said Mum.

"Matthew and I are playing poker."

"He's fourteen, Stanley. You're giving him beer?"

"I didn't know it was poison."

"I forgot," she said. "You're not the health expert around here."

Mum stormed off. Dad watched her. It was all my fault. At least, that's how I felt. I wanted to throw the table across the room, watch everything go flying, make Dad have to clear his mess up.

"Sit down," he said.

I did. "What's wrong with her?"

"Your mother? Well. Have you heard of a tortured artist?"

"No," I said.

"That's what she thinks she is. Only she can't paint."

"I thought she liked it. Isn't she happy?"

"Drink your beer," said Dad.

"It's horrible."

"Drink it!"

"It's not fair."

I got up. I didn't even want his stupid beer in the first place. Mum would've been fine if it wasn't for him.

"Matthew," he yelled when I was at the door, but I ignored him and ran up to my room.

A few minutes later there was a knock at my door. Mum never came up. She always left my ironing on the stairs and made the cleaner do my room along with the others, so I knew it wasn't her. It was a clammy night, and the stench from the beach filled my room. I pulled the covers over my head.

"Anyone there?" said Dad.

He came in and perched on the bed, same as that time with my atlas, when he caught me practicing headstands. It made me think of Mr. B, of Sid, of them leaving for Brighton. I didn't want them to go. We'd only just started being friends. Dad pulled the covers off my head. Suddenly there were two stenches: seaweed and whisky.

"You didn't guess how much was in the boot," he said.

"Three trillion."

"Come on."

"Mum hates me. It's not my fault and she hates me."

"Don't be daft. You're her boy."

He leaned over to touch my hair or something. I lurched away, upsetting my pillow. Something fell between my bed and the table beside it. He reached into the gap. "What's this?" he said, coming back up, showing me what he'd found – one of the envelopes. He pulled out the innards. "The Heart of Hawaii?"

"Yeah, that's my . . . my next project. Geography." Then I said, "Thirty-eight pound fifty."

"What?"

"The boot," I said.

"Oh," he said. "You sure?"

"Positive." I was waiting for his head to rewind to the part where he saw the brochure cover and exploded, but he didn't. It was late. Maybe he was tired. He didn't put the brochure back in its envelope, but he also didn't get knocky. He just dropped it on the bed.

"I'll count it and let you know," he said. "Now get some kip."

"All right."

He smiled. "And no dreaming of mermaids."

"No."

"Oh." He stopped, put his hand over his mouth, and squeezed. His eyes went a bit wider. "Those Jap kids. I got carried away. I shouldn't've."

Then he got up and left. Soon as the door closed, I crept out of bed and went over to make sure. Standing with my back against it, I could feel my heart pulsing through the wood. I went to sleep that night imagining a heart the size of a door.

34

The next Monday I bunked off school for the afternoon and hid in the pillbox up Winterpit Lane, not far from the girls' school, so I could get down there for last bell. Winterpit Lane was the main drive to the Glades, our local loony bin. It had its own brickworks and pig-gery, and cut through a straggly arm of the forest as far as the ham-mer ponds. The Glades' main claim to fame was its annual sports day, which always took place on August Bank Holiday. They had a mar-quee and a fête. Who knows, Lucy might have ridden Nutmeg there. People came and ahhed as they watched the cream of the loonies race against teams of visiting loonies. I don't know if they did the steeple-chase, but they chalked out a running track on the front lawn and had a brass band for support. They might've held an egg and spoon race, with no eggs. Whatever they did or didn't have, it was a big fundrais-er. We never went.

Everyone said the Glades was haunted, but then they said the same about the pillbox, which never once gave me the jitters. The only strange thing about it was the musky twilight that greeted you no matter what time of day you were there. Not so dark that you couldn't see your hands, but without a torch you'd have a hard job reading the spray-painted walls, as if any were worth reading – just the same Ter-ry 4 Jane crap in every loo cubicle. The thick concrete walls were as cool in January as they were in July, which probably didn't help the overall smell of damp. Someone else might have said the pillbox was dingy and stank of wee, but it wasn't, and it didn't. And I never once saw a turd.

If you lit a candle and huddled over it, or cupped a fag in your hands, your life closed in around you and somehow sent the damp away. I'd often make a twig-and-leaf fire to break up the boredom. The only problem was that the narrow firing slits didn't let out much smoke, so if the leaves were wet, the box, which was no more than eight by six, with a low flat roof, filled in no time, choking you out. And apart from finding a tree trunk to sit on in the woods, there was nothing else to do up there. The Glades was private property; if they caught you sniffing about, they'd treat you to a free lobotomy and put you to bed. Forever.

As I got closer to the girls' school I saw a few older boys from our school having a smoke by the gates, looking hard, waiting for their birds to come out. Some were on mopeds – 50cc Fizzys with engines the size of a shoe. I stayed back and found a tree to hide behind. It started to drizzle. I didn't mind. I clung to the tree and pretended I was in a film, one of those late-night French ones that always seemed to be on BBC2 when I couldn't sleep. Did all the French pick their noses in traffic?

Come ten to four, a thousand green-and-white clones poured from the building and made their way across the playground to the gates. A few filed out of the gym doors at the end in their netball kits, and looked nervously at the sky. Some held their palms out. As if on cue, it pelted down. The girls who were dawdling in the playground scattered, most of them back towards the same doors they'd just come out of. The netballers ran inside. Others didn't care about getting wet. In no time there was a bottleneck at the gates. I couldn't hug the trunk tight enough. Rain aimed for the gaps in the branches and skated off the leaves. In the first minute, the sky turned so dark I thought the sun had gone out. It was funny to watch the panic. About three of the thousand girls had brollies; the rest used their schoolbags or cardigans. Any one of them could have been Lucy. It was a waste of time. Even if I'd seen her and followed her, she lived so far from the school she would have got on one of the girls-only buses. And despite what Vi said about my eyelashes, about how Mum had always wanted a girl, I wasn't one. Even the bus driver would know that.

The next week, Dad sent me round to Miss Jinny's to dig up a bush that was in the way of the new larchlap fence she'd ordered, which I told her would need a professional to put up. (I gave her Roy's number.) She only lived a few minutes' walk from the girls' school, so as soon as last bell rang I went round there. The bush seemed harmless enough, and probably would've been if she'd had any tools worth using. Instead she gave me a pickaxe with a loose head that slid down the shaft when I raised it. And every sliver of wood I wedged in the gap between the head and the shaft split on first blow. Her spade looked like it had clocked up at least a thousand miles of ditches, and a few canals too. But it was that or nothing. Three days running I went round there after school to attack the bush, telling Miss Jinny at the end of each day that she'd be better off phoning Roy, who was bound to know how to get it out. "Is he expensive?" was all she said. When I got round there on the third day and took the spade from the shed, the raw skin on my palms hurt the instant they closed on the handle. Plus it had started to rain. So I put the spade back and knocked on Miss Jinny's door. When I showed her the state of my palms, she was horrified. "What on earth have you been doing?" she said. I told her to phone Roy.

A group of girls went by. I couldn't wait to walk behind them. I was just about to leave Miss Jinny's when I saw Lucy coming down the road, on her own, violin case in hand. At first I couldn't believe it. But then this scared feeling came over me, the kind you get when you know something's about to happen but you don't know what or when. It was too strong to ignore. I waited for her to go by, then followed. When she went into the bus shelter on the corner of Depot Road, I kept walking. After a while I started to run, realising I had to get to the next stop before the bus. I felt sick when I got on it. "Where to?" said the driver. I was stumped. I hadn't bothered to check where it was going; all I cared about was that Lucy was on it. "Where to?" he kept saying. He must've thought I was deaf. "As far as it goes," I said. He gave me a funny look. It cost me a fortune. He gave me an even funnier look when I followed Lucy off the bus after ten minutes. "We're not there yet," he shouted after me.

Lucy took a left on New Street, walked fifty yards or so, and then turned up a garden path to a house that looked like all the other houses in the road. It was drizzling and windy. I sat in a bus shelter and read *Confessions of a Window Cleaner*. Then I got bored. If I wasn't going to talk to her, which I couldn't bring myself to do because in my head she was the local equivalent of Jane Seymour, why waste my time? So I caught the next bus home.

Rubbing away a circle of mist, I put my cheek to the window in the hope that the judder from the road and the engine would vibrate all thoughts of Lucy to dust. Instead it had the opposite effect: a rod-on. As we came into town, I counted how many shops were still open. The bus stop was just past the Candy Box. I was waiting for the bus to slow down enough so that I could jump off without sliding on the wet pavement and breaking my back, when I spotted Lance, under the shop's canopy, picking sweets from a bag. What if I didn't go straight home but hung about with him for a while, tried to talk things over? But just as I was deciding, Zoë came out of the shop. She grabbed Lance's waist, as though carrying on a game they'd been playing before. The slimy git. How come he hadn't said anything about seeing her? And what was she doing with him? When the bus slowed and the doors opened, I jumped off and ran up the road. It was true what they said about Zoë. She'd do it with anyone.

35

I was on evening duty in reception while Dad did the bar, serving an annoying guest who was drunk and who kept shouting for no reason. At first I thought he was upset about something and was having a go at Dad, but now and then he'd let out a dim grunty laugh which, stupid though it sounded, was still a laugh, and laughs weren't exactly ten a penny at the Remora. Not that it made the *Argus* crossword any easier, mind. I'd never even heard of Liza Minelli, so how could I guess what character she'd played in *Cabaret*? Or the All Blacks fly half? But I did know the capital of Mongolia. The phone rang as I finished the second A in ULAN BATOR.

"You've got something to tell me," said the voice, a girl's.

"Pardon?"

"Your message. I got it."

"Oh. Is that—?"

"What do you want?" she said.

Just then I heard Dad in my other ear, calling me into the bar. I was trying to come up with an answer for Lucy when he appeared in the doorway, beckoning me. Something had got him going. I was stuck between him and the mouthpiece.

"Er, I'm a bit . . . Can I phone you back?"

"No. I'll phone you," she said.

"Is that Lucy?"

She hung up.

I went in. Dad was behind the bar. A bloke in a suit jacket was slumped on a barstool with his back to me.

"There he is," said Dad.

The drunk customer tried to turn around but for some reason couldn't. "Where's the boy?" he asked.

"Matthew, meet Colin. Mr . . . What was it, Colin?"

"Paleokastritsa," he said, counting the syllables off on his fingers in case he'd left one out. Then he laughed at how funny he was.

"Colin takes people up in hot-air balloons. He's a qualified pilot. Where did you say you're from again?"

Colin drained his whisky, set his tumbler down harder than he meant to. The bang made him jump, then giggle.

Dad showed me a business card. "He's kindly offered to let you go up for free."

"Why?" I said.

"Why?" said Dad. "Because it would be terrific up above the world, that's why. Don't look so bloody glum."

"You should go," I said, knowing he hated heights more than I did.

"You could go on the train," he said. "I'll organise it."

"Great," I said. "Is that it? I've got a life to get back to."

"You ungrateful sod," said Dad. "Go to bed."

That was all I wanted. As I left, Colin was slurring something about his beautiful balloon.

It was probably the only thing he could get up.

36

Lucy rang again the next Monday. I was up in my room gluing plate lips to my latest creation Mawenzi Sarong. When Dad buzzed me on the intercom, I ran downstairs.

"Hello?"

A scratching sound came down the line.

"Anyone there?" I said.

"It's me. Lucy."

"What's that noise?"

"What?"

"The scratching?"

"Oh. Cyril."

"Cyril?"

"My gerbil Cyril." The noise got louder. There was a metaly squeak. I pictured a busy head and a tiny pink nose at the mouthpiece. "Say hello, Cyril."

I said, "Can he talk?"

"Sometimes. But he's shy."

"Can I meet Cyril?"

"Why?"

"I don't know. Because he's nice."

"You don't know him."

"Well, I would if I met him."

"He can be difficult."

"I don't mind. What about the pier, Saturday? About one?"

"I'll ask Cyril." When she went quiet, I could hear him squeaking. "He says only if you're nice."

"I am, tell him."

"You tell him."

"Cyril," I said, "I'm very nice."

"He heard."

She hung up. I sat with the dial tone in my ear, wondering if that exchange with Cyril constituted an arrangement.

37

At the far end of the pier, a short flight of steps led to a lower deck, a sort of landing stage, though nothing landed there. No one seemed to know what it was meant for, but everyone fished off it. Two kids who looked like brothers were arguing about bait. The older one was telling the younger one to use lugworm, that's why he'd gone down to the beach early to get it. But the younger one had his own supply of worms in a Kiwi tin. He wanted to stick as many as he could through the hook. "I like hearing them pop," he said. "You won't catch anything," said his brother. The younger one sounded hurt when he said he didn't care. In their bucket was everything they'd yanked out of the sea that morning, mostly dark squiggly things that hadn't been alive more than a week. There was one proper fish. The younger one said they were after squid, and that they'd heard a big one lived under the pier. He leaned over the railing and pointed.

"How deep d'you think it is?" I said.

"Hundred foot," he said, without a doubt. His brother, who was fiddling in his bait box, heard us.

"That's a hundred-foot deep down there," I told him.

"No it ain't. Don't listen to him."

His brother didn't care; he knew the secret, and no one could tell him different. "He don't know nuffing," he said. Then they elbowed each other for a while, getting more and more excited, putting their weight behind it, giving each other violent shoves. That's when I saw Lucy plodding up the pier. I was boiling in just my T-shirt. She was wearing an anorak. Not just an anorak but one of those knee-length quilted footballers' coats that hang like a wet blanket and weigh half a ton. She looked like a dumpy oven.

She was sucking her bottom lip. When I put my hand out to shake, she stared at me like I was a Martian, and kept her hands in her pockets.

"You should've stayed in bed," I said.

"Why?"

"You're all—" I patted my forehead. Hers was sweaty, her hair stuck to it.

Compared to her, I felt like I'd just stepped out of a fridge. It must've been eighty degrees. The whole town was in shorts – apart from the crumblies. Was she raising money for charity?

"What do you do when it's cold?" I said.

"None of your business. Anyway, what's that?" She pointed at my T-shirt. "Deputy Dawg?"

It was my favourite. I'd worn it specially. I felt a sulk come on. I turned away and looked along the coast to Brighton, counting the groynes down the beach until they became so bunched in the distance that they blended into one. "Only babies suck their lips," I said.

She stuck her tongue out and walked off. I wasn't going to be part of her day after all. I didn't care. At least I'm not flat-footed, I thought, watching her go.

A waft of salt and vinegar hit me as I caught up with her. Walking around the arcade building at the end of the pier, I heard laughter, which for a second cut the bad air between us, at least for me. The first thing I saw as we turned the corner by the fish and chip kiosk was Sid, and then Gary, and then Sandy Sangeet, clutching their chip cones as they laughed at the wind, which was blowing Sandy Sangeet's hair all over the place. The way she ducked and shook her head to stop it from getting in her face, and the wildness of her hair as it blew around her, made it seem like she was being pecked at by a swarm of birds.

Gary gave Lucy a slow up and down. It was obvious he'd clocked her coat by the way he nudged Sid, who pretended to ignore it. Then, totally unlike him, Sid said, "Is that your sister?"

"No," I said, angrily, without looking at Lucy. They'd think she was ugly. I tried to forget she was there. "I haven't got a sister. You know I haven't."

Gary smiled, not at me but at what Sid had said. They all knew I was the only Bowen. Suddenly it was funny?

Without a word, Lucy wandered off. I grabbed the chance to get away from Sid and his brother by following her. Glaring at Sid to let him know he hadn't bothered me, I felt like my whole bodyweight was sitting on my shoulders and trying to bury me.

As I followed Lucy, the smell of chips made me feel lonely. I didn't try to catch up with her. I wished she'd go home. God knows what she thought of me, what a mug they'd made me look. The whole weird encounter brought back memories of when I was younger, when I wandered around for no reason, with nothing to do, wishing I was on my way to the camera club, or the chess club, or wherever it was people went to be with other people. But joining those sorts of clubs seemed impossible. Imagine the first time you walked in ...

I peered through the gaps in the deck. The sloshing water below made me feel wobbly, like I was standing up in a dinghy.

Years earlier I'd gone barefooted on the pier, a shoe in each hand, my socks tucked inside. It was early evening in summer. A weekday. I was eight or nine. After tea I'd gone out on my bike. Two boys and two girls, sixteen or so, came towards me, muttering to each other. I thought nothing of it. Then the boys stopped me. "You can't walk on here with no shoes on," said one. There's no law against it, I said. Thinking they were just showing off in front of the girls, I tried to go round them. "Think you're funny, do you?" said the other, blocking me. No, I said. What those girls were doing with a couple of knobs like them was anyone's guess, but they didn't say anything. Next thing I knew there was a tug at my hands. The boys had snatched both my shoes. They jogged a few yards up the pier, stopped, and turned around. One had my shoes by the laces.

"My dad'll kill me if I go home without them," I said.

"Aw, diddums," said the other kid, flapping his bottom lip. Then he dangled my shoes over the railing.

"Don't you want them?"

Er ...

"Well you ain't gonna get them standing there like that."

"Come and get them," sang his mate, like we were playing hide-and-seek.

"You'll drop them," I said.

"He doesn't want his own shoes," said the singer to his mate.

"You've got to three," said the other. "Ready?"

I'd practiced punching in the kitchen mirror a thousand times. I had the stance and everything. Fast hands. I could've been a boxer. This was the moment I'd trained for. But I didn't move.

"Going ... going ... gone." The kid let go of my shoes. One watched me, not sure what I might do. The other laughed. Apparently watching my shoes fall to the water made his day, his week. He'd be talking about it for years.

"Woops-a-daisy."

To punish myself, I walked home along the beach, my toes curling around every pebble as if it would make me weightless and stop them from crippling me, but it didn't. I felt like a pilgrim.

I caught up with Lucy. She lifted her chin out of her zipped neck and said, "If you could come back as someone else, who'd it be?"

It was on my mind, so why not say it? "Pussy Galore."

"I'd come back as the Yeti. Do you know who he is?"

Yes, I said.

"I'd live in the Himalayas," she said, "in a cave."

"That anorak'll come in handy."

She bent her head, as if hearing a voice in her coat. "What was that?" she said.

"What?"

"Cyril says you're not funny."

As soon as she took him out of her pocket, he dug his claws into her coat and scampered up her arm. Except for his pink eyes, everything about him was white. He had twitchy whiskers. "He's a champion," she said, stroking his side with the back of her nail, or what was left of it.

"Not for long," I said. "Look at his heart." If you plugged it into the grid it would power the town. "Shouldn't he calm down?" I said. I didn't want to be there when he burst.

She half bent and half raised him up so they were on the same level. "Two years ago he won the National Gerbil Society competition for his class, which is Himalayan."

"The Himalayas again?"

"Yes."

"That's a long walk on those legs."

"Cyril says you don't know what you're talking about so shut up."

She put him back in her pocket and then pulled something from her jacket sleeve. A sewing needle. "Can you fit a needle between your front teeth?"

"I wouldn't know," I said.

She bared her top teeth, which weren't gappy, and slid the needle in. It wasn't exactly hard. Pulling it out again, she jabbed her lip with it and sucked. I felt a spiky pang behind my ears.

"Try it now." She handed me the needle.

"What'd you do that for?"

"What?"

"Your lip?" I mimed her jabbing.

"It's just a prick," she said. "If you were a diabetic you'd have to inject yourself every day."

"No chance. I can't even watch my mum darn my socks. Well, not that she does."

"Pain's like anything. You get used to it. It's easy."

When I went to take the needle from her, she jabbed my finger. "Ow!" I took my hand away and looked to see if there was any blood. There wasn't, just a red dot, but it stung. "What was that for?"

She laughed, then jabbed her lip again. "So what was this message about my brother?"

I was hoping she wouldn't mention it. "Oh that? I just...I heard some kids talking about him by the lockers. Tony, right?"

"Yes."

"Right. It sounded serious, like he'd really be in the shit if he didn't stop what he was doing."

"Like what?"

"It's really awkward," I said. "I don't want to—"

"Just say it," she said. "I want to know. Why else do you think I'm here?"

"All right. But this isn't me, right? I just heard it. Well, apparently some kids found this big clearing up the forest, with trees around it. There's trees everywhere, but in this bit all the leaves and wood were pushed to the sides to make a big circle. But everywhere else was normal forest – trees and stuff. In the middle of the big circle was a small one, sort of carved into the ground, and they'd...they'd used this dye or something, paint, to make the shape, the witchy thing. Course, they reckoned it was blood, what with the bones laid out how they were and—"

"What's all this got to do with Tony?"

"Well, that's the thing. They went back up there after school, a few days on the trot, see if they could see anyone. That's when they saw him. He was on his own. He had a spade. They watched him."

I paused to catch myself up.

"He started digging. Your brother, I mean. In the small circle. He dug for a bit and left. They went back a couple of days later and there he was again, only now the hole he'd been digging was...more like a, well, a grave."

"My brother, digging a grave?"

"I don't know," I said, like I didn't believe it either. "That's just what I heard. I thought you should know. In case...I don't know. If he's in trouble or something."

She frowned. "How do you know him?"

"I don't, that's what I'm saying. It wasn't me. I just heard."

"But how did you know about me?"

"I'm a worrier. Always have been. I thought his family would want to know. But I don't trust mums and dads. So I asked around to see if he had any brothers. Everyone said he didn't. So I looked for sisters."

"Oh," she said, her frown more of a daze. "Thanks."

I'd finally reached the end. My muscles slackened. My temples tickled with sweat.

"I hate him anyway," she said. And then straight after that: "Are you double jointed?"

"Not that I know of. But I've got a photographic memory, if that's any good?"

"Liar."

"Watch." I stood in front of her and stared, fighting not to blink. Then when my eyes hurt too much, I blinked, making a shutter-clicking noise. "There," I said, tapping my head. "All stored. If I want to remember you standing there I just blink hard three times and it plays in my head like a film."

"It's like me," she said, pressing her palm down on her thumb tip. "Every time I go somewhere, I stick one of my hairs to the bottom of my door, my bedroom door, one end on the side that opens and the other on the frame. If anyone goes in my room when I'm out, I can tell."

"How?"

"'Cause the hair won't be stuck to the door. When you open the door, it pulls the hair off but leaves the frame end on."

"What's the point of that?"

"Are you deaf? I just told you."

By then she'd bent her thumb so far I couldn't see how it would ever spring back. My body went tight again, anticipating the crack. I wanted to pull her hand away before she snapped the bone, left her thumb flapping like gristle. "Don't," I said, reaching out to stop her: "it's horrible."

"It's natural," she said. "Everything to do with the body is."

"How come I can't do it then?"

"You've never tried." She released her thumb, let it spring back. "See? Give me yours."

"You're joking."

"I won't hurt you."

"I'm not bendy."

"You don't need to be."

Before I'd thought to resist, she grabbed my hand. Her thumbs were raw from chewing. She'd eaten all her nails too. I bet her toes were gruesome.

She did the same thing to my thumb, using her palm to ease it back, more gently than she'd done with her own. Her palm was warm and dry. It felt nice on top of my thumb, for a while, till she forced it back. I told her to stop.

"It's like yoga," she said. "Your body needs to be told what to do, not the other way round."

"Ow."

"Don't be a baby."

"Stop."

I could've kicked her. I closed my other hand around my thumb as though it were spurting blood. She was smiling. Anyone walking by would've thought me a baby.

"I said stop."

"It doesn't hurt," she said.

"It bloody does." Shouting only made it throb more.

"You get used to it. Wait here. I'm going to the loo."

She did a little skip and walked back down the pier. I clutched my hand and watched her, wishing she'd trip and crack her shoulder. Then I could tell her it was only natural, that everything to do with the body was.

A hundred yards or so past the pier, two windsurfers were going full tilt across the water and then taking off, gliding for ten, twenty, thirty yards before crashing back down. I pretended they were the two world finalists and that I was the head judge. The one in the black-and-blue wetsuit was the winner, hands-down; he stayed up more often when he landed. The other one was too cocky. And if he was cocky on the water, he'd be cocky in person. I knew I wouldn't like him. You can't give awards to people you don't like.

Lucy was back, sucking her lip.

"D'you know what I think?"

"I've no idea," I said.

"The sea's like a diary, only it writes itself. It's always changing, but you'd never know it 'cause it keeps everything in here." She poked herself in the chest. "Do you like diaries?"

"I don't know."

"Are you still sulking about your thumb?"

"I wasn't in the first place."

"Not much."

It went quiet. Gulls dive-bombed, skimmed the surface, pulled away. Foam washed the pilings. When the breeze died down, the sun felt double strong.

A few seconds later she said, "Haven't you got one?"

"What, a thumb?"

"A diary, you ninny."

"To write what?"

She looked at me oddly. "Anything."

"I prefer pictures," I said.

After the business with my thumb, I wanted to outstare her on principle, but the more I tried, the harder she stared. My eyes watered. She'd think I was about to cry, which would mean she'd won again. I couldn't think of anything to say. We stood like that for a while, quiet, watching the horizon.

Then she said, "We're all turtles, but none of us go in the sea."

She was one big riddle. When she said she had to go to feed her horse, I nearly slipped up. The word Nutmeg flashed so bright in my head I thought I'd have to shout it out loud to stop it.

38

Healeys and Interceptors filled the parade from the pier to Denne Gardens. It was the first year of the Jensen rally. The prom was packed. Lance said he'd meet me down there, wanted to know what time. I hadn't told him about Lucy – who she was, how I knew her, what she was like. I'd stopped telling him anything. But I couldn't give him a time because I didn't want to cut things short with Lucy, especially if it was only to meet him. "You would if I was a Paki," he said, all hard done by. "Give it a rest," I said. "I've gotta help my dad." During the phone call, he went on and on about how doing the things we used to do wasn't good enough for me anymore because I thought I was special. At one point I put the phone down on the reception desk and went into the kitchen for some milk. When I came back he was still yapping. And then after all that, just before he slammed the phone down, which was usually how our talks ended by then, he said, "Oh, I just remembered. Harry's taking us to Longleat to see the lions. Laters."

Everything shone – bumpers, door handles, trim. I'd only seen Jensens in magazines. The Interceptors were lower, longer, and heavier than I imagined, and big enough to sleep in. The Healeys were like nice small toys. More ladyish. Still, I wouldn't've minded.

I was thinking about Lucy's hair on the door. Why tell me that? If she wasn't so obsessed with sucking her lip she might've seen the goose-pimples on my forearms when she mentioned it. So what if she knew her door had been opened while she was on holiday? I'd left everything as I'd found it. Besides, that was assuming she'd done the hair thing before she went. What if her dad had been shouting at her to hurry and she hadn't had time? Then she'd have nothing.

"Don't I know you?" said a bloke with a thick tigery beard, gawping.

"I doubt it," I said.

"Yes I do. You're Stan Bowen's boy."

"Who?"

"Stan Bowen," he said.

"My name's Brian," I said.

"Brian Bowen?"

"No, Wormley."

"Brian Wormley? Come off it. Are you sure?"

"Course I'm sure," I said. "You know your name, don't you?"

If it wasn't customers in town asking how Dad was or Mum was or other B&B owners asking about trade, it was Bill Turret asking me how things were at home, at school, at the meat factory, at the dog track, or in outer fucking space, or Lance's mum phoning to ask why I'd fallen out with him, what had he done, you were so close. It drove me up the wall.

He shook his head. "Well, you could've fooled me." He still wasn't convinced as he walked away. When he did a double take, I caught him.

39

Freewheeling into Vi's road one Sunday morning, I heard the echo of kids playing football in the rec at the end. The voices got trapped between the tall rows of houses and seemed to pinball up the road to meet me. Except for a bloke washing his Maxi outside his house, the road was dead, which was why the shouts carried. It sounded like a fight. The noise was worse than our playground.

I'd been for a bike ride up the steep windy road to the golf course, the same one that Lance wanted to join when he was older so he could land some quality skirt. Grinding my way up the hill, barely moving enough to stay on, I was nearly ditched by some bald prat in a Rover who clipped me with his wing mirror. He cut in to avoid an oncoming car. I lost momentum and put my feet down. He kept going. I stuck my fingers up at his rearview. He took longer to disappear than I expected, which left me feeling a bit of a goon, standing in the road, jabbing my fingers. I pushed my bike the rest of the way, trying to keep the dust he'd thrown up from filling my mouth. The morning was so sharp and clean in those hills, just as it was at dawn on deliveries, that it almost felt good to be human.

Even though I was starved, I was too full of the day to go home. Vi never minded me popping round; visitors make all the difference, she'd say, even when she was in the middle of something. The odds of a bacon sandwich were good, especially on a Sunday. As long as the weather was decent, her door was open to all. That's how she knew everyone's business. Her house was a gossip shop. I don't know why she didn't make the most of her talents, like renting a stall next to Len's Wet Fish and setting up in business. The seaside equivalent of Mystic Meg. She'd make a mint.

Uncle Norm was definitely round – his grey Cortina was out the front. I wheeled my bike down the passage, opened Vi's back gate, and went in. The smell of fresh washing blew over the wall. I said hello to Mrs. Menzies, who was pegging out a sheet. The connected row of walls and gardens and the identical backs of the houses always made me think of those wartime photos when gardens were full of everything, including chickens. Vi's was still like it. There wasn't a stamp's worth of ground she hadn't planted. Or Roy hadn't. You'd think that with no front garden, she'd have a nice bit of lawn at the back, a couple of chairs to sit out in, but she had Norm's sensitive skin. Quick to burn.

I poked my head in the door. "Hello? Any chance of a haircut?"

Voices. Scraping of chairs.

"It's Matthew," said Norm.

When I went inside, Vi, Roy, and Norm were at the table. Norm was half out of his chair. He looked like he'd seized up. It was so quiet I thought they'd been doing a séance. On a Sunday morning? Not even Roy was that keen.

"Mornin'," I said.

Vi was smoking and shaking. She wouldn't look at me. Eventually she did, and I saw her red puffy eyes. There was a bottle of Bells on the table. Some tumblers. Vi's was empty.

"If your mother sent you round here you can sod off."

"Vi, Vi," said Norm.

"No," I said, "I just...I was out on my bike."

"Give you the money, did she?" said Vi.

"What money?" I said.

"It's all right," said Norm. "Your auntie's a bit...upset. Out on your bike, were you? Where'd you go?"

"Nowhere."

"Tea?" said Roy.

"No thanks."

"Seat," he said, nodding to the settee. I sat down.

I'd lied about the haircut. A couple of weeks before, Mum had told me not to go round Vi's because of the trouble she was having with her head. When she was like that, she said, there was no telling what she might say or do. She couldn't be trusted. That's why she'd probably need a spell in the hospital. What, the Glades? I said. No, Mum said. The General. Mum would kill me if I came back with a haircut, unless I told her that Lance's mum had done it, which she had once or twice when I was round there and she was cutting Lance's, sitting us next to each other like at the barbers. But Lance's mum had just been on the phone about my not going round there anymore, hence Lance's moping, so that was out too. Anyway, I didn't even want a haircut.

I said, "You know that hilly bit you were talking about with the long grass where you found the pelvis? I counted sixteen rabbits this morning. You wanna get your gun up there."

"Not allowed," Roy said.

"A thousand pound," said Vi. "Here." She picked a piece of paper off the table and waved it at me. "Read this." Norm reached up and took it. "You tell him, then," said Vi.

Norm looked like he was trying to mend a boiler. He let out a big breath. He looked to Roy for help, but Roy just did one of those don't-ask-me's with his mouth.

"It's your Uncle Ernie, Matthew," said Norm.

"The Australian one?"

"Right."

"Bet you didn't know that Melbourne's in the exact same bit of Australia we are," I said. "In England, I mean."

Norm cleared his throat. "It's ... he's not well."

"Not well!" said Vi, reaching for the Bells.

"He's got cancer," said Norm. "They only just found it. They're giving him three months at best. Your auntie here's gonna fly out to see him."

"Thanks to Norman, I am," she said. "That mother of yours wouldn't give you the drippings off her nose. Her own brother."

I'd had a nice ride. It was sunny out. I wasn't in the mood for episode three thousand of Vi and Mum.

"How's your head trouble?" I said.

"Matthew," said Roy. Like his head was any better.

Vi splashed whisky into her tumbler. "It's gone on long enough," she said. She looked at Norm. "If you don't tell him, I will."

"Not now," he said. "It's not the time for it."

"It's never been the bloody time for it. Tell him."

Norm appealed to Roy, but again with no luck. I don't know why he bothered. He'd have more luck if he bribed him with a new soldering iron.

"It's not our job," said Norm.

Vi gulped her whisky and set her glass down. Ash curved from her fag. She looked at me. "Your dear mum was already carrying you when she married Stan."

"So?" I said. "You can't always get babysitters."

"Not carry carry: in here." She patted her belly.

"I'm off," I said, getting up. "The Moscow State Circus finished last night. They've packed up their big tent. You find watches and everything."

"Yeah, and say hello to your dad while you're down there," said Vi.

"Vi," said Norm, like a warning.

"For your information, he's at home," I said, "doing the path."

"For your information, he's not your dad," she said.

"That's enough!" said Norm, rising in his chair.

"You're as bad as the rest of 'em," she said to Norm. "Won't face a bloody thing. How come I'm the only one going to see Ern? Go on. Ask yourself. You can afford it. She can afford it. And I'm the one getting my nose rubbed in it? At least I was born with a spine. At least I—"

"Cunt shit wankers," I shouted. Then I ran out the back door.

I queued for a lolly at The Rock Shoppe under a string of miniature flags, betting there was no one within a mile of me who could name more of the countries. Jamaica, Austria, Wales, Norway, South Korea. People poked at Wicked Willie T-shirts, danced with inflatable sharks. Three charter coaches were parked along the prom – Houndsditch, Catford, Penge. I couldn't be arsed with the circus. You never found anything anyway. Even if you got there before the sun came up, it was too late. They'd beaten you to it. I got my lolly and looked for a quiet spot. There was no one on the rocks, so I wheeled my bike over and ate my Strawberry Mivi there.

40

Napoleon was proud and ugly and didn't like the English. He called us a nation of shopkeepers. What he didn't know was that shopkeepers are a very important part of an economy, especially ours. Every holiday-maker that comes to the seaside buys something from us. They rely on them to make their holidays happy. Being a shopkeeper is a public service. It also provides lots of jobs. Not only do holiday-makers buy things from shopkeepers but everyone else does too, like loo roll. Napoleon was too bitter about being short to see that.

41

And then all of a sudden, Sid stopped helping with the ant city, stopped having anything to do with me except for the odd time we saw each other in the corridor, when he only said hello because he couldn't avoid me. I tried to ask him a couple of times but he more or less snubbed me, which wasn't like him at all. Well, it was; he tended to avoid everyone, but not me, not since we'd become mates. The only reason I could think of was jealousy. Lance had been allowed back to school, and Sid didn't like it because it meant he'd have to share me again, which wasn't true anyway. By then I'd had it up to here with Lance, and was much happier with Sid. The school had accepted the court's recommendation that Lance be given another chance as long as there was no repeat performance and that he continued seeing his shrink. Lance thought it was a game, that they were stupid, that if he told them what they wanted to hear he'd be home and dry. With this medal on his chest he was unbearable. I kept trying to shake him off so I could spend time with Sid, who now blanked Lance altogether. But it seemed I was stuck with him. What made things trickier was that Lance still got bullied by Massimo, who'd found out that he'd tried to pin the fire on him. So, much as I wanted nothing to do with Lance, he needed me, not that I was handy or anything, but simply as another body, as two instead of one, something for Massimo to think twice about. If he ever thought at all.

I came out of the history block one lunchtime to see Sid watching a kick-about on his own. He looked sad, as though he wanted to join in but knew they wouldn't let him. Thinking he'd be glad of the company, I went over.

"I thought we were friends," he said.

"So did I."

"So why didn't you tell me about that meeting? Everyone else knew."

"What meeting?"

"Your dad's meeting. At the pub."

It wasn't that I'd forgotten, I just thought the whole thing had blown over, seeing as his dad had come round all friendly that night with a pot of pudding, telling Dad how glad he was to be leaving the B&B game and moving to Brighton. I was happy for them, but pissed off with Sid for not telling me. "It wasn't my fault," I said. "How many more times have I got to say it: he's a wanker."

"I heard it was full of people who hated us."

"No it wasn't."

"You should know. Do you hate us too?"

"No. Look. What was I s'posed to do? My dad tells me to get dressed, I'm going with him. I can't exactly say no, can I?"

He was fiddling with something in his blazer pocket. Another of his dad's animals? I thought he was going to bring it out and show me, but he didn't. The football went past us. Neither of us moved, even when Darren Russell shouted for us to kick it back.

"What have I done to you?" he said.

"Nothing, I just said. And anyway, how come you never told me you were moving to Brighton?"

"I only found out the other day. I was going to tell you."

"It's a bit late now."

"I don't want to go. It's my dad's idea."

Silence. Our talk had taken the wrong road from the start. Now it was getting darker and we'd passed all the signposts and the lights from the nearby town had faded. I didn't know him. He might as well have been a mute hitch-hiker I'd taken pity on. Now I regretted picking him up.

He had a little fit, threw his arm down. "And there's me inviting you round to meet my mum and dad. Didn't that mean anything to you?"

"Look!" I said. "I've always been on your side. I didn't ask for a dad like him." I don't know where it came from, but out of nowhere I added, "You can't know it if you haven't lived it."

"Know what? I'm glad you never told me any stories about your family."

"I'm warning you."

"What, to move out before your dad and his mates burn our house down?"

When my punch landed, the force of it shot through my wrist and up my arm, fuzzing my shoulder. Sid was half curled up on the ground, covering his face. Blood trickled through his fingers and down the back of his hand.

I stood over him, put my arm out to help him up. "I didn't mean it. Please. Honest I didn't."

He rolled onto his back. "My nose," he said through his hands.

The kick-about stopped. A couple of kids shouted Fight! Fight! and then ran over. More followed. In no time there was a circle around us. Someone kicked Sid, like it was a free-for-all. I ran at him, rammed him in the chest with both hands. He went flying.

I put my hand out again to Sid. "Come on. We'll get some loo roll and clean you up."

He rocked left and right, as if the pain was getting worse. "Leave me alone," he said.

"Come on. I can help. Best mates. Please. Take my hand."

But he wouldn't. He got up on his own and didn't look at me before he staggered off across the playground, clutching his face. I watched him until my eyes welled up so much I couldn't see.

"Girly pants, girly pants," someone shouted from the circle when they saw I was crying. I couldn't move. I just stood there with my head down hoping the ground would open and suck me down.

42

The last time I'd been in the bowling alley was more than a year ago. That day Lance had been showing off to his Uncle Daz, who was two years younger than us, which probably would've made sense if I'd asked him about it, but I wasn't interested: he'd only think I was taking the piss and launch into me, like he did with everyone else. Daz was from Portsmouth. He dreamed of being a sailor. Every one of his stories involved drinking, fighting, and smashing things up – usually at least two of the three. The day him and his mates pushed a bloke in a wheelchair down a slipway and into the harbour; the day his mate's brother dragged a girl off a bus by her hair; how they went queer- and/or Paki-bashing on Sundays... All I could do was watch him make a tit of himself by trying to answer brainteasers such as Where did the sun go at night? Why was the sea full of salt? What kept islands afloat? It was priceless watching them argue over whether the Romans or the Normans had filled the sea with salt so that we'd die if we drank it. Why either invader might have done that they didn't say, but it was definitely one or the other. (Daz said the Romans, so that was that.) As for the sun, it sat just over the horizon and slept like the rest of us till it was time to get up. And for keeping islands afloat? Balloons, massive ones, so high in the sky we couldn't see them.

It was a dodgy game. If Daz got it in his head that you were taking the piss, he'd brain you. He was primed to explode as it was. Hair-triggered. He'd rear up at a lollipop lady if he didn't like her tone. And Lance, who threw himself at signs that read Make An Arse of Yourself Here, did what he was told. The more Daz egged him on, the stupider Lance acted.

That nightmare day's bowling had ended with Daz betting Lance that he couldn't throw a ball clear across one lane and into the next. Course, Lance took him up on it. It didn't matter that the family in the next lane had been nice to us – the dad and son had shown us how to use the new scoring system, in the nick of time. Daz's frustration at not understanding it almost made him smash the console with a bowling ball, as though the world of electronics had singled him out as being particularly dense. Man or machine (or lollipop lady), it was all the same to Daz. Punishment was due. The manager saw him and went loopy. Game over.

Smack on top of the bowling alley was the town's biggest multi-storey car park, all eight levels of it. As I waited for Lucy I couldn't stop my mind's eye from roaming all the dark rows of cars above me, gliding up and down the echoey slopes, veering around the bumper-scuffed corners, breathing in the stale fag smoke on the stairs. No roof was thick enough to stop all that from caving in. How could those kids and parents stuff their faces with burgers when there was a huge concrete cake poised to bury them?

My eyes took a while to adjust to the dimness – the reverse of going outside after a matinée. I stood inside the door, getting my bearings amid the music and the woody chock of skittles. At first I didn't twig that it was Lucy coming towards me, even though I should've guessed by her Bobby Robson coat.

She peered into my face. "It's me, remember?"

"Sorry," I said. "Can you see all right?"

"Yeah, why?"

"This light."

"It takes a while to get used to it."

My eyes adjusted as we walked along the main floor overlooking the lanes, most of which were occupied by groups of kids, though there was one evergreen in a satin jacket and a bowling glove who seemed to be doing the rounds, making small talk, showing incompetents how to stop their balls from sliding straight into the gutters, wheth-er they wanted help or not. The last group he'd chatted to definite-ly didn't, but they couldn't shake him off, even when they conspired to ignore him. It was as though he had a quota of jokes to crack and wasn't leaving till he'd cracked them.

Nothing had been said about actually doing any bowling. I'd brought enough money to pay for a couple of games, if it came to it, but some-thing told me Lucy was even less of a fanatic than I was. As long as she could prick her lip and suck it she was fine. But we weren't talking. I was happy enough with quiet, but I kept hearing this nagging voice in my head telling me to say something, anything, to remind her I was there before she got fed up with feeling alone and went home. I said,

"You must be boiling in that."

"Stop going on about my coat! If I didn't like it, I wouldn't wear it."

I stuck my hand in my pocket and quietly hurt myself as much as I could with my door key. Lucy watched a punk girl with a red Mohican, who bowled so hard she almost flew down the lane with her ball. She didn't get excited about her strike, but then it didn't look like it was her first. She was sitting with her mum and nan, maybe her brother too, none of who had Mohicans, though her nan's hair was greeny-yellow like a parrot's. She went back to her seat and lit a fag, blew her smoke out and looked around. Her gaze ended at Lucy, who was still watching her. They looked at each for a while before the punk girl smiled, put down her fag, and got another ball.

Just then came some yelling from further up. A bunch of kids from school were arguing over something, like whose turn it was to use the brain. Orson Pike was among them. When the group broke apart, I noticed a girl. It was Zoë. Typical. Just when you could do without it, Farthing shrunk to a hamlet, with Zoë as its mascot. Luckily, Lucy was still watching the punk girl and hadn't noticed. Even though she must've gotten my message from Zoë, I didn't want Zoë to see us – she'd only say something to show me up. I could do that myself. Already had. To get Lucy away from there, I asked if she fancied a milkshake. "Only if you're buying," she said.

We sat at one of those module tables with moulded seats and dealt with our shakes – both chocolate. Even the great sucking Greg Chubb would've had trouble. My cheeks and head hurt. "This is hard work," I said.

"If I'd just killed someone and was on the run," said Lucy, pulling her straw out and licking it, "I'd come here. There's so many dark places to hide."

A woman walked by with her little kid. She had her hand flat on his head while he tried to get the hang of his yo-yo, which he couldn't, so he banged it instead. I hated the bowling alley and wanted to get out. The dim light made everyone look ill. And that air. Did it come out of a barrel?

Lucy finished her milkshake then checked her watch. "I need some help." She rummaged in her coat pocket, brought her hand back out. "It's embarrassing. Promise you won't laugh?" She opened her hand. A syringe and a dumpy bottle.

"What's that?" I said.

"My medicine. I'm diabetic."

"How come?"

"There isn't any how come."

"How'd you get it?"

"I didn't *get it*, it just—" She sighed. "Look. If you don't want to help me—" She looked back in the direction of the punk girl. "I'll ask someone else."

"No, that's all right. I can help."

"Come with me," she said.

We left our milkshakes and went over to the pool tables in the far corner, where some older kids were smoking and playing. The ladies' and gents' loos were side by side. Lucy tugged me towards the ladies. The door opened. A girl came out. I saw a bit of a sink and some mirror.

"What if someone's in there?" I said.

"I'll check."

She went in. I looked around. From where I was standing, the whole place went fish-eyed – all curved and lurchy. As a kid I used to get down on my belly by the front door and put my cheek to the carpet, then look all the way down the hall. It made everything completely different. I felt a bit like that by the loos.

"Pssst!"

Lucy was holding the door open and waving me in. With one last look at the kids by the machines, I went in. It felt better than my first ride on the Ghost Train. An instant rod-on. Four sinks, four mirrors, and no long tin urinal like you get on the prom. Strange dispensers. Lucy unzipped her coat. "Down here," she said. There were four stalls – whoever designed it thought in fours. I followed her to the furthest one.

"Eurgh!" she said, when we were inside. "That's disgusting." She slammed the lid and flushed.

"I thought only blokes did that," I said.

"Lock the door."

There wasn't even enough room to swing Cyril, not that she had him with her. Her coat was like a third person between us. She reached into her pockets and got what she needed, then wormed her way out of her coat. "You'll have to put this on," she said. "But I'll die," I said. She looked behind me at the door. "There's no hooks," she said. "And I need my hands." I took the coat. Putting it on was like *It's a Knock-out*. My knees dipped at the weight. Her body smell wafted from the lining – part soap, part BO. Nothing flowery that stuck in your throat. It was nice.

We were facing each other, so close that my own space, the see-through bubble we walk around in, mixed with hers to form one bigger bubble. I felt like I should touch some part of her, but I didn't know which. "Hold this," she said, handing me the bottle. I took it. It had a stopper instead of a lid. The bottle was clear. She took the orange cap from the syringe tip and drew out the plunger. "Give me the bottle." As I gave it to her, outside noise rushed in. Lucy's eyes widened; she put a finger to her lips. Whoever had come in went into a stall. First the lock, then the rustle of trousers. Hiss. The rattle of the loo roll holder, the tear of paper. Flush. Trousers. Lock. After the taps ran and the paper-towel holder clattered, there was the same outside noise as before. She'd gone.

Lucy took the bottle and turned it upside down, then dug the syringe needle into the cork and through. She tapped the syringe with her fingertip before pushing the needle into the liquid and drawing out the plunger. "Right," she said, pulling the needle from the cork. "Take this." I took the syringe. She turned and faced the wall, then bent forward and pulled her jeans and knickers down to the cut of her cheeks. "Inject me."

I felt like I was about to be breast-fed by Kate Bush.

"I'm not a doctor," I said.

"For God's sake, you're as bad as my brother. Just jab it in then push the plunger all the way down."

"What, does he do this for you?"

"He used to. Now, Matthew. Please?"

"Where d'you want it?"

"Here." She put her hand on her left cheek. "Where's yours?"

I rubbed my palm dry on her coat. She replaced her hand with mine.

My Hand On Her Arse. My Hand On Her Arse. Repeat till fade.

"Stick it in, will you! I'll have a fit."

In it went. She sounded as though she'd finally unscrewed an impossible lid. The syringe hung in her cheek. With my right fingers spread across her cheek, I plunged. It all went in. I pulled the needle out.

"See," she said. "It wasn't hard, was it?"

I rotated the syringe in my hand, studied the needle. There was nothing on it. Then I put my hand on her cheek again, across her crack. If I could just—

She banged the top of her head when she jerked away. "Ow! What are you doing?"

"Nothing. Sorry."

"You better not."

She pulled her jeans up and arranged herself. "Open the door."

I slid the lock open and went out. I don't know what I was expecting when I looked at her again – something that registered what we'd just done, how close we'd been.

"Give me my coat," she said.

"That was weird," I said, shrugging out of her coat. I felt two stone lighter.

When we got onto the main floor, I said I needed to get out, that the airless air was killing me.

"I like it," she said, looking across to the lanes. "I'm staying."

"All right. Well, will you go out with me?"

"Not yet," she said.

43

We were down the lock-up that Sunday. Dad wanted to waterproof the bottom corner of the walls, see where the mice had been getting in and nibbling our greens. I swept while he went over the place with his torch. In no time he found a hole big enough to slip his hands in. "I bloody knew it," he said. "We need to fill that bugger up."

Out in the hot oily breeze from the railway, we unloaded a bag of sand, one of cement, a few cans of sealant, plus a shovel, bucket, and a diamond-shaped trowel. Dad looked around for a mixing board. Being Sunday, the next-door businesses – car parts, toolmakers, the new chemical place – were closed. No one came by.

"This'll do us," he said. He scraped at the ground by a pile of old pallets, his moves quick secrets, like a kid scared of getting caught. Where did he hide it all?

He split the sand bag with his shovel, tipped it out. Then he chipped open the cement, drew out a heaped shovelful, folded it into the sand.

"Ever see this?" he said, twisting the shovel in the middle to make a hole, scraping out a clean centre before heaping the sides.

I said I hadn't.

"You might learn something. Get the watering can."

I filled the hole with water till he said woo.

"Now watch," he said, bending to scoop a shovelful of mix from the outside, then letting it slide from the shovel just above the water so as not to make a splash. "Be careful." He scraped the next load from a different spot. "Don't take too much from one place or the wall will burst. No point robbing Peter to pay Paul."

"Do what?" I said, not sure if I heard him right.

He slid the second load off the shovel then stood upright, his face red and beady with sweat. "All right," he said, gearing up for a lesson. "Say you owe your mother a tenner. To pay her back, you take a tenner from me. What's happened?"

"Er, Mum's got paid and you've lost a tenner," I said.

"Right." He nodded slowly at the ground. "But what else? What about the tenner you nabbed from me?"

"Depends. Do you know I nabbed it? If you don't know I nabbed it, it doesn't matter. Does it?"

His mouth stretched with disappointment.

He bent and swept up a biggish load from the wall. "What I mean is," he said, holding the shovel over the water to slide the mix in. Only this time it caught and fell like a rock, sloshing water to the brim. He waited for the water to calm. "I mean that now you owe me a tenner instead of your mum. So you're no better off."

"But what if Mum's skint and you're loaded? She'd be better off, I'd be happy paying her, and you—"

"Soddin' thing!" The wall sprung a leak. All arms and legs, Dad rushed to scoop a bit here, a bit there, but the patch-up wasn't working, and now water was running under his boots. He gave up trying to stem it, just folded everything he could into the middle and started turning the mess over at triple speed to soak up whatever water was left. Once he'd got it all mixed, he dragged the shovel back through the slosh towards him, leaving a row of smooth watery furrows on the top. Upright, both hands pressed at the small of his back, he looked proudly at his work, at having made even a pile of pug seem pretty.

Inside, on his knees at the hole, he used the trowel to make fresh patterns in the pug. "It's all ready and waiting for you, you know," he said, as though picking up on a conversation we'd been having outside. But I knew what he meant. If I played my cards right, I could be going up to market five or six nights a week for the rest of my life. On my own. "You already know the business like the back of your hand." He slapped more pug in the hole.

"I don't know," I said. "I haven't thought about it."

"Well, you'd better start. You're not gonna be an astronaut, are you?"

"Shouldn't think so."

"Waving a telescope at the stars won't make you a living."

His shirt rode up as he bent closer to the hole. I fought back a smile, thinking how mortified he'd be to know that the crack of his arse was showing. "It's a hobby," he said, "keep it like that." His forearms were flat to the floor, his head jutting above them. "There a rag laying about?"

I got up, wandered around. There was a dusty old vest beside some crates. I handed it to him. "What about Patrick Moore?" I said. "He's famous."

"He's soft in the head. Besides, it was different in his day." He wiped some wet pug from his jumper sleeve. "Weren't much call for that sort of thing. Got in at the right time."

"I wasn't thinking of doing that anyway."

He nodded. "Good lad."

I'd learnt to end our chats with something he could nod his head and say "Good lad" to.

Later, when he'd completely bunged up the hole, I washed out the bucket and swept away the last of the mix, losing it in the grass. There was a dark stain on the road.

He came out, studied the sky. "What's the chances of rain then, Patrick?"

I looked up. It was clear as a bell except for a couple of vapour trails in the east. Paleokastritsa? Torremolinos? Magaluf?

"Slim, I reckon."

"You're right there," he said. "Tell you what. Sod the waterproofing. What we need's a nice mug of tea."

44

Tindall's was our one posh department store, the one place you could forget as you walked around it that you were anywhere near the seaside. It sold everything from curtains to hacksaws, from earrings to pickaxes. If there were no other shops in town, it wouldn't have mattered. Well, except for a greengrocer's. Other than fruit and veg, Tindall's had it all. Not being a shopper by any stretch of the pocket, Dad only ever went to the local cash and carry to buy stock for the Remora at trade prices, and in ridiculous bulk. If you asked him, though, he'd say Tindall's was the best shop in town. All because it was family owned, and had been since it opened. It was our second most famous landmark.

The fourth-floor caf was a favourite with the crumblies. Value for money. They did school dinner-type food, laid out in tin tubs under heat lamps – gammon, egg, and chips; crispy fried cod; cottage pie and beans. Once you'd slid your tray along and picked your dinner, you could sit in there for hours. No one minded. Plus it was warm.

If you went to school within a ten-mile radius of town, there was no avoiding Tindall's. All the schools chose it as their sole supplier of uniforms, as if its reputation for quality might somehow rub off on the pupils. As soon as you grew out of your old trousers, you'd be down the outfitting department full of retirement-age bachelors in thin ties and V-necks – a school uniform for grown-ups. The school uniform-buying trip was a golden opportunity for mums to get their own back on their kids by publicly humiliating them. And no matter what day or time you got dragged in there, there would always be someone you knew. Always. But instead of making you feel better about not being alone in your measuring tape-cum-borderline-fondling ordeal, it made you feel even worse.

It was Lucy's idea. In a month she'd pulled me into the library toilets, the town hall toilets, and the grotty ones in the precinct, where two kids had followed us in. While one tried to break down the door, the other climbed to the top of it and tipped a whole pint of milk over us as we put our full weight to the door. It was traumatic. Lucy had to go without her injection.

Even though she still hadn't said she'd go out with me, I was seventy-nine percent certain it was love. We saw each other every Saturday, and sometimes after school. It bothered me a tiny bit that we spent most of our time in toilets, but I didn't say so. There were her medical needs to attend to. And I liked the new feeling of being trusted.

My fifteenth birthday was a special occasion, she said. With her leading, we went into the Pavilion foyer and snuck into the toilets. After she'd made me inject her, she turned around and kissed my cheek and said "Happy birthday." Then she guided my hand between her legs and moved the edge of it back and forth over her hairy moundy bit. (Lance was wrong about his bald Vs.) My thumb kept prodding her bumhole. I didn't think to bend it. She was damp. I felt her lips give. I could've cried. And then, in the middle of it all, she pushed my hand away. "You can't stop now," I said. "It's not fair." She pulled up her jeans. "My body is up to me," she said.

"You're weird," I said.

"Try looking in the mirror."

Her smell stayed with me for days.

The ladies' toilets in Tindall's had two cubicles, side by side as you walked in. As usual, we were in the one furthest from the door.

"Let me," I said, as she pulled her jeans down over her bum. I had the syringe ready.

"Don't you listen?" she said. "It's not time."

"How much longer?"

"Never, if you don't stop going on about it. He who asks doesn't get."

"You must want to."

"Oh yeah, Matthew, I really do," she said, taking the piss. "Have you done it yet?"

I jabbed the needle so hard into her cheek that she yelped, and backheeled me in the shin. I pulled the needle out and shoved her forward. I didn't mean to do it so hard but my shin was agony. And I hated when she took the piss.

She turned around. "Don't you dare! You don't know what I can do."

"My shin!"

"Serves you right for stabbing me like that."

Half reaching down and half lifting my leg, I rubbed at the skin that I could feel was broken. The shoes she always wore with the thick wood sole looked ideal for kicking. And they were. She took the syringe from me, reached around me, and unlocked the door. As we walked out of the loo, two crumblies were coming in. They looked confused.

Lucy wanted a cake, so we went over to join the queue. That's when I saw Mum and Turret. She was sliding their tray along the display. He had his hand in the small of her back.

"What're you gonna buy me then?" said Lucy.

"Nothing," I said. "We're going."

"I want a cake."

"Shut up."

"Don't tell me to shut up."

The exit meant walking parallel to the counter. Mum and Turret were ogling the cakes in the self-service display.

"Let's go," I said. "Now!"

I rushed past the counter and the tables and swung a left to the exit. Whether Lucy was keeping up didn't matter: I had to get out of there. I hadn't told Mum about Lucy.

We were outside on the pavement. It was bright and windy. A postman rode by. He had more energy than me. I felt heavy and sick. "I'm going to the gardens," I said.

"I'm going home then," said Lucy.

"Please yourself."

I walked off. But she followed, shouting my name. By the entrance to the gardens, a boxer pup came over to sniff me. I shook my leg at it to get it away.

"He only wants to play," Lucy said

"Well he can find another bloody dog to play with, can't he."

Lucy sat just up from me on the bench. I stared at the tennis courts. The nets had been taken down for the season. It was just a fifty-by-thirty-yard slab of grey tarmac, enclosed by a tall wire fence. I rolled a fag. Lucy wanted to try, so I pulled out a Rizla and pinched off enough tobacco for a small one, and said watch and learn.

"Why were you in such a rush to leave?" she said.

"Because."

"If you're just gonna sit there and sulk, I'm going home."

"Do that."

She threw her unrolled fag at me and got up, stood there for a minute to see if I'd apologise, to see if I had anything to say worth hearing, but I didn't. So I lit my fag and sat there, and watched her walk off. That stupid flat-footed waddle.

45

When it came to siphoning petrol from the Princess, I just copied what I'd seen Dad do when he topped up our Suffolk Punch, which was a proper mower, unlike Miss Jinny's. I threaded one end of the tubing I'd pinched from chemistry into the tank, held the other end low, and sucked. Tasting the first drops of petrol, I put a finger over the end and felt for my Lucozade bottle, fed the tube into it, and let it fill.

Wednesdays were dead so Dad always took Tuesday nights off from going to market. If I didn't get petrol out of the car that night, I'd have to wait till the next Tuesday. That was too late. Once I'd decided to do something, it pecked at my head until I finally did it. There was no putting it off.

Three in the morning, damp and quiet. Orange light from the lamp-posts smeary with mist. Crouched by the car, still half-asleep, I was having doubts about the route I'd picked for the mission, even though it was as under-the-radar as I could get. I was so busy talking myself out of it that I forgot what I was doing. Petrol spilled over onto my hand. I whipped the tube from the tank. The drive was probably covered with it. If Dad asked, I'd say I had as much idea of how it got there as he did. I might even push it and make him feel guilty for blaming everything that went wrong on me. I screwed the filler cap on and put the lid back on the bottle. I went over to the drain and poked the tubing through the grate till it was gone. I took the rag from my pocket and wiped the outside of the bottle, then pulled the carrier bag from my pocket and wrapped the bottle in it. I zipped the bottle inside my coat and got on my bike.

At that time of the morning the law were bound to be suspicious of anyone, let alone a young kid riding his push-bike on the pavement with no lights. So I cut through Albion Terrace and took the alley to the duck pond, or Nature Park, as they called it, since they'd put a path around it, and then through the grounds of the old seaman's hospice, which used to be a retirement home for fishermen and sailors until the council sold it to a builder who converted it into retirement flats that went for a quarter of a million apiece. I bet the sailors weren't expecting to be all at sea again. The hospice overlooked the prom, and once I'd reached the far end of the grounds I had a quarter-mile sprint to go.

When I got to Turret's stall, I crouched out of the wind for cover, took the bottle out of the bag, unscrewed the lid, then tossed both away. I dunked the rag in the bottle till it was well soaked, then made a wick, squeezing the wetness out. My hands were useless. Getting that wick in the neck was like threading a needle in the dark. I lit the wick and waved it till all of it flamed, then launched the bottle at the base. Fire splashed up the stall. The flames were killing it. My face was tight with heat. Against the sea's blackness, the fire was magical, just magical. No wonder Lance was addicted.

I didn't hear the siren until I'd passed the pier on my way home. A law car came belting down Middle Street, lights flashing, a fire engine on its tail. All the shop windows in Middle Street looked alight. I darted up Collett's Alley and into Bilson Street, which was narrow, with concrete bollards. They'd have to be Allan Wellses to catch me. The side street cut across three small roads before it dead-ended at St. Mary's cemetery. I stank of petrol. If the law got within fifty feet of me, they'd know.

The main gate to the cemetery was on the other side, by the church. I lifted my bike over the wall. I had one leg over when headlights hit the trees, followed by a blaze of coloured lights. I pulled my leg back and ducked. It was just me, my heart, my panting. Poking my head up, I saw the law car drive into the cemetery. Graves glowed in the headlights; trees shone at the end. I yanked my bike back over the wall. Then another set of headlights, riding high up the lane. The odds were quickly getting worse.

After cutting through side streets and car parks and alleys, I got to Fray's Yard. No one would look for me there. Fray did heavy machinery – cranes, diggers, dump trucks...Lots of hydraulics. That was the working part of the yard. The other half was full of bizarre rusting hulks that he must've just liked collecting – there was no other reason for them being there. He had a scaled-down submarine, two train carriages, and what looked like a prototype combine harvester. Along with several derelict tractors were a dozen or more army lorries that looked like they'd been there since the war. Lance and I used to sneak in after school to smash windscreens.

Fray had sold some of his land to developers who'd built an indus-trial estate full of warehouses and small-business units. Plus he leased an area to a truck rental firm, who parked their fleet of shiny white Transits in a line as if waiting for emergencies. Against the backdrop of rust, the mass of white vans couldn't have looked odder. Lance had trouble getting his head around all that whiteness. He wanted to blow the vans up. If we did a couple, he said, the rest would go with them. He was serious, but I wasn't up for it. So he gave it a miss.

I hid in the submarine till it was light.

When I got home, Mum was already up, and washing the bin out in the kitchen sink. Half her arm was in it. She saw me. By the coal bunker was a dumped pile of bricks that Dad got from Norm for the path. (After getting that chip in my eye, I refused to clean any more.) I went over and restacked them.

"Matthew? What are you doing?"

Mum was pulling off her Marigolds in the doorway.

"Nothing."

"It's six o'clock in the morning. Where have you been?"

"Nowhere." I thought for a second. "Out."

"Out where?"

"Er, Jupiter."

"Matthew."

"They just dropped me off."

She sniffed. "What's that smell?"

"Dunno. Dads?"

It was about two seconds before the penny dropped. When it did, she scowled then did a marching-band turn and went in. I counted to ten before skirting the wall as far as the window and putting an eye to the corner to check where she was and whether I could run through unchallenged. As I bent to untie my shoes, it felt like a kids' tea party was going on in my head. All sharp noise and jumping.

I left my shoes outside the door and made a run for it. Mum pre-tended I wasn't there.

In my room, I pulled the shower curtain back and anticipated all that water. Then I thought: why? I didn't care if I smelled. I left my clothes where they'd fallen and put on my uniform just to get out of the house without an argument.

"Where d'you think you're going?" said Mum when I went through the kitchen to get my shoes.

"School."

"Not with no breakfast you're not."

I opened the back door and went out. She came after me.

"Don't ignore me. You've got another two hours."

I did my laces up and wheeled my bike around to face the alley. Mum blocked me. I had to get away before my tears started – I could feel their fat blobs on my eyelids. "I'm warning you," I said, gulping, my voice stony and strange. "I'll charge." I shoved my wheel forward to show I meant it.

"Just calm down," she said. "Talk to me."

"Three, two—"

"I'm not moving until you answer me."

I shoved my bike at her, ran to the coal bunker, leapt onto it, then onto the fence. The dry wooden panel broke free of the post. (Dad must've used all the creosote up on the barrow.) I fell into the alley and ran along the back of the gardens to the garages at the end, then into the allotments.

The pillbox up Winterpit Lane. I spent the day sleeping and smoking and scoring every grown-up I could think of on a scale of one to ten according to how much I hated them. Then I smoked and slept some more. At one point I woke up with a stone stuck in my cheek. From time to time I sat by the gun slits and stared at the undergrowth. The day didn't move. I felt like a hostage.

Stand on your head if you have to, but don't say anything. Ignore their ranting and raving. That's what was going through my mind outside Brain's Electrics as I waited to cross. And that's when I heard the tooting. A palm on the horn. It was Norm in his Cortina, across the road. He'd pulled up on the chevrons. His face as he worked to lower his window was brilliant – my first laugh of the day. "Get in, quick," he shouted, to me and his mirrors. When the light changed, I went over. I'd never been so happy to see him, no matter what happened next. Getting in, I felt half as heavy as I had all day. It was like climbing into an ambulance.

"Send you to do her dirty work, did she?" I said, shutting my door.

"Bloody hell," he said, waving his hand as though I'd farted, which I hadn't.

"What!"

"Fumes!" he said. "And put your seat belt on."

In the seafront caf at Goring he bought a ham-and-pickle doorstep for me and a pot of tea for two. He ate at half past seven in the morning, at quarter past one, and between six and half six at night depending on how late he had to stay at the shop. It was half past four. He'd make do with a cup of tea and a fag. He took our tray out to one of the picnic tables at the top of the beach.

The doorstep was doughy and soft like a bap, but huge – a meal in itself. It plugged every gap in my teeth. Norm poured the teas then rolled a fag. His collar rim was blood-specked from shaving. And he'd missed under his nostrils.

"I ran your auntie to the airport earlier," he said. "Gatwick. Guess what the Australian national airline's logo is?"

"A kangaroo," I said, "and it's a mascot."

"Poor old Ern," he said. He brushed ash from the table, raised his chin, and looked at the sea. He smoked slowly. "Families, ay?"

"Yeah."

"You might think you had a hard time not having any brothers and sisters, but I'm not so sure. Look at our lot. You'd only end up piggy in the middle like me, trying to keep everyone apart. Ern had it right. I should've listened to him. 'What's there to stay here for?' I remember it clear as day. Having a pint down the Station, we were, the day before he went. 'Carpets?' he said. 'What's the attraction?' It's a job, I said. People always need carpets. Know what he said? 'People always need everything. Heating, electric, kitchens. Get a trade.' Old Ern. Always right."

"What sort of cancer's he got?"

He tapped his chest. "Lung. Too much of this." He showed me his fag. "Don't you be stupid like me."

"I won't."

"You see some people, smoke till they're ninety, not even a cough. Miserable buggers too. Then you get the likes of Ern. Salt of the earth. Forty-three." He shook his head. "I know what I'll be doing when this tin's gone."

"You say that every time you come round."

"Ah, but saying it and meaning it is two different birds." As if to prove it, he flicked his fag towards the sea. It didn't go far. He sipped his tea. "All right?" He meant my sandwich, which I'd just finished. "Lovely," I said. It was. "Drink your tea," he said.

It went quiet. Everything moved to the front of my head and pressed against it. My forehead must've been bulging. I couldn't keep it in.

"I already smoke," I said.

"You what?"

"I already smoke."

"I thought you just said you didn't."

"Yeah."

"Why say you don't when you do?"

"Dunno."

By then I didn't care what he thought or said about it, I just had to say it. It could've been anything, but it was that. As soon as I said it I felt the bulge of my backy in my pocket, like it was reminding me that I needed it. I pulled out my papers and what was left of my Golden Virginia and put them on the table.

"Silly sod," he said. "Well, who'm I to talk?"

"Mind if I have one?"

"I'm not saying," he said. "Just don't go up in flames."

It was strange. As I rolled my fag I felt embarrassed for letting him down, but at the same time it was as if I'd stepped out of my old self and left it behind. Like growing up five years in a minute. When I lit my fag, Norm rolled himself another. We smoked.

"So what's going on?" he said.

"Like what?"

"Like a fish stall catching fire in the middle of the night?"

"Dunno."

"You're on the front page of the paper, you know that?"

"What, my name?"

"Not your name, you goon. Your handiwork."

"I'm not a goon."

"Your mum's not daft, Matthew. She smelt your clothes. You don't have to be Columbo to put it together."

"You watch *Columbo* then?"

"Yeah."

"What about *Banacek*?"

"I'm being serious," he said. "Look. Your Auntie Vi. She shouldn't've gone shouting her mouth off like that. She had no right."

"At least someone did. You all knew. I bet everyone in this stupid town knows."

"No they don't."

"Says who?"

An old couple came out and looked at the empty tables, meeny miny mo. Norm watched how they sat down and then leaned across the table. "It's been hard on everyone," he said quietly. "Especially your dad. Well, and your mum. All of us. No one wanted to lie to you, Matthew. Your dad . . . he didn't want anything said. You can't blame him. He didn't ask for it."

"What? What didn't he ask for?"

"To have it all brought up again. Bygones and all that. It was decided. For the best. Your mum was only protecting you."

"Yeah, and sharks are only fish." My roll-up had gone out. I reached for Norm's lighter. "Anyway, forget it. I've got other things to worry about."

He laughed. "Oh yeah? Such as?"

"None of your business."

He held his hand up. "Just— Please, Matthew. Just hear me out."

46

Back in Mum's younger days, when she was trying to make a go of the Remora, and when her and Vi were still partners, Turret had the fishmonger's on Dulwich Street. He was older, and married, with three school-age kids. On Mum's weekly visits to his shop, they got to talking. He was charming, and Mum was only too happy to take a break from her daily grind. Before long, small talk gave way to heart-to-hearts. Mum vented her frustration with Vi, and Turret opened up about Linda, his wife, who'd been diagnosed with a bone disease and was confined to a wheelchair. Turret couldn't cope. His kids did what they could, but it didn't help. It seemed that every free minute he had was spent taking care of Linda, lifting her in and out of the bath, driving her to the seafront in the evenings so she could get some air. He'd had no training for any of it. He'd never even used the twin-tub. He was angry – not at Linda exactly, but sort of. Not that he blamed her. They didn't come any kinder, and she'd always looked after him. But now there it all was, this *problem*, piled on his plate. And he had no one to tell. Until Mum.

One day he plucked up the courage and asked her to join him for a picnic, to Bodiam Castle. With a name like mine, he joked, where else? It was something he and Linda had done before she was ill: Sunday picnics, a new castle each trip – Lewes, Bodiam, Pevensey, Hever, Amberley, Arundel, Leeds... Some were more ruins than castle. A single standing tower. Grandness didn't matter. They were all special. And Turret missed them. I'd be delighted, said Mum.

They fell in love. A month after their outing to Hever Castle – Turret's favourite of all – Mum found out she was pregnant. When she broke the news to Turret, he was torn. He'd have to leave Linda; he couldn't. He'd have to; he couldn't. He would; he wouldn't. But his life was with Linda. In sickness and in health. Not to mention the kids. It was impossible. Mum reacted to his decision with vodka and a handful of Aspirin. If Vi hadn't been stood up at the Odeon that night, she wouldn't have been back in time to save Mum. The ambulance came. At the General they pumped Mum's stomach and kept an eye on the baby. All seemed to be well. Mum made a full recovery. And she'd done some thinking. If she couldn't be with Turret, she'd keep his child as a reminder of what they'd had, of what might have been. Her first job when she came out of hospital was to find a husband. And sharp.

Enter Stanley Bowen. Mum was his customer too. (Once a customer, always a customer – another of Dad's sayings.) A nice man, Stanley. Smart. And kind to a fault. He was single and going places. And he was short, like Turret. Look no further. Mum lit a fire under him, cooked up a whirlwind, and had a wedding band on her finger before she showed. She must've carved off the days on her bedpost till it was safe to break the news. Finally, the announcement was made: a baby was on the way.

At first Stan adapted to his role by putting in long hours at the shop. Building the business for everyone. To him, crying was chaos, or close to it. Every new outburst sent him scurrying to the lock-up, where he could find comfort in order and numbers. When the baby eventually resigned itself to being alive, and settled down, Stan warmed to it. Matthew was now a little human. He could listen. He was teachable. Stan could fill him with what he knew. Handily for Mum, Stan didn't warm to his role so much that he badgered her to try for a brother or sister. It wouldn't have mattered: Mum had no intention. Imagine pushing a Punch and a Judy around a town full of nosy grannies: "Ooh, they're like chalk and cheese, Mrs. Bowen."

Five or six years later, Stan was arguing with one of his customers, Harry Sykes, who refused to pay for stock that he claimed was damaged. Something about nibbled greens. Dad was tired of Sykes. He'd done nothing but moan and pay late from the start. In the heat of the argument, Sykes said things about Vi, about how he'd seen her singing and staggering through town in the middle of the afternoon. "You leave my family out of it," said Dad. "This is between you and me."

"What about you and Bill Turret, then?"

It was a small world. Dad had heard Turret's name, but he didn't know him.

"Meaning?"

"Him and that kid you adopted—"

"Adopted?" said Dad. "A bloody check up from the neck up's what you need. Now sod off."

"I'll tell you what I don't need," said Sykes. "I don't need anyone telling me what kid's mine and what isn't. Unlike some people."

"You're soft up here," said Stan.

Stan brushed it off, put the outburst down to Sykes's small brain and big mouth, both of which he was famous for. But try as he might to forget, those words kept coming back. They were there when he woke up in the morning, and then at night, on his long drives to market, they rang so loud and clear in his head that it was as though Sykes were there in the passenger seat, saying them over and over.

Adopted?

The next time he met Norm down the Legion for snooker, Stan told him about his blow-up with Sykes. And as he told the story, he watched Norm's face for signs, flickers, anything that seemed off. But Norm's life, for want of a better word, was in Shoreham. He only drove into Farthing to see Stan and Jean and young Matthew, and Vi once in a while; he didn't know any Harry Sykes. "So you wouldn't know anything about a fisherman called Turret either, then?" Stan said. And the second the words left his lips, Stan saw them working on Norm, goading him, prickling his skin, making him clammy. Norm was lining up a slice on the brown. He had his chin to his cue. But instead of taking the shot, he stood up, cracked his neck left and right as if the tension had been messing with his sight, then shook his head. "Nope," he said.

"Come off it," said Stan. "It's written all over your face."

Norm looked at the table. Three reds over pockets, six total. Pink on the top cushion. "I don't know, Stan," he said, irritated, trying to wriggle free.

"What about Jean? Does she know him?"

"Stan. Don't put this on me."

"Who else am I gonna ask? I need you to be straight with me."

"You're putting me in a real—"

"Norm, I'm not asking for the key to space."

"I know you're not, Stan."

"So—" Stan softened his voice. "How does she know him?"

Norm leaned his cue against the cushion. "All right. If you must know. They had a thing. It was before you. There. I've said it."

"A 'thing'?"

"An affair. There was some trouble."

"This 'trouble'. It didn't by any chance involve—"

"For Christ's sake, Stan. Yes! Was it Matthew? Yes! Is that what you want me to say?"

Stan was stunned. He didn't answer.

Norm packed up his cue, collected his keys and tobacco. He looked at the unfinished snooker game on the table, at having been forced to leave it while he still had a chance.

He said, "I really wish you hadn't made me say that, Stanley. Really."

47

When it comes to stopping invaders, castles are second in importance only to piers. Here in Sussex, and next door in Kent, there's loads. The fort at Pevensey, which the Romans built, was strengthened and used as a base by William the Conqueror, who started his conquering there. But the Battle of Hastings wasn't a fair fight because King Harold and his army were knackered – they'd just run all the way from York. William only conquered us by luck. Then he built castles.

Hever Castle is famous for being where Henry VIII went out with Anne Boleyn. Her family owned it and she grew up there. It's lovely. I was made under a bush in the Italian Garden, on a sunny day. My mum and real dad, who's not my real dad now, were there for a picnic. His name is Turret.

48

When we got back home, I asked Norm to come in with me, even though the Princess wasn't in the drive, which meant Dad was still at the shop. Mrs. Hodges must've heard the front door open because she was hurrying towards us when we went in.

"Jean around?" said Norm.

"She's in her room."

"Do us a favour and tell her we're here, would you?"

"She's not well."

Norm told me to wait in the kitchen. I followed him and Mrs. Hodges down the hall and went through the swing door. On the kitchen table was the edition of the *Argus* Norm had mentioned. I was more worried about my bike, until I saw it out the back, leaning in its usual spot. At least that hadn't changed. The headline read:

FISH FRY ON SEAFRONT AS TURF WAR HOTS UP

Under the headline was a black-and-white photo of Turret's stall, or rather what was left of it by the time the fire brigade had got their hoses out and blasted half of it to France. The article, written by a Paul Soap, read:

> Fire investigators have confirmed that last night's fish stall blaze on the seafront was an act of arson. Said Sergeant Dougal McCreery, "We found traces of an accelerant and pieces of shattered glass. The fire was deliberate." But when asked to commit himself further, McCreery was reluctant. "If you're after the arsonist's name, I can't help you." McCreery also refused to speculate about the motive, saying it was too early to tell. But many locals with seafront businesses weren't surprised by the attack. "It's been brewing for ages," said one, who asked to remain anonymous. Indeed, most Farthing residents are unaware of how bitter the feud between local fishermen has become in recent months. And while some reject the notion that last night's arson attack represents a turning point in the feud, others are less hopeful. "It's a turf war," said retired fisherman Jack Selby. "It's been on the cards for years. I'm just glad I got out when I did." As to who was behind the

attack, Selby wasn't sure, but he had some ideas. "I'm not pointing my finger, but someone ought to keep an eye on the youngsters. They're a law to themselves."

A few minutes later, Mrs. Hodges came through the swing door. "Your mum wants to see you."

The curtains were drawn. The only light in the room came from the standard lamp with the tasselled shade next to Dad's bookcase. Mum was in bed. Norm had pulled a chair up beside her as though she were in hospital, which she was doing a good impression of – flat on her back, head propped on pillows, face blank. Norm waved me in. I stood at the end of the bed and leaned on the footboard, not sure if Mum had seen me. The olive branch clock that Ruth had brought Mum back from Spain ticked on the telly. It seemed to take forever till someone spoke.

"He's a very nice man, Matthew," Mum said. The words started her crying. She pulled some tissues out of a box I hadn't noticed at her side. "You shouldn't've had to hear about him like that."

Norm turned to me and gave me a strange look, like he and I ought to be encouraged by the fact that Mum had spoken, that she hadn't been stripped of all her faculties since earlier that morning. I felt no need to say anything. Norm would've filled her in.

"I'm going to ask you something," Mum said. "Your dad . . . this dad," she opened her hand to his side of the bed, "he stayed with you, Matthew. He's a good man. Don't make him explain. He couldn't—" And then her crying cut her off.

When I got up to my room, the clothes I'd left on the floor that morning were sitting on my bed, washed and ironed. There was no trace of petrol. I took off my school uniform and hung it up, then jammed a chair under the door handle and went to my cubbyhole, pulled out Sandy Sangeet's knickers and Mum's tights. After stripping naked, I put them on, and lay down on my bed. I must've been dead to the world because I didn't hear a sound till the next morning, when a bird on my windowsill woke me up with its chirping.

That night I found Soap in the phonebook – his name made it easy: there were only two in Farthing, and only one beginning with P. If he thought it was all right to lie just to get his name on the front page, he had another thing coming. As if the real story wasn't meaty enough.

Then I set about making my last creation.

As an infant, Priscilla Daggermouth was so badly crushed when her dad backed over her in the driveway that she never fully recovered. Her surviving at all was a miracle unfathomable to science. Her skull resembled the excavated remains of a missing evolutionary link that lay boxed and shelved in a basement. Over time, the assembled team of world-class surgeons restored her skull to an approximation of the original. The leading surgeon likened the process to peeling an under-boiled egg and then refitting the shell with watertight precision so as to encase the gluey interior. Her face, alas, performed poorly, leaving Priscilla with a buckled surface of ridges and dips. Her eye sockets were uneven: the crowded left eye was twinned with a fully boiled and fully peeled egg of a thing on the right. Not to mention the tooth-and-hair cyst in her neck. In short, had we been living in the days when carrying a cabbage in public after midnight was enough to send a woman to the Glades for life, Priscilla would've no doubt been condemned to a pen in the piggery. Instead she got life in the world.

Using old copies of the *Argus*, I cut out all the letters I needed, little and large, and wrote my kidnap note:

I set fire. Lies kill trade. Stop now or pay. The Arsonist

I clipped the note to Priscilla and posted them the next morning.

Lance phoned about the fire. He'd been down there. It wasn't great, he said, only one stall had been burnt. The good thing about it was that it'd had enough time to burn properly, leaving just a pile of charred wood and whatever ash hadn't blown away. He said he'd meet me down there after school if I wanted. As far as I was concerned, we weren't talking. If he thought he was punishing me again over Sid the same way he always punished me when things didn't go his way, he was wrong. I told him I was busy. Then, just before I put the phone down, I said, "Oh, can you give Zoë a message for me?"

"Zoë who?" he said.

49

It was Mum's birthday. She was poaching eggs in the kitchen. Dad was reading the paper. He looked up. His eyes widened when he saw my card and present.

"Good news all round, it looks like." He closed his paper. "See the movers' van outside the darkies'?"

"No," I said.

"They're all out there, loading up."

"Happy birthday, Mum." I put her card and present on the table.

"Well I'm blowed," she said.

She came over with the eggs. I sat at the table and poured a mug of tea. Mum sat down.

"You shouldn't have," she said.

It was the only card on the table. She and Dad didn't celebrate birthdays, or anniversaries. Sometimes they bought something small for each other at Christmas, sometimes they didn't. As she opened her card, Dad took his wallet from his back pocket.

"I nearly forgot." He put five tenners on the table and slid them to me.

"What's that?" I said. I poured milk in my tea and stirred it.

"The boot," he said. "You were right. I rounded it up to fifty."

"How lovely," said Mum, after reading her card. She stood it on the table in front of her. Dad picked it up. He read it and smiled, put it back on the table. He nodded at the money. "Get yourself a nice camera with that. Take some cracking shots of the market."

Mrs. Hodges walked in as Mum was unwrapping her present. She stayed just in front of the swing door, hands clasped in front of her, waiting, as always, for permission to speak. Mum and Dad had their backs to the door. Only I could see her. She kept raising her brows at me and then darting her eyes at Mum and Dad. She was trying so hard to recruit me. I ignored her.

"Seiko?" said Mum, examining the moveable dial on the top that told you your up from your down. "It looks expensive."

Dad was suspicious. "Matthew?"

"I found it. Under the pier. Same place I found the boot."

"You sure?"

"Cross my heart and hope to die."

"Oh Matthew," said Mum, sadly.

"What?"

"That's a terrible saying."

Mrs. Hodges coughed. Mum turned around. "How long have you been there?"

"Oh, no time." She was about to say what she was doing there when Mum turned back to the table.

Dad banged his ear a few times. "It belongs to the Crown then," he said. "The Queen owns the beaches."

"That's not fair," I said. "She's loaded. Why should she have it?"

I wasn't planning on taking Dad's money, but when he defended the Queen's claim to the beaches I grabbed it out of spite. I hated the Queen after what Sid had said about the Koh-i-noor diamond.

"I can't keep it," said Mum. "It's lost property. Someone's lost this." She turned the watch over and held it to her eye like a jeweller. "There's something on it."

"Give it here," said Dad, reaching for it, but Mum cupped her hands around it.

"I'm looking," she snapped. "Initials. Second letter's an R. The first—" She tilted it this way and that trying to catch a glint of the letter. "—an A? Yes, A. Could be a B, mind."

Dad took it from her, held it up in front of him the same way. "A. R." he said, matter-of-factly.

Mrs. Hodges developed a severe tickly throat.

"The police should have it," said Mum.

As soon as Mum mentioned the law I felt a hot wave across my cheeks. They'd know it belonged to Mrs. Rafferty, and then they'd be round asking questions. I'd have to get rid of everything. "You can't," I said. "Finders keepers. It's yours now."

"They've got a lost property, haven't they?"

"Yeah," said Dad, "their Christmas bonus. You hand that in and the guv'nor's wife'll get it in her stocking."

Mrs. Hodges' presence annoyed him, the way she stood there with her hands clasped, all sorry and small.

"What is it?" he said

"Don't give it to them," I said. "You've got more right to it than they have. It's not fair."

"Sorry, sir," said Mrs. Hodges. "Mr. Fletcher in room four wants to know if he can get a bus from here to Devil's Dyke."

Dad pushed his paper aside. "Drive a bus now, is it? Honestly." He got up, went over to the swing door, and brushed past Mrs. Hodges on his way out. She waited till he'd gone and then followed him.

Mum put the watch on her wrist. Then she tilted her wrist again to see if it did anything when the light caught it. "Well, thank you, Matthew," she said, pulling her cuff down over the face. "It's the thought that counts."

Everything went quiet for a while. For what felt like an endless minute, our house could've been mistaken for any other. I admired the watch as much as Mum did. It was so quiet in the kitchen that I sat back in my chair and put my hands behind my head and imagined not having to get up to do anything, not having the rest of my day divvied up between washing the Bedford and clearing out old crates and boxes from the lock-up. Just spending a quiet day with the family.

50

I peered out the lounge window and saw the movers' van in front of the Bhargavas'. Chairs and boxes and bedsteads were being ferried by Indians I'd never seen – the relatives from Kashmir, I supposed. Then Sid appeared with a sink, a chunky old porcelain one. You could see it was heavy enough for two. For a second I thought he might drop it. Without consciously deciding to, I looked down at my feet to see if I had any shoes on, which was odd because in our house shoes were illegal, except for guests. I watched Sid struggle to the pavement, bend his knees by the van, and let the sink down on its side. Then he went back in.

Upstairs I folded a sheet of notepaper in half and put Mrs. Rafferty's diamond earrings in the fold, bent the top over, and tucked the ends in. Before slipping that into a proper envelope, I wrote *Here's your diamond back*. On the front of the billing envelope I wrote *Dear Sid*, and wrapped the tiny packet in Sellotape.

It was a Sunday and Dad needed my help to move some shelving in the shop. All day we were at it. I wasn't much use. I couldn't get my mind off of Sid's leaving.

Between measuring up and banging away, Dad prattled on about the new sign he wanted done for the shop, about why Dick Tolly would milk everyone dry if he was voted in as the new mayor, and then about the fundraising drive for the new stand they hoped to build at the local football ground, which he said was a waste of money because it wouldn't make them play any better – they were always third to bottom – or attract any new fans. It was funny hearing him waffle on about the state of the football. He'd never been to a match in his life. But knowing what was going on in town was all part of the job. His regulars loved a chat. He needed to have an opinion. It wasn't something he had trouble with.

We stopped for lunch. I went up the Spar for sandwiches and crisps. That's when I saw Lucy and Zoë on the steps by the precinct, Lucy on a lower step in front of Zoë, clamped by her legs. My lung gurgled. I moved closer. Peeking round a poster in a bus stop, I watched as Zoë lifted and gathered Lucy's hair into bunches. Instead of her sweaty coat, Lucy was wearing a dark bomber jacket I'd never seen before, not even in her wardrobe. What was she doing? She hated people. All people. She told me. We were turtles. What if she needed an injection?

Back at the shop, Dad insisted on quizzing me while we ate.

"Right," he said. "If you made eighty percent of your turnover in three months, how would you make it last the whole year?"

"I don't know," I said.

"Don't know won't get you far."

"I don't." A slice of tomato fell out of my sandwich. I got off my stool, picked it up, threw it in the bin. "Save, I s'pose."

"Good lad. But think. You're sitting there twiddling your thumbs from October to May. Then wallop, all of a sudden the coaches start showing up and the prom starts filling with punters. Spend, spend, spend. Twiddling over. You need more staff, and you've got to make room for stock so you don't run out—" He battled with a mouthful of beef and mustard. "You start working twelve-, fifteen hour days, seven days a week. How d'you think you'd feel pulling rakes of cash out the till at the end of the night?"

"Terrific."

"Too right you would. But it's not all yours, see. Why not?"

I finished my sandwich but was still hungry. I wanted to go home. "Do we have to do this?"

"We do."

"'Cause you've gotta pay your suppliers first," I said mechanically.

"Good lad. What else?"

"Bills, staff, rent. Everything's gotta be paid before you see a penny of it."

"There's hope for you yet. Well, not that you can't draw *a modest wage*. I mean, you've been working your goolies off, you want something to show for it. A *reward for your efforts*."

"Only if there's enough to pay for the next load of stock," I said.

"Why?"

"How much longer?"

"I'm asking."

I blew out a load of air. "No stock no business. If you don't pay yourself, it doesn't matter. Not for a while. Hang onto the money and stick it back in the business. You'll make tons more. Then you can take an even bigger cut."

"Good lad," he said, screwing up his sandwich bag and tossing it in the bin. "You should work in a bank."

I waited till dark that night to go round to Sid's. The big van was still parked outside. The sink was still on the pavement. All the front lights in their house were on. When I knocked, his mum opened the door.

"Is Sid in?" I said, holding the envelope behind my back.

She gave me a sour up and down. "What do you want?"

"I just wondered if he was in."

"He doesn't want to see you," she said. The hiss of a catfight came from the side alley. Maybe it was the same cat with the chewed-up ear and the manky leg we used to throw in the air. Sid's mum didn't seem to hear it, or if she did, she didn't flinch.

Sid came to the door and stood beside her. They both looked at me without speaking. I felt like the taxman.

"What're you doing here?" he said.

"Nothing."

"You're not welcome."

"I said I was sorry!"

I waited for him to say something, anything, but he didn't, he just stood there with his mum, looking like he didn't know me. And neither of them said anything when I turned and walked back up their path. I heard their door close.

I started to walk home. Ten yards on I stopped and looked back at all the lights in Sid's house, thinking how they'd be switched off soon and the place would be empty. In the light from the lamppost I pressed the soft, taped envelope, then read the front again. *Dear Sid.* I went back to his door and dropped the envelope through his letterbox, pausing for a moment in the hope that he was watching through a dark window and had seen me come back and wanted to apologise for being mean. But when his door didn't open, there was nothing else for it. So I went home.

51

Not only is basketball not Pareto efficient, nor is living by the seaside if your livelihood depends on it. The reason for this is because Pareto efficiency means that the most efficient way of going about things is if one side benefits but not at the expense of the other side. Mrs. Thatcher's way of running the country isn't at all Pareto efficient because the rich have done very nicely thank you at the expense of everyone else, especially independents like us who rely on the seaside trade. Because so many people go to Spain and Corfu nowadays for the sun, no one comes to see us, which means we don't get the business we used to. All our money is going to Spain and Corfu, who are very Pareto efficient because their holiday trade people aren't benefiting at anyone else's expense, except ours, which doesn't count because they don't need to worry about us because we're a different economy. Heretofore lies my definition of Pareto efficiency.

52

For the first time in my life, not counting Christmas or birthday cards, I got a letter in the post. It was handwritten in green ink, with a Farthing postmark. I opened it in my room. In the envelope was one torn-out sheet of lined paper, folded in half. It was a neat fold, corner to corner, like I would've done. When I unfolded it, there was a newspaper clipping stuck to one side. At the top of the clipping was a black-and-white photo of a boy, about my age, with long dark hair. He looked familiar. The first part read:

> In loving memory of Antonio Fortino, son of Rocco and Luisa, and brother to Lucy. His tragic and untimely passing has been deeply felt by all. He will be forever missed. The Lord sanctions his passing according to His glorious design.

It didn't say how he died. Under the obituary, in the same green handwriting, was a message: *Tony Fortino died three years ago, 12ᵗʰ March. Oh dear.* It was signed *Liza Radley.* Under the signature was a face, drawn in the same green ink, with no hair, ears, eyes, eyebrows, or nose. Except for the dagger mouth, it was blank.

That Tuesday after school would've been our next date. We always went to Lucy's music lesson together on the bus. I'd wait for her in the nearby caf. Lesson over, she'd meet me in there for milkshakes and flapjacks. But the next Tuesday I didn't go to the bus stop to meet her. Something told me she wouldn't phone to find out where I'd got to. And I was right. She didn't.

53

The tide was out, the sand hard and ridged. I was prodding a cuttlefish. A woman jogged by, whipping spray from her heels, trying to avoid the shallow pools. Her collie didn't care, it just ploughed straight through. I took the cuttlefish out to the water, which was miles. It swayed when I lowered it in. I stood there for ages, sea covering my toes, just watching the water, thinking how much of it was out there waiting to come in.

By the pier, and downwind from Turret's stall, I could smell the remains of the fire. As I got closer, I saw a shape bobbing. Then I spotted his washed-out red cap. It looked like he was sweeping.

The concrete base was covered with charcoaly smears. Turret was loading the burnt wood into a wheelbarrow with red grips and a skinny wheel. He had a real bucket and spade with him, and some lengths of four by two.

"Did a pretty good job," he said, standing, holding his lower back.

"I s'pose." I nodded to the bucket. "Want me to fill it?"

"Why not," he said.

I started down the slope of the beach with the bucket, my feet slipping on the pebbles.

"Matthew," he shouted. I stopped, turned around. "It's entirely up to you. You can walk halfway to France if you want or," he pointed behind him to a short post, "you can use the tap." We both laughed. I walked back up the beach.

"My back's not what it was," he said. "How about I tip and you sweep?"

I gave him the bucket, he gave me the broom. I stood aside while he tipped the water over the base, then I rushed at it, as if it were in danger of drying up. When I'd finished, the smears were gone and you could see some of the screw holes. Others were still clogged with ash.

"Can I ask you something?" I said.

"As long as you're not after a loan."

"No."

"What're you waiting for?"

The longer I waited, the harder it would be to start. So I bit the bullet.

"Well, if you had a friend, one you really liked, but you'd been really stupid and ruined it, and it didn't matter how much you said sorry and wanted to make everything right, they still wouldn't talk to you, what would you do?"

"Such as?"

"I didn't mean it. I mean, I *did*, but it was his fault too 'cause he wouldn't listen, which is what got me angry 'cause I only did it for, well, there was a reason, but he didn't want to hear it, and now he hates me and won't be friends 'cause what I did was really horrible and I don't know why – well, I do sort of, but he won't have it. I mean, he might, but he doesn't know 'cause he won't let me explain, but if he did I know he wouldn't hate me so much and we could be mates again."

He went over to his toolbox and picked up an old Thermos and pointed to a small wooden fishing boat just up the beach. There was a black square on the front side with 96 in white numbers. It had flags too. I followed him over to it.

"The office is flooded," he said, nodding at the water in the bottom. "It's better like that. A man thinks more clearly with his feet in water."

We climbed into the boat. There was a bench at the back. The water in the bottom stank of slimy weed. We sat down. He pulled the plastic cup off of the Thermos and unscrewed the cap. Coffee steam rose between us. "Do the honours," he said, passing me the cup. He poured coffee into it. The cup got hot so I took it by the handle. "Taste it," he said. I did. "What's it like?" he said. "Hot," I said. "Strong." I gave it back to him. He sipped at it. "Strong's the word. Now, slow down and go back to the beginning."

So I did. I told him how Dad would've skinned me alive if he found out I'd been friendly with Sid, let alone been in his house. I told him about the Anchor, about how I used to think that what Dad always called "the strength of your convictions" really meant something. I told him some of the history with me and Lance, about how he'd stitched me up, and about smacking Sid for saying I'd been on Dad's side all along when I'd stuck up for him against Lance and would've stuck up for him by the church that day if I'd been on my bike and not in the car with Mum. Which was and wasn't true. But when I looked up and saw Turret staring out at the horizon, I thought he was tired of my droning and had switched off. So I stopped. Before long, he asked what I'd stopped for. Keep going, he said. I'm listening.

"So now I've got two dads and no friends," I said. "What use is that?"

"That's for you to work out," he said. "I can't give you the answers. All I can tell you is they're out there. You might look in a lot of wrong places, but you'll find them. And remember: they're looking for you too."

Something about the tide being out and all that space around us made my voice seem painfully loud, to me at least, as though I were shouting. I couldn't gauge it. But when I tried to speak softer, Turret told me to stop mumbling. "It's a good job you're not on the boats," he said.

My thoughts regrouped. I was ready to tell him about Lucy – not the breaking in to her house part but the having her for a girlfriend, sort of – to see what advice he could give me on whether I should let bygones be bygones, as Dad liked to say, or whether I should phone her and apologise for what had happened that day in the gardens.

"When it comes to women," he said, "always apologise. It doesn't matter if you're right. You'll make life easier for yourself."

I was about to ask him what he thought I should say to her, when the sound of crunching pebbles came from behind us. Turning around, I saw two coppers, an older woman and a younger man. She had stripes on her sleeve.

"Speak of the devil," said Turret.

"Doing a spot of rebuilding, then?" said the woman copper.

"I'll be here till doomsday if I wait for the insurance."

"It was insured then, was it?" said the man.

"No, son, I'm pulling your leg." Turret got his Players out and lit one. "Why would I insure a crappy pile of wood?"

"I wouldn't know, sir."

"So, have you found the buggers?" said Turret.

"Who's your friend?" asked the woman.

I forced a smile. "Hello."

Turret slapped me on the shoulder. "This is my lad."

"What's your name, son?" said the woman.

"Matthew."

"Turret, I take it?"

"Didn't I just say?" said Turret.

"There's no need for that, sir," said the man.

"Isn't there? What you questioning my boy for when you're s'posed to be finding who did this?"

The two coppers looked at each other.

"We just wanted to update you," said the man. "Someone's claimed responsibility for the fire."

"About bloody time. Who?"

"We're still investigating. But there does seem to be some sort of pattern. He's no stranger to crime. We've had our eye on him for a while."

"He?" said Turret. "Are you sure?"

"Ninety-nine percent," said the woman.

She put her hands over her face and sneezed. I waited for her to check what she'd caught but she didn't. I bet she was dying to.

"'Scuse me," she said, watery eyed. "As a rule, women don't go around setting fires. It's almost always males. We put it down to testosterone."

"Ah," said Turret. "Bit hard on the teeth that."

"Very good, Mr. Turret," said the man. "When we hear anything, we'll let you know. In the meantime, you might consider—"

"What, getting a security guard?"

"No, sir," said the man.

"That's all for now," said the woman. "We'll leave you to get on with your day."

"Very kind of you indeed," said Turret, slinging the last of his coffee over the side of the boat.

"Goodbye Matthew," said the woman.

I said bye.

The coppers walked to their car. Turret smiled as he put the cup back on his Thermos. "Put a flea in their ear."

We sat there, in his boat, on the beach, watching gulls dive at wriggles on the sand. The tide was creeping in. My heart wasn't so hectic. I turned. The coppers were pulling away. I tried to look anywhere but at Turret, and found myself staring at the sea end of the pier, then back up to the Pavilion.

We were both quiet for a while until Turret broke the silence.

"I loved your mum, son. Still do."

A bunch of bright, bulky, flat-bottomed clouds went back to the horizon, receding like hill after hill, only they weren't rolling, they were perfectly ordered. It was as though someone had told them to get in position and stay there.

"Did you hear?" he said.

"Yeah."

"Ask me anything you like. Anything."

I probably should've had questions, should've wanted to know the ins and outs of what had gone on over the years, but I didn't. Questions meant getting answers, and I already felt like a suitcase stuffed with unwanted things, strapped so tightly that it was only a matter of time before the seams gave way from the strain. All I could think of to say was, "Could you stop doing French?"

"French?" he said. "French what? Impressions? I knew I should've been on that stage." He laughed, nodded towards the Pavilion. "Here, that miming bloke? What's his name?"

"You know what I mean."

He stopped laughing. "I'm not sure I do, son."

"Evening classes. At the school."

"You're not mixing me up with your mum, are you?"

"No."

"I think you are. The French? I wouldn't even touch their wine."

My head hurt across the eyes. I shut them, pressed my thumb and forefinger to my lids, but then that hurt too. The boat shifted. Opening my eyes, I saw Turret climbing out. I handed him the Thermos, then climbed out too.

"You ready?" he said when we were both on the beach.

"For what?" I said.

"For building the new stall you owe me."

54

I waited till Dad left for market, grabbed the torch, then scooted off on my bike till I got to the prom. It was three in the morning. The town was dead. October, and they still hadn't raked up the seaweed, which by then didn't smell freshly sour the way it did in summer, but rank as old veg.

At the back of the Pavilion were a stack of beer crates and a bunch of barrels. I leaned my bike against a barrel and went looking for a good window. Eyeing a head-high two-window block, I spun a barrel back on its rim and stood it under the window. Climbing onto it, I smashed the glass with the end of the torch and reached in.

Fifteen years in that town and I'd never set foot in the Pavilion, except for that one time in the toilets with Lucy, which was different. So much for Dad's keeping tradition alive. I hadn't even gone to a Christmas pantomime as a kid, let alone seen the likes of Ken Dodd and Max Bygraves when they'd come down for the summer season. Dad went on and on about them, but we never saw any of their shows.

Walking through the backstage area, I waved my torch at each and every door, looking for a way through to the auditorium. What I came across first was a door with a star on it. Above the star, Dawn Rose was scrawled on a scrap of paper like an afterthought, like she'd just pulled up and was on her way in when they wrote it. She was always playing the Pavilion. I went in and shut the door, turned the light on and my torch off. Talk about bright. A bit like in Sid's house, there were white bulbs around the mirror. Yellow dots danced before my eyes. The dressing table was crammed with powder puffs, moisturisers, coloured glitter, eyebrow pencils and lipsticks, eye shadows and mascaras, and a ton of squirty perfumes...the same stuff you find on all dressing tables, just more of it. Oh, and a jumbo-size box of tissues. What with all the bouquets and ovations you get when you're a star, it made sense. Crying was part of being famous.

Most of the lipsticks were in a wicker bowl; others seemed

thrown down in a rush. One by one I pulled off the lids and compared their shades – everything from coal to buttercup. I tested a few by drawing lines on tissues. Cinnamon would've been perfect for my Anastasia Bulimia, who'd grown up in the Spice Islands and had exotic tastes. So I went with that. But when I pressed it to my lip, my hand wouldn't stop shaking. The tip strayed. After wiping the colour from my Hilda Ogden mouth, I started again, carefully lining the tip of the stick against the outside of my lip, drawing it one way and then the other, slowly, feeling the new waxy tightness as I went, watched over by my giant looming shadow on the wall, spooking me into thinking that the trapped spirit of some old-time star was in the room with me, watching as I painted my face for more razzamatazz. If I just opened the window…

It took a few tries to plant a real smacker on the mirror. I put more Cinnamon on my lips and kept trying till I got it right, a real film star pucker, with crinkles. Over the kisses, in the same Cinnamon lipstick, I wrote *Eliza Bradley xxxxx*. With any luck I'd be in the *Argus* again. Hopefully they'd remember their CrimeWave article of a while back, put two and two together, and get Paul Soap to write the story.

The corridor smelled of fabric and wood, but not any old wood, like the sawn four-by-twos that Turret had used to build the new frame, more like the sort you'd smell in a castle library, or if you sniffed the beds in a vicarage.

After trying several doors, I continued along and came to a set of steps. Following the torch beam to the top, I wound up skirting a step ladder, some rolls of cable, and then a long, thick, heavy curtain, like velvet. My torch landed on a drum kit, flashing its pearly finish onto the walls and curtain like a mirror ball. There were microphone stands, speaker cabinets, keyboards, but no guitars. Maybe they were back at the hotel. The Lancaster, probably. I thought of Dad dropping off mushrooms in the morning for the band's omelettes. I went over to the main mic, front centre, and smelled the gauze. If anyone ever mentioned Dawn Rose in Dad's shop, I could tell them she had a hundred lipsticks and metallic breath. I shone the torch at the rows and rows of tipped-up seats, waving the beam like a spotlight high in the rafters tracing figure of eights over the crowd.

I picked a row halfway up and scissored my way to the middle. Then I switched off the torch. Was the dark hot or cold? I couldn't tell. But soon enough I began to feel the high airy cool of the space around me. I felt a long way back in my head, watching the people as they came and went, came and went, just as they always did. And as I sat in that cool airy dark, images began coming to me of that night at the Anchor, of the crowd yelling for Dad on the podium, and then of Judge Gavin, the jeering he got over Dad's petition. Then I remembered wishing that God's hand and white sleeve would come crashing through the ceiling and sweep me off to a fatherless place. There, in the auditorium dark, I wondered what a fatherless place might be like, and if such a thing existed. I used to think it was the closest thing to heaven imaginable. After all, it hadn't done Lance any harm. But then, on second thoughts, it hadn't really done him much good, either. Now I had two dads to his none. I had no idea what to do with them, or what they might want from me. Two could easily be better than none. You work with what you've got, not with what's missing. How about that? My own saying. Who knows. It could be the first of many.

Printed in the United States
201525BV00004B/667-708/A